Stumbling
Book One on The Fool's Path
© 2018 C. M. Martens
www.CMMartens.com

Stealing Shade Productions
Clearwater, FL 33760
www.stealingshade.com

Cover Design by Jason Piraino
HavenTattooArts.com

To all those unsure:
Keep at it.

C. M. Martens

Chapter One

Silvery light from a full moon filtered through the clouds, illuminating the stone markers of the dead as pinpricks of reflected light. Stretched out before her, these lanterns coaxed her past the metal entry gate. Though locked, the obstacle didn't break her stride. A foot taller than her, the vault to the other side was an easy feat of agility.

When her feet hit the graveled drive over the threshold, she paused to consider her options.

-Really?-

Her inner-voice's sarcasm made a joke from a passing thought: a cemetery was where she'd been led. Could it be more cliché?

Her lips even twitched upwards towards a smile, despite the pain that radiated through her. Centered most heavily in her right arm, the throbbing of her injuries seemed greater now that she'd stopped her forward sprint.

What was she even doing there?

Her almost-smile was erased by an exhalation of breath that puffed out her cheeks.

Expression set against the pain that radiated from her every cell, she squared her shoulders before clutching her arm more tightly to her. The blood dripping from her in a steady splash increased its flow.

It was a lot of blood.

The part of her that recognized how dangerous this was was ignored. First aid could wait. What mattered now was what lay ahead.

-Right, because you're *the person to deal with this thing.-*

And who would the right *person be,* she wanted to shoot back, but an argument with herself wouldn't draw helpful conclusions. A conversation with herself might not even be healthy for her deteriorating state of mind.

Still, the sarcasm pierced the veil of surrealism settling over her and it drowned out the terror that poked at her.

Even in this quiet wake of the chase, she struggled with the reality of what had happened—what *was* happening. Attacked on the silent streets of her home town, this was the first moment she'd had to consider what it was she'd given chase to.

She had no name for it. At least, no name she was willing to say out loud. Saying it out loud meant forcing herself to consider that she really might be crazy. Or that reality was much different than she'd believed.

Neither seemed like the better alternative.

Regardless, here she stood, at the threshold of a graveyard, in the middle of the night, short hair tossed like some mad scientist as she bled from a gash that ran from wrist to elbow, body aching like she'd wrestled a speeding train.

-Guess we should have made good on our promise not to go out so late.-

Easily ignored, the tug of guilt this idea sparked was overridden by the panic of what lay in front of her.

Even as crazy, as surreal, as this all was, something about it tugged at hidden memories. Something about the thing she chased. Something about the night.

A year ago she'd been attacked and she'd been forced to crawl home, glad the only friend left her in the world still lived in this boring town she'd grown up in.

She couldn't be sure it was the same thing. She couldn't be sure that night hadn't been some insane nightmare.

-*How many creatures of the night do you think there are?*-

She ignored the question, understanding the absurdity in thinking there was more than one kind of scary, yet on the same train of logic, if there was one, why couldn't there be many?

-*Unless there are none, and you really are insane.*-

Washed suddenly in the heat of fire, her blue eyes no longer saw the cemetery stretched before her. Instead, she saw the inferno that had taken the house in the woods she had no memory of going to; only the vague memory of leaving, knowing she'd somehow escaped the death that had taken her friends. The sharp smell of chemicals, the brightness of the blaze, surrounded by an overwhelming confusion as to where she was wrapped her senses in the recall.

With considerable effort, she shook the images from her mind to force leadened feet forward.

After only a handful of steps, she stopped. With one arm useless, and no experience with fighting, she wasn't sure what her next move should be. Maybe lure the thing home so she could show Mike?

-*What? Trap it in the basement?*-

It was a stupid idea, but how could she prove it was real? Proving she was *not* out of her mind seemed as important to her as surviving. Maybe more so.

-*Take a picture?*-

She stifled a burst of laughter at the simplicity of it, then again when she realized her phone was missing. Most likely back where she'd been tackled, her mind conjured an imagine of it lost forever in the thick brush where the thing she chased had ambushed her. Another image, this one of a sweatshirt with pockets that zipped things like phones safely away, laying uselessly on her bed brought her teeth together in a frustrated clench.

-*I'm sure fitness clothing designers had assault-and-battery in mind as key marketing points.*-

Annoyed by her bad luck, she found no humor in her head's wit.

More bad luck, brought on by ineptitude, had the creature attack at that moment.

Driven by instinct, she ducked and rolled so the creature flew over her. It landed in a graceful coil that brought it back to its feet as she flopped to the ground. Searing pain from incurred injuries brought spots across her vision.

-You're going to die.-

Teeth clenched against the silent announcement, she forced her legs to push her from the ground.

She spun to face the creature, but it had run off. A zig-zagging gait made attempts to trace its path impossible in the shadows of the tall hills. Rather then want to fight her, it seemed more eager to play.

-A game? Cat and Mouse? Who's who?-

She ignored the voice's implication. She was the one chasing here, making *her* the cat.

-Maybe this game is cat and cat? Or cat, and bigger cat?-

She ignored her self-mocking, eyes studying the lay of the land, as if something in the topography would give her some insight into what she was doing. Unable to maintain a visual of the creature, she was wary of moving forward. Turning to make an exit seemed an equally bad idea. It had snuck up on her twice while she was looking for it. What would happen if she turned away?

Staring ahead, frozen with indecision, she tried to remember the reason she thought this chase was a good idea to begin with. This thing could kill her, and she had no skill to ensure it didn't succeed.

Pure instinct had compelled her to follow it. At a dead sprint she'd pursued without thought. Reason hadn't returned until she'd stopped inside the cemetery.

-What? Don't think your heightened strength and speed is enough to take it head-to-head?-

More to run from the voice in her head than that she had formulated a plan, she took a tentative step forward, then another, eyes frantic to penetrate the too-shadowed area.

Each unhindered step instilled a layer of confidence. As a blanket of surrealism wrapped her thoughts, pushing thoughts of pain and death to darkness, she allowed the reminder of what she'd become to strengthen her resolve. Holding on to this, she let this moment of empowerment take a turn at manipulating reality.

Maybe she *could* take this thing.

Movement farther in the cemetery, ahead and to the left, caught her attention. The arms of a concrete angel beckoned her forward, welcoming her towards victory. Believing this a sign that her chase was motivated by some redeeming cause rather than misguided instinct she focused her attention to that spot.

She crept through the shadows, intent on surprising her prey, but when she reached the spot of attack, there was nothing to find. She stared stupidly at the neatly tended plot, grass inked black by the night.

Continuing to crouch, maintaining silence, she listened like she'd never listened before.

-You're not very good at this.-

A car at the far entrance distracted her attention, the crunch of tires telling of its turn onto the unpaved paths that curved through the cemetery.

Her attention was taken from this new problem when the old's rushing force met her in another surprise strike. The creature's enjoyment of tackling her was pissing her off. Whatever this game was, it needed to end.

Its body slamming into hers brought an exclamation of air from her lungs. Hissing growls sent panicked chills across her skin even as she fought to get her arms free from an iron-like bear hug.

Attempting to rip her arms from their trap only served to instill more carnage on her already battered body. The shredded skin of her damaged arm pulled away so she wasn't sure what might be left to hold it together.

The sharpness of the pain overrode all thought and she tightened her muscles in a body-sized cringe before going limp in defeat.

-Really? Just go fetal and hope it gets bored?-

Adrenaline surge overrode the pain of her many injuries, and she was suddenly free, tossing the creature away with a push of legs. Something wet ran down her face. Shutting off the part of her brain that wondered if the creature had managed to take a bite out of her for after she survived, she focused on completing her getaway.

Rolling to its feet in a display of agility that left her jealous, the two squared off, both panting heavily as they stared each other down.

She noted its ratty jeans, coupled with a fraying t-shirt that suggested the creature's beginnings as human. So thick was the layer of grime covering it, she wasn't sure what its original skin color had been. Its similarly filth-dyed hair was matted so tightly to its scalp, only thin wisps protruding from the knot allowed her to tell there was hair there at all. But mostly, it was in the eyes; something just off about its facial structure that defined the thing as not human. Did its eyes bulge just too much? Was its brow-line retracted just so that the forehead sloped too sharply? Were its limbs elongated beyond their normal reach?

Whether one of these, or all of them, it was too subtle to pin down in her current distress.

The creature pounced.

Rather than get out of its way, her great idea was to take it on.

-So much for your getaway.-

Insides jarred by the clash of bodies, she found the air she'd just regained pushed back out of her torso. They were motionless, pushing against each other in a test of wills.

The distraction of keeping her skin from its jaws was enough of a disadvantage that she lost her forward momentum. She fell backward, forearms crossed against the creature's chest to keep it from making a meal of her face.

More pain exploded through her as her body slammed into the grass. Whether this pain was from a fresh wound, or old, she hoped to survive to find out.

-This seems familiar.-

It was exactly what had happened in the initial attack. Loping through town on her nightly jog, earbuds playing her favorite songs directly to her brain, she experienced a moment of missing time followed by a solid collision with the Earth that sent her rolling through the trees that lined the road.

Instinctively warding her face with raised arms had probably saved her life, though not her forearm. The creature had clamped down on the part she'd offered up, working it like a dog would a bone, before she'd managed to get her legs between them and vault the thing off her.

Hoping the move would work again, she leveraged her legs beneath her, managing to get one in a position to kick out at the thing snapping at her face. Her arms burned with the effort to keep its mouth from fastening on her, while pain threatened to send her into unconsciousness.

She threw all her will behind that one-legged kick.

Free, she scrambled onto her stomach, pulling herself through the damp grounds of the graveyard in a half-crawl, half face-shimmy. She didn't make it far before her leg was caught by the thing that may, or may not, have been human.

Groping in desperation, her hand settled on a piece of broken tombstone. It was all she had to fend off the snarling vestige intent on ending her life. With a secure grip, it dragged her towards it. She swung...

-*You are so going to die.*-

...feeling the bone of its head cave under the mass of the stone. The snapping sound of the impact echoed in her stomach, sending her senses to war. Willing herself not to throw-up, she maintained a tight grip on the makeshift weapon, swinging for a second blow.

Another snap, this time from a facial crack, and she was free. Scrambling on a hand and knees until she could get to her feet, she tripped on steps that propelled her faster than her balance could maintain.

Stumbling, she sensed the creature line up for another leap. In the recesses of her brain, she wondered how she could still be conscious after so much blood-loss, while a more primal part of her maintained control of her physical movements. This instinct paid more attention to the wrought-iron fencing buried in a season of overgrowth than on her encroaching death. This instinct allowed her to grab the new weapon, rise, and spin to meet the next assault.

As if choreographed, the two met, becoming one as the metal post pierced through the creature's body. Its face shrieked in surprised defeat while its fangs clamped open and closed mere inches from her face. Letting go, she kicked it away before she, too, dropped to the ground.

Out of danger, the emotional torrent adrenaline had kept at bay flooded over her, manifesting as silent tears. Already on her knees, she heaved the contents of her stomach into the damp grass.

Gasping from both physical and mental trauma, she rolled away. With cheek pressed to the damp earth, her eyes fluttered closed.

Darkness took her.

***

Hamal had had no trouble finding her and even less tailing her over the last few days; his job made simple since the girl rarely left the house.

Whoever she was, she was clueless that anyone had any interest in her. No security other than a lock on her door. No awareness of her surroundings as she left each night to trek her jogging path through town. He didn't worry that anyone would catch him snooping around, especially the girl he watched.

Possibly the most boring person he'd ever seen, he still had no information to suggest she was worth this much trouble to anyone, especially to one as powerful as the one who'd sent him.

Desiree Galen. Small-town girl, living in a degraded upstate town, complete with the small-town life.

As far as Hamal was concerned, Adam's Center, New York was the center of Hell. If Hell was the most mundane place one could think of, anyway.

Her only friend, a Mike Nolan, hung around for reasons Hamal had yet to discern. Mike's work took him out of town more than he was ever there, but he'd never officially relocated. A romantic relationship between the two would have explained things, but Hamal had found no evidence they were anything but good friends.

Hamal smirked. *Idiot.* He couldn't understand the use of a female friend, especially not one who kept him living in a place like this. Hanging around a place like this for *anyone* was senseless.

The only information he had managed to collect was that Mike called Desiree, Dee. Hamal had made a notation of this, the words close to slicing through the paper from his fervent tracing of the note in an outlet for his obsessive boredom. That, and a detailed map of both her house and Mike's, along with their surrounding properties, was all he'd been able to add to her file.

He laughed to himself at the ridiculousness of the assignment. Didn't they have drones and satellites for surveillance jobs like this? Way below his pay-grade, Hamal had only agreed to take it because Zi had personally asked.

As Dee came jogging around the corner of the night darkened street, a fact about her flashed through his mind. A fact that could be interesting. A fact that could be nothing. A fact that ate at his pride so he couldn't just forget it.

He drummed his fingers against the leather steering wheel of his luxury SUV, annoyance at her outperformance of him coming through in this tick of motion. Nothing in her file suggested she was anything other than some random girl, but the fact that she had an endurance far superior to his own ate at him. Finding this out on his first night, when he'd failed to tail her, festered in his mind.

He sighed, a huff of air that expressed his annoyance at a mission barely started. Not that anyone was monitoring his mood, or would care if they were, but it made him feel just a little better.

To circumvent this problem of tracking her through town, he'd set up cameras along the girl's jogging route, tuned to give him live-feed of her progress from her front door, through her journey, and back again. His gamble that she traveled the same path each night had paid in full, which helped heal his wounded ego.

Parked in the center of this course, as far from the sparsely placed streetlights as possible, he waited. In a town like this, everyone was sure to know everyone else, so his SUV would look suspicious. Proactively, he had stopped by a few of the local haunts to drop hints that he was in town doing some work. If he was noticed, seeds of explanation had been sown. Not that she would hear any town gossip. As far as he could tell, she had no contact with anyone other than Mike.

He'd noted this with more heavily traced marks in her file.

As she moved closer to his position, he relaxed into the bucket seat, ensuring he was obscured in shadow. As unlikely as it was, there was always the chance she would notice him sitting there. Whether or not she recognized his truck as out of place, someone hanging out in the middle of the night in their vehicle would draw attention.

The portable screen he was using to view the camera's video sat in the seat next to him. Tented by a thick, dark cloth to keep the light of the viewer from reflecting to the exterior of the vehicle was something else that might garner a look.

He held his breath.

When his presence went unnoticed, he let out the air he'd been holding, then glanced at the screen to watch her turn the corner behind him.

Anticipating another eventless night, he picked up her file from the center console to keep his hands busy. As many times as he'd been through it, he still hoped some nuance of information would clue him in to what he was doing there. These late night jogs were weird, but they were nothing that required the level of attention his presence indicated. Especially nothing that explained the secrecy stressed around him being here.

Flipping the folder open, he stared at her picture. Short, dark hair framed a nice face. Pretty even. Her cerulean eyes held sadness as she looked away from the photographer to some faraway point.

Eyes flickering from her file to the monitor, he noted nothing of interest. Settling more comfortably, he dragged the file onto his lap.

Five foot six. One hundred forty-five pounds. Athletic. Hair cut in a sort of naturally tousled look, though it had grown out a bit since the picture was taken. Dropped out of college after her father died at the end of her sophomore year. Being an only child, she'd inherited everything, though she had turned the operation of her father's company over to Mike, who'd expanded the very profitable construction firm into consulting as well.

Mike's head for finance was the reason for Desiree's growing accounts. She was worth over one-hundred million dollars. From what her file told Hamal, she didn't use much of it. The house was paid off. She had no extra-curricular activities and rarely traveled. The occasional night out with Mike, which he usually paid for, was the only time she spent money on anything outside her utility bill and groceries. Running shoes seemed to be the only thing she splurged on with any consistency.

What was more strange, though accountable to grief, was that as soon as the papers were signed that gave up responsibility for her property to Mike, she'd dropped off the grid. For four years she seemed to vanish, never touching her father's money.

Hamal knew it was in this unaccounted history that he'd find the answers to why he was here. If only he were allowed to approach her, Hamal was sure he'd get all the answers he needed. He had no doubt she would be putty in his hands. If not for the parameters that forbade him from making contact, he'd be talking with her right now. Possibly between the sheets of her king-sized bed.

He shook that thought away. If the assignment had come from anyone else, Hamal would have ignored the decree and reached out to her. As hard as his curiosity pulled at him to figure out the mystery, he wouldn't cross that one. Not even for this.

Instead, he was left to watch, wondering who this girl was and how she might have garnered the attention of one who pulled so many strings.

His eyes moved back to track her progress on the monitor while he leaned over to change the infrared view to night-vision. The red, blue, and green of the screen turned to a green-tinged world where her form shone brightly against the background of the night.

He'd noted the wireless earbuds in her ears as she'd passed and couldn't help but wonder, from a strictly professional point-of-view, how she could deal with running at night after cutting off her strongest working sense. What if something came at her? There was no way she could see that well in the night that she should risk blunting her sense of hearing.

Maybe the girl had a death-wish.

He straightened in his seat.

If she did have a death-wish, and something happened to grant that wish, was he supposed to stand by and document what happened? His directives were clear; he was there merely to observe, but should he interfere in this case?

Not for the first time since arriving, he fumbled with his phone. Another clearly laid parameter had been not to make contact with home-base under any circumstances.

He'd never been on such a troubling case. How could such a dull girl be the focus of such a confusing mission?

These were questions above his pay-grade. If he was here merely to observe, then observe was all he would do. If the girl wanted to die, then maybe that was all he was supposed to find out.

Slapping the thin file closed, he tossed it aside and nestled back into the seat, wishing he hadn't already finished his coffee.

Lids heavy with boredom, he almost missed the blur of movement that cut across the screen. He jolted forward to manipulate the video to rewatch what happened.

Had she just been attacked?

He watched the video in slo-mo to be sure.

Completely unprepared, the second hit to his ego since arriving, he leapt from the vehicle. Sprinting, shotgun in one-hand, night-vision goggles in the other, he made his way to where his mark was most assuredly dead.

He hated being right, especially when he hadn't expected to be this right.

The thing that had ambushed his mark was the last thing he'd thought to see turn up as a player. If he'd had more time to wonder about the nature of its appearance, he might have re-thought his forward pace. There were things he was good at, and there were things above the ability of his DNA to accommodate. What had attacked Dee was one of those things he wasn't sure he'd be able to help with.

Eyes accustomed to looking for the barest of clues, Hamal saw the phone lying in the ditch where she'd been ambushed, right alongside the scuff marks and battered grass that told of the struggle the pair had shared before racing off into the night.

He gazed down the path the two had taken, curiosity peaked that she had chased it. He allowed the fact that she lived through the attack to filter quietly in the back of his head as other questions raised by the event were pulled forward, the most important being: if Zi had known the players involved, would he have sent Hamal? This was a job for someone much more durable than Zi's favorite human pet.

More questions raced through his head as he followed the trail of blood, knowing he'd arrive too late to be of any use.

He knew the speed of the thing that had attacked, but still wasn't wrapping his brain around the idea that she'd met its pace, despite every clue pointing to that fact. If she'd been a Soldier, Zi would have known. If she were another form of cast-off, someone would have been aware of her, wouldn't they? She wouldn't have been left to her own devices. She wouldn't be living this benign existence watched by someone like him. Right?

Questions he couldn't answer were forgotten as he caught the sign ahead: *King's Quarry Cemetery*. Laughing ironically to himself, he couldn't help look around to see if someone was setting him up for some elaborate joke. A cemetery was where the fight had gone to? C'mon!

The sound of bodies colliding brought his attention from his possible candid camera debut, mocking thoughts overrun with the panic of a possible failed mission.

Hiding in the shadows of the hills and sparse groupings of trees, he watched, helpless, as Dee fell to her knees while the creature lined up for a final attack behind her. A part of him wanted to move forward, but he knew there was no way he'd arrive in time to save her, even if he thought the intercession might help, or be allowed. When she pulled a shaft of metal fencing from the brush, turning in time to impale the creature's final attempt at taking her life, his mouth fell to his knees.

All he'd seen over the last few miles suggested she was capable of this, but his brain struggled to align the dull girl he'd been tailing on previous nights with this new persona more akin to the creature who'd attacked her. Whatever the answers, why he'd been sent to watch her was finally clear.

This new perspective on the mission sparked excitement in him he hadn't felt in a long time. As he continued to watch, his mind whirled with possibilities and what they meant for the true nature of his mark.

This excitement was tempered when the girl fell to her knees, followed by her throwing up violently. When the sounds of retching faded, Dee seemed to think about pushing herself to her feet; instead collapsing to her side. Finding something to be excited about, only to lose it so soon was enough to send him forward.

"Shit. Shit. Shit." The word was his mantra as he made his way to her, using as much shadow as he could find on a full-mooned night to cover his approach.

He knelt next to her, eyes scanning the Revenant that would not be getting up. Its skin was already shrinking in on itself, showing a glimpse of the husk it would become that always reminded him of a mummy he'd seen in a museum when he was a boy. He noted the head wounds that told the story of their fight, impressed she'd bludgeoned the thing as she had. Not near the power of the ones he worked for, these Revenants were still nothing to laugh at. He wasn't sure he could have wounded one in such a manner, and he definitely wouldn't have survived the ambush she had.

His ego survived these observations. Matched against any human, he was the best, but when compared to the things that were more, he never tried to compete. He'd seen too many lives end from that kind of pride.

This was all processed in a scan of eyes as he knelt next to the one he couldn't lose like this. What would his reputation be if the girl he was sent to watch died as soon as things got interesting?

Fingers searched for a pulse at her neck as his eyes scanned the damage done to her body. Her wounds were severe. He'd never have guessed she would still be alive if shown them in another context.

As he continued to check her over, he noticed the blood that moments before had been flowing liberally from multiple lacerations was slowing. Her heart-rate, thready and irregular only seconds ago, was a steadier, stronger pulse against his touch.

He took off the night-vision goggles to look at her with his own eyes.

Athletic muscularity was easily recognized through tight running pants. A tank top, mostly torn away, showed the athletic bra underneath still intact. Blood seeped at her knees, and there were tears in her thigh, ribs, and most especially, the arm he worried she would never use again, mangled in a way that suggested she should have bled out from the wound long before she made it here.

He winced at the dichotomy of her clean bicep and untouched hand book-casing her forearm. It made the injury seem more traumatic with her hand laying there, almost as if detached from the rest of her.

She moaned, pulling his attention from cataloguing her injuries. How could she recover consciousness already?

Who was this girl?

Stumbling: Book One on The Fool's Path

Chapter Two

Dee was sure she'd heard a voice curse; felt fingers on her neck. When she finally managed to pull her eyelids apart, there was no one. Only the shriveled face that had been her attacker staring at the sky, metal fence-post sticking from its chest.

-What's with that thing looking like a mummy?-

She giggled with delirium at the observation.

Her weight shifted, flooding pain through her, and there was no more laughter. There was no more anything as moving took all her focus.

She managed to get herself to a kneeling position without using her arms. Head hanging to her chest, she paused to gather her will, body fighting her desire to stand. She was one giant hurt. As one fought for attention over the others, another she hadn't even known about rose to take top place. Her right arm was held close to her stomach by the left, and she vaguely remembered the creature using the appendage as a chew toy. The bleeding had stopped sometime while she'd passed out, though a fresh current was now leaking out of her, spawned by her movements.

-Eww.-

It was only through masterful compartmentalization that she didn't pass out. That, and her inner-voice making light of the serious wounds tethered her sanity.

This tether was too thin.

The reality of her staring at her own shattered bone through her own shredded skin slammed into her, bursting through those things that had been sheltering her.

Then, she was throwing up.

Through her dry heaving, she remembered the light touch that had brought her back to consciousness, focusing on the sensation to better determine the truth of it. Someone checking her pulse? Had that same someone cursed, thinking they'd found a dead body in the cemetery? What did they think of a mummy lying there? Who would even be out at this time of night, and where had they gone?

-Maybe a ghost checking who was disturbing its territory?-

She might have rolled her eyes if she had any control over her movements. Dry heaves continued to wrack her body.

When she once again had control of her actions, she leaned back on battered knees, cradling her arm as she panned her surroundings. Seeing nothing out of place, she slowly, gingerly, rose on unsteady legs.

Thoughts of nameless strangers and ghosts left her head when she stepped on a phone laying in the grass. Her phone.

Picking it up, she looked at it as if something on its surface might reveal its appearance, too late to be of any use.

Another shaky step forward had her kicking the body of the thing she shouldn't have forgotten. Ignoring its withered form, forbidding questions of the hows and whys of its posthumous physiological changes, she pondered what to do with it. She couldn't just leave it here, could she? Would someone be able to trace it to her if they found it? And what would they find if they ran tests on it?

Did she even care?

-I'm pretty sure you'd be a lab rat if anyone ever figured out anything about you. Don't leave this body here.-

The idea of someone learning how much of a freak she was brought her attention from the shriveled husk at her feet to the question of how she would get home. Exhaustion pulled at her, so she was tempted to lay back down in the damp grass. She was miles from Mike's, which was miles closer than her own home.

Her head hurt, pounding from blood loss. Chilled to the bone, she was sure she was using the last of her energy reserves to concentrate on the strangest of problems. Wiping absently at her battered arm brought her attention to the fact that it was still trickling blood, and the hand of that arm was numb in a way that even staring at it brought her no sense that it was a part of her.

Fighting hysteria, she returned her attention to the corpse at her feet. Her battle with fatigue made it impossible to hold onto more than one thought at a time, so she'd forgotten this issue that needed a solution before she could work on getting home.

Her eyes glanced into the dark landscape again, remembering the lingering touch that had fluttered over her neck, searching for the someone she was now sure had been here. Had that someone been watching over her? Had this same someone saved her last year when she'd almost been killed by something that could only be similar to the corpse at her feet?

-No one saved you from this thing. You killed it all by yourself.-

That was true, but it didn't mean no one had helped her before or hadn't been here tonight.

-Seriously? Like a guardian angel or something?-

She panned the cemetery, tired eyes losing focus among the silvery stones reflecting the moon's light. What should have taken mere seconds kept her standing there far longer. Still, she was sure she'd be able to see if anyone was out there.

***

Even knowing there was no way she could find him nestled in the shadows, Hamal slid more securely into the darkness. The way her eyes probed the area shouted at his subconscious to be less visible. Her movements were too precise, even in her dazed state, for someone who was struggling to see in the night.

Putting back on the night-vision goggles in preparation to follow her through a canopy of trees to her house, he carefully monitored her movements, barely breathing. Shocked, he stared wide-eyed when she grabbed a leg of the husk, easily dragging it the hundred feet to the far side of the grounds where a steep hill dropped sharply. At her level of blood loss, exhaustion, and simple lack of mass, she shouldn't have been able to drag that much dead weight so casually.

His brain raced through possibilities, both practical and unlikely, that might explain all he'd seen this night from the girl who, until minutes ago, he still hadn't believed was worth his time.

Forcing himself to pay attention, he watched her stare after the fallen corpse, her expressionless face motionless for several minutes. The fact that she was conscious said much about her mental fortitude. He reiterated to himself that she should be dead. The ulnar artery in her wrist was severed in multiple places. It had been her blood that had laid such a clear path for him to follow. That she was staring off in a daze seemed natural for someone who'd been fatally wounded.

Breathing relief when she lifted her phone from a pocket, he was curious who she would call. Was there someone who knew about her strangeness? Someone she could go to who would help patch her up?

It had to be Mike. There was no one else, as far as he'd seen, she could call this late. There was no one else she could call, period.

He couldn't hear her conversation from his position but watched with studious appraisal. When she began her journey out of the graveyard, pace more plodding than usual, he followed carefully.

Staggering a step here and there, she made it to her destination with no more drama, confirming Hamal's thoughts that Mike was in on her secret. He was disappointed that there wasn't some unseen place or person that might shed more light on her surrounding mystery, but there was still time for those kinds of things.

Chapter Three

"This better be good." His voice cracked from the hangover of sleep.

She almost laughed, but a lack of energy stopped the expression from forming. "I got a little banged up."

She heard him come fully awake. "A little banged up?"

His tone was accusatory, and she might have flinched if her body had the energy.

"Yeah. I just need a little help." Her tone was apologetic.

She sensed his nodding, so continued, "I'll meet you out back in twenty minutes."

She wasn't sure if he spoke after that. She hung up, not trying to be rude, just forgetting, in her dazed state, to see if he had anything to add. She headed towards Mike's, forcing her pace beyond that of a walk, ready for a bed in a way she'd never known.

***

When they'd traveled far enough that he was sure there wasn't some new, secret place she was headed, Hamal advanced to settle into a position he would be able to overhear any conversation. Risking the extra time to pick up his bag from his truck, he was glad he took the chance. The only place for him to spy was from the cover of the tree-lined property, too far away to hear anything without aid.

Positioning his night vision gear more comfortably over his face, he quietly slid the small shotgun microphone from his pack, eyes scanning the moon tinted landscape for signs of the injured girl. The fuzzy black material surrounding the four inch, tube-like device, screwed into a collapsable pole, was the perfect color and shape to blend with the night dark trees surrounding him. Connected to a pair of high-end headphones, he would be able to hear whatever was said more clearly than if he was standing right next to them.

The metallic rattle of a doorknob drew Hamal's attention to the back of the house that juxtaposed the surrounding country with modern urban style. He watched Mike step outside, his thin frame hunched slightly with the vestiges of sleep. Hamal noted the thick towel the man held just as his expression of sleepy annoyance was replaced with genuine concern.

Hamal's gaze followed Mike's as he moved quickly down the few steps of the raised deck to meet Desiree in the grass, wrapping the thick towel he'd brought around her as he drew her in close. "Dee, what the hell. You said a little banged up."

She leaned into Mike, allowing a second of connection before stepping out of his grasp to move towards the house. "Guess I'm not crazy."

What did that mean?

From Mike's expression, Hamal knew he understood their meaning too well.

Then they were in the house, cutting Hamal off from any information their conversation might give.

Annoyed he'd decided not to bug Mike's place as he had Desiree's, he weighed the risk versus reward of creeping towards the house. As long as they stayed in a room near a window, he'd be able to pick up their conversation without difficulty.

＊＊＊

Guess I'm not crazy.

She knew the words would hit him like a slap to the face. She knew this whole event would conjure memories from another night, just over a year ago, when she'd found herself curled up against his front door. Blood, whether her own or her attacker's, she still didn't know, splattered across her. Mike's expression of unbridled fear was forever burned into her memory.

He hadn't let her out of his sight for weeks.

"No doctors." She'd quickly read what he was thinking from the set of his eyes.

Her statement broke his seething silence. "No doctors? I don't know how you haven't bled out already! I'm taking you to the hospital!"

"Exactly, I haven't bled out. I'm fine. Doctors will only ask questions I can't answer."

Her voice sounded impassive even to her ears. She watched Mike's face crease as his mind raced to find an argument to contradict her.

She knew he'd given up trying to come up with a reason to haul her to the hospital when he guided her into the kitchen. He pulled out a chair for her to sit in before moving to the bathroom where he collected towels and hot water, antiseptic cream and bandages.

Dee listened to his rummaging knowing she'd be able to sleep once he was done mothering her. She knew she needed to give him this time so he would feel better about not taking her to see a doctor. He needed to see she was alright.

Making his way back to the kitchen with a collection of meager first aid tools, Dee sat up, stifling a groan.

Her smile was forced, but her voice even. "Relax. I really am fine. Super exhausted, but fine." A yawn slipped out, before a glance at her arms hanging loosely in her lap brought attention back to the obvious. "Considering."

"Considering it looks like you were mauled by a pack of wolves."

"Yes, considering that." Voice thick with underhanded sarcasm, she sat straighter in the chair, as Mike went to work on her.

"Always with the jokes. Even like this. Never listen to anybody—"

Desiree let him have his muttering, closing her eyes to lay her head on the back of the chair while Mike patched her up. Neither of them had any experience with first aid that made them adequate to handle cuts and bruises, let alone wounds that would make a trauma surgeon cringe. Still, Mike had seen enough that he wouldn't push the doctor issue. Even if he was too weak to acknowledge it, he wasn't stupid enough to ignore it.

She was changed. Even if they wouldn't talk about it, it was real.

A year ago, when she'd come home, propping herself on his front porch half dead, she'd allowed him to convince her she'd been the victim of a mugging, not the victim of an attack from a creature that only existed in fiction. But he'd seen the injuries she'd sustained. He'd seen the recovery that defied explanation. And now this.

Would he finally allow himself to wake up to the idea that what she claimed was true? Would he finally accept the idea that she had been attacked by a vampire?

She winced from the word, wishing she had another to label the thing as. But the more she tried to squelch the word from echoing through her head, the louder it became. It's what she had called it then, though she couldn't remember why. Over time, her memory of what had happened to bring her home had gotten cloudy.

Still, it's what she was calling the thing she'd seen tonight, though, as the strange evening made its thousandth re-run through her head, she wasn't sure if it was an accurate enough description of what had attacked her. Had it tried to drink her blood?

-Was it going for your neck when you put your arm in its mouth?-

Maybe.

***

Hamal lay against the pillows. In the background of the tiny motel room the television played re-runs of a sitcom he'd never heard of. It didn't matter. He wasn't paying attention. His thoughts were rushing over what he'd seen in the cemetery and what he'd overheard at Mike's.

Not even he could guarantee coming out alive against the creature she'd run down. He wouldn't have tried to run it down.

There were so many layers to what the encounter suggested, yet he focused on the surface of it. For now, replaying the image of her pushing the creature away from her after impaling it on her makeshift weapon was enough to think about. No mere girl could have taken the force of that attack, let alone stabbed it by pulling a piece of wrought iron fencing from the earth.

His mind trailed to all he'd heard and the little he'd been told directly about Revenants. He'd never heard there were any roaming free, unaccounted for out in regular populations. That they were even allowed to live was a point he didn't understand but was never stupid enough to ask. That one would be so close to a settled population was unheard of, and he was sure he'd never heard of one used as an assassin. Even so, it was the only way he could explain the coincidence of his mark running across the path of one.

Maybe not an assassin. Maybe a test? A creature of supernatural strength without skill was the perfect probe to see just what surprises lay under the surface of the supposed normal girl.

Both scenarios suggested that someone knew about her and had reason to think she was more than she seemed. That someone wasn't Zi. Hamal wouldn't have been sent if they believed she had any of the skill he'd seen from her tonight.

Whoever it was, Hamal would have to be more careful. If another party was watching her, they'd see his interference and he was too easily linked to Zibanitu's House, though his humanity kept him separate enough from them that they couldn't officially use him as a link. It was what made him such an asset.

Sitting up, he grinned at his reflection, the mystery of why he'd been sent to watch her made clear.

More at ease from his deductions, Hamal replayed the girl's romp in the graveyard. He conceded that luck had played a large part in her success, but despite trying, he couldn't deny what her success meant. His excitement continued to escalate. He moved to his feet, pacing across the small space, wanting to call in what he'd seen, but knowing it was too early to break his order of no communication.

Another parameter of the mission was answered. Communication was an easy thing to intercept and Zi didn't want any link to this girl getting out.

The next question was whether she was some odd, naturally occurring anomaly, or someone's misplaced creation.

Whatever her origins, she was strong-willed enough to chase down the thing that had ambushed her. That, on top of her being a natural fighter, even if some training was necessary to bring up her competency, had Hamal itching to begin her training.

Chapter Four

Fire beckoned her closer, even as flames licked painfully over her skin, singeing hair from her face and arms. Still, she continued forward, drawn by a compulsion so strong the fire burning her wasn't enough to turn her away.

Then, a crash; a loud crack of wood splintering before she was buried in smoldering fire...

Gasping, Dee sat up fast, clutching the sweat-soaked sheet to her. As her brain released the last of the dream, she fell back to the pillows.

When Mike left the house that morning, she'd crawled from his guest room, limping gracelessly through the trees like some prison escapee to her own home, to settle into her own bed.

Now, late morning, she had every intention of sleeping for a week.

As she was drifting back off, her phone rang, startling her.

Mike's voice was in her ear before she'd found her voice, "You're not here."

It must be lunchtime. Of course, he would waste the break in his day to check on her. She squeezed her eyes shut. She could have at least let him know she'd gone back to her place.

"Yeah. I just wanted my own bed." Her voice, laced with shame, sounded pathetic even to her.

There was silence on the line for a few seconds, and Dee held her breath, waiting for Mike's hurtful, yet justified, response.

"I don't know how you can stay there." His voice was quiet; distracted.

It was a running conversation that Mike thought Dee should sell the house. He couldn't understand why she surrounded herself with a shrine to the man whose absence continued to shape her life.

"I just like it here."

Mike grunted, a response that said both nothing and everything.

Silence stretched again. Dee closed her eyes, falling back to lay against the pillows, sadness replacing the gladness that her friend wasn't mad at her. He might not be angry, but the chasm that existed between them was real. And that was all her fault.

"I'll swing by with dinner, okay? It'll be late though."

-*Why he doesn't just write you off, I'll never understand.*-

She made a mental note to make more of an effort to be a better friend. The *best* friend.

-*You're going to give up your nightly jogs? The thing you actually promised you'd stop doing, but kept doing anyway?*-

"I'll be here." She hoped her voice sounded natural.

Sensing he wanted to say more, she held her breath, but he hung up after a quick goodbye.

Dee flung her phone down, watching it bounce forward on the bed like a skipping stone before resting near her feet, its silver exterior a shining mark against the charcoal of the bedding.

Her first instinct was to ask how things had gotten so bad between them, but she already knew. She was the reason. Her leaving, taking off for so many years with barely a whisper of where she was, or how she was doing, ruined any relationship between them. He'd been like a brother to her. A best friend. And she'd abandoned him, too caught up in her own existential dilemma to worry about anyone else.

She took a deep breath, then another, forcing her mind to a place where getting out of bed would be possible.

Her naked form moved slowly across the room to the window whose heavy curtains, colored the same charcoal as her comforter, kept the daylight locked away. Blinking at the onslaught of sun, she stared across the front lawn that ran fifty yards to the tree line.

Fall. Last night, she'd been thinking of fall. How the humidity of these last days of summer would thin out into perfect nights.

Then, she'd been hit from the side by the creature no amount of wishing could make just a dream. Closing her eyes, she traced the night's events, focusing on details she'd lost as they were happening.

She'd been lucky.

She should be dead.

-You should be dead.-

She didn't like that her inner-voice agreed with her.

Shoving the thought into one of many compartments in her mind, she pushed past the frightening idea and on to another.

Vampire.

-Does vampire *really explain what that thing was?-*

What should *we call it, then?*

Great, now she was having full blown conversations with herself.

She sighed, moving to the connecting bathroom to start a shower, thoughts continuing to repeat last night's adventure.

Were there more of those—whatever they were—nearby? Should she go after them? Protect the town?

-Now chasing after them is a good idea?-

She couldn't ignore the point. On the other hand, if someone got hurt by one of those things, it would be her fault. Did she want that sitting on her conscience?

-It's not your responsibility.-

Letting the spraying mist gather heat, Dee took a seat on the pillow top chest that housed the thick, long towels she spoiled herself with. She was still so tired, though the throb of her injuries had faded to a dull background pain. Had she healed so much overnight?

Her eyes slowly moved to the gauze on her arm. Having prolonged the moment when she'd be forced to acknowledge the limb that would never be the same, she now unwound the thick layer of porous material. As the binding slowly came loose, she wasn't sure if she was more worried the last of her wounds would be healed, or wouldn't be. If she was healed, it would mean her *powers* might not be something she could continue to ignore. But if the wounds weren't healed, could she admit she was in trouble? Who could she ask for help against a creature that wasn't supposed to exist?

Unwrapping the last layer, she flung the tangled material away. Smooth, clean scars zigged and zagged, intersecting around the skin from elbow to wrist. The marks were all that remained of an injury that should have crippled her permanently. Less than a full day for her body to repair shattered bone, torn muscle, and build new skin.

Clenching and unclenching her hand to loosen the tightness she knew should be much worse, then rotating her arm to probe how the muscles reacted, she was ecstatic, and frightened, by her recovery.

Closing her eyes, she took in a shaking breath.

-*Let's not get overdramatic. This is a good thing.*-

Sure, this was a good thing. Too good. What the hell was she?

-*Who cares. You're like a super-hero.*-

She'd known about her superior strength, heightened speed, and fantastic agility, but her self-testing had never involved severe injury recovery. She knew she'd heal on her own. She'd gotten other scrapes and sprains before, but never had she thought one night of sleep would knit bone, muscle, and skin back to almost new.

A spike of adrenaline surged through her, so she forgot her exhaustion, and the running shower. She sprinted down the stairs and ripped open the front door. Once on the wrap-around porch, she stopped short. Where was she going? There was no one to tell. No one to ask about what was going on. Nowhere to run.

-*And you're naked.*-

Lifting her face, eyes closed, she allowed the humid rays of the sun to bask her in their nurturing light.

Thankfully, the voice in her head allowed her the quiet moment.

Stumbling: Book One on The Fool's Path

Chapter Five

Dee picked up her pace, as if running from the truth of her thoughts was a real thing.

She'd been running the darkened, vacant streets of this town almost every night for the past year, and until two nights ago, she'd never had a problem. It seemed overly paranoid to stop doing the one thing that made her happy after one bad experience.

-Even though it goes directly against your promise to Mike?-

Her speed intensified as the thought proclaimed itself, arguments why her broken word was valid warring against her guilt.

If there were more of those things out here, she needed to know. She needed to stop them before any innocents got hurt.

Of course, this was not a point she mentioned to Mike. Rather than debate her refreshed pledge to him, she'd quickly agreed. She knew he'd chain her up if he had the slightest inkling she might go out to purposefully risk her neck, even if her reasons were altruistic. He still didn't quite believe her, but he couldn't avoid the fact that she'd been attacked. While the attack didn't prove the existence of a supernatural world, her amazing healing attributes forced questions she knew he'd rather avoid. They were questions *she'd* rather avoid.

She'd spent day after the attack sitting around, debating this single thing, trying to find the argument that would let her make good on her promise. But she kept coming back to the same conclusion: if someone got hurt, the guilt of it would be more then she could bear, even at risk to herself.

So, here she was. Running through the darkened, wooded landscape despite having said it was something she'd cease doing.

Distracted by a tingling in the back of her skull that had been slowly growing over the last few minutes, she slowed her pace. Like a word on the tip of her tongue, the semi-familiar feeling was just outside memory. Had she felt this the other night just before she hit the ground?

-*There!*-

There.

She dropped just in time for the attacker to sail over her. She stared stupidly as the creature refocused on its mark, launching itself back at her. Bracing herself, Dee managed to use its momentum against it, throwing it past her into the woods that surrounded the country road.

As if detached from herself, not sure what to do, Dee followed its path with her eyes. She peered into the dark in anticipation of a third attack. Feral hissing pinpointed the creature's location and her eyes snapped to its face.

Even in the dark, she noted its hateful stare. Its ferocity spiked the fear riding her body, freezing her movements. When the thing spoke, the hair on her body stood on end. "He thinks it is you, but all I see is a girl. He wastes his time."

Shocked by the words, too surprised to hear their meaning, Dee stood transfixed as the creature prepared to launch itself back at her.

Quietly, as if locked in some backroom in her mind, Dee was aware of a voice suggesting she pay attention to what was coming, but her brain was processing everything in a detached slow-motion, even as the rest of the world continued at its break-neck speed.

He? What he? Who?

Could she convince the creature to have a conversation with her? Would it tell her what was going on?

Crunching footsteps from the road brought her attention back to her surroundings. Her turn to see what else had shown up halted when the creature used her moment of distraction to rush her. The sound of steps stopped, closely followed by a loud blast that pushed her attacker to the side. Whipping her head towards the sound, Dee saw that the explosion had come from some guy's shotgun.

-What the hell?-

Dee turned her full attention to the newcomer, eyes flashing upwards as movement in the trees gave away the position of a second creature dropping behind him.

The man turned quickly and fired another loud blast that echoed through the woods as this second body found its head scattered among the leaves.

The gore of the exploding face set off her gag reflex. Before she could give-in to the instinct to throw-up, the first assailant's angry rush drew her attention. Injured, but not out, the creature dove for the newcomer who was checking that the body of the second attacker was out of the fight for good.

Dee lunged, tackling it before it could reach him, rolling in the earthy bramble to find herself straddled by the thing that, it was clear now, had once been a woman. Her long, thinning hair was a strangle of wispy threads that only emphasized the minor changes in her face. Her pupils dilated to completely take over the color of her iris and her teeth reached too far from her gums, pushing out her lips. Her fingers seemed just too long. And most especially, the look on her face that spoke of something more base than any human mind could reach. All this created a scary picture of violence.

-Was this your plan?-

Struggling to keep the snarling mouth away, Dee agreed with her inner-voice that this seemed, again, all too familiar. Maybe she had no business being out here with these things. Sure, she was as strong as them, but strength had nothing to do with fighting skill. Her last encounter had said much about her luck, not her ability to battle, and it seemed her luck had been used up.

"Don't move."

His words were unnecessary. Dee couldn't move, locked in perfect balance with the strength of the creature whose snarling face pushed down towards her, fangs suggesting that maybe it had never been human; that maybe vampires were real.

Another boom from the shotgun blasted all thoughts from her mind, forcing eyes closed against first, the shot, then the warm wetness of pieces of the creature's face raining down on her.

The warm goop was the straw. Her psyche caved.

Hysterically, Dee crab-walked out from under the dead pressure of the thing that had attacked her, continuing away from what was left of the body until her movement was forced to stop against the pressing inertia of a tree. The thing's head was sprayed into the brush, though its body continued to twitch with remaining nerve impulses.

Eyes blinking too fast, brain trying desperately to see anything but the gore in front of her, she rolled to her hands and knees, retching an empty stomach into the bramble of the forest floor, hoping the man with the shotgun wasn't there for her as well. There was nothing she could do until the bile finished its release from her stomach.

Energy sapped, eyes blurry with tears, she was finally able to look up at the man who had waited, patiently, for her to regain control of herself.

She hadn't noticed his calm acceptance of her reaction to having blood and gore rain down on her, or his quick check of the bodies to make sure they wouldn't rise again, despite their lack of brain matter. When she finally glanced up, rolling slowly away from the puddle she'd just made, he was checking his weapon.

He put a hand out to help her up.

She ignored his offer, and he flashed an amused smile as she rose to her feet.

-*Kill this guy!*-

The thought was earnest, though she pushed it from her mind. Rather than kill him, or run as her panic insisted should be the second option, she willed herself to look at the man more carefully.

Deep-seated arrogance wound tightly around his medium build. The tight, long-sleeved shirt he wore showed off a muscular frame that was functional rather than bulky. His over-six-foot height was too close, so she took a step back, eyes following the scar that ran down the left side of his face from his temple, skirting the edge of his eye socket before jutting out slightly to follow his cheekbone to end at the corner of his mouth. The scar hid an attractive face behind a sense of menace, and the short haircut screamed military, enunciated by the black tactical clothing he wore.

His eyes scanned the gore littering the ground before returning an expression of amused contempt to her. "Interesting choice."

Dee raised her eyebrows in question, his comment making her defensive. To hide her reaction, she used the edge of her shirt to wipe her face as best she could, holding her breath against the smell, refusing to throw-up again. Using the dark to trick her eye, she repeated to herself that it was mud. It was only mud.

-Mud despite the fact we haven't had rain for weeks?-

The man was pointing to the wooden stake Dee had shoved into the pocket of her sweatshirt in case a situation like this came up. She'd forgotten about it, and it now lay on the ground, useless. Telling herself she'd lost it before she could have used it allowed her to meet the stranger's humored gaze with a challenging frown. "Yeah? Guess I figured blasting the whole state into alert with a shotgun seemed overkill."

The stranger swept his eyes over the two bodies that would have been gnawing at Dee's bones right then if not for his interference. "You think this was overkill?"

She shrugged, a wave of exhaustion sapping her energy for more banter. Dropping her hands from the failed attempt at cleaning her face, she looked around. She just wanted to get home, climb into bed, and claw these images from her mind.

-Kill him. Take his weapons. He can't know about you.-

What could he possibly know? And why was her inner-nag so intent on killing this guy? It wasn't like she'd done anything to pique his curiosity except get her ass kicked.

-I think the fact that you're out here at all is curious.-

That might be true, but he was out here too.

-If you kill him, there will be no worrying.-
I'm not killing him.

She ignored his amused expression while he waited for her to sort through her thoughts.

Refusing to feel self-conscious under this gaze, Dee stood taller, meeting his arrogant expression for the first time, almost daring him to laugh at her, frowning when laughter filled his eyes. She wasn't sure what she would have done if he'd chuckled out loud.

Then it hit her, the obviousness of his presence that meant he knew what these things were.

She softened her expression, floating her eyes away from his to survey the carnage again. Taking a deep breath, she asked, "What are these things?"

The bloody mess scattered before her triggered another gag response. Afraid she might throw-up her actual stomach if she let her brain focus on it any more, she brought her attention back to his face. A small tremor had started in her hands, and she needed something to focus on that wasn't the image of brains splattered over the forest floor, some of which was drying to her face.

"Is this the first time you've seen these things?"

She was too distracted by maintaining calm to realize he'd ignored her question.

Did it matter if she told him about her? Maybe she should. Maybe, it would be a good idea to let someone know. Someone who knew more than she did about these things.

-No! No! No!-

She closed her eyes against the raging in her head, allowing the paranoia to grip her so she wouldn't start blabbing her life story to this guy. The weariness settling over her wasn't helping her senses. Trusting her inner-voice, knowing she wasn't in her best mind, she shrugged, opting for a non-answer.

He walked to one of the bodies and kicked its leg. "They're called Revenants. I've never heard of them being so close to human populations." Mumbling to himself, he said, "First time for everything, I guess."

He turned back to her. "Guess you were just lucky enough to run into them."

She stared blindly, remembering the night in the cemetery. "I saw one the other night."

"Yeah? Where?"

Dee stepped closer. "Two nights ago actually. Tackled me out on the road near here."

His surprise seemed genuine. "Really? That's hard to imagine. What happened to that one?"

Dee looked down, wondering how much she should say. It seemed prudent to lie, but she wanted more information from him.

She didn't catch the smile playing at his lips as she said, "It's dead."

A different smile came over him. An expression Dee couldn't read. "I see. As are these two. You think there are more around?"

-Don't start trusting this guy.-

The voice in her head was ignored while she watched the man, his athletic body pressing against his shirt. He obviously knew how to handle himself. A part of her wanted to invite him home to pick his brain, while another part agreed with the voice's suggestion that she kill him to resolve any future problems. Yet, she sort of owed him her life.

She shuddered at the thought that her life really had been in danger. Focusing on his words kept the panic at bay. "You're lucky. Not many come within their reach and live to tell about it."

"You seem to be alright," she said, turning away from him.

He smiled, a genuine reaction to her words. "My life is not like most."

These words brought her attention back to his face, her smile matching his. "Neither is mine."

"That's obvious." His eyes roved her face, more thoughts wandering through his eyes she couldn't decipher.

She frowned, the crickets and frogs creating a wall of sound around them.

"Do you actively—hunt—these things?" She wasn't sure the word to use, gesturing with her hands as she searched for vocabulary. If she'd thought chasing some creature from a bad horror movie through a cemetery was surreal, having this conversation in the woods with some mysterious stranger needed its own adjective.

"Not so much. I'm as surprised as you to see them here."

Her eyes sparked at this before squinting slightly in distrust. "So, then, what are you doing here?"

Smiling, the expression holding a mischievous edge, he met her eye. "I could ask the same of you."

-Kill him!-

He hadn't stepped forward, but the look in his eye and the tone of his voice gave the illusion he was suddenly closer, a looming presence pushing against her. She stepped away, eyes scanning the darkness for the most localized path of retreat.

Dee was surprised when he spoke again before she figured out how to respond. "There're not so many of these things to warrant actively hunting. I've never even heard of them being this close to where they might hurt anyone."

She nodded, eyes distrustful, not looking at him as she scanned the darkness.

-If you're not going to kill him, at least get out of here.-

Ignoring the voice in her head, she mulled the strangers words over. "You said that."

The cocky expression on his face was hard to interpret. She was annoyed with herself when she couldn't meet his heavy gaze.

"Why are you here then?" Her attention remained on the trees.

"I'm not sure you'd believe me."

She frowned, head turning so her eyes could come back to his face, her expression clearly saying, *don't screw with me.* "Try me."

He shrugged apologetically, glancing down at his fingers. "I don't know you well enough to tell such secrets."

Her eyebrows rose in disbelief at his brazen attitude, and she was reminded of a friend lost to the fire. He'd also been obnoxious in an arrogantly joyous way that had grown on her. She almost smiled, but wouldn't give him the satisfaction.

Still, the annoyance flashing in her eyes was real. "Fine." She turned, walking away from him into the woods, in the opposite direction from where she needed to go. She didn't know him, and getting near enough to him that he might pull something would have been stupid.

"What's your name?" he called after her, halting her steps before the darkness swallowed her from his vision.

Her head tilted, but she didn't turn around. "Dee."

"Dee, glad I was here to save your ass. I'm Hamal."

She spun, eyes flashing anger, simmering to annoyed humor when she saw the smile on his face. "Hamal? I think we're even."

He called after her retreating shadow, voice laughing, "How 'you figure?"

She waved a hand in a gesture that could have meant anything, this time not stopping to answer.

Stumbling: Book One on The Fool's Path

Chapter Six

Hours later, Dee was still awake, thoughts moving from the idea of tracking Hamal down to kill him to wishing she'd invited him back to her place. Even if he wasn't right for information, it'd been a long time since she'd spent the night with anyone.

-Really? The guy blows two bodies to pieces in front of you, and you want to get naked with him?-

She admitted it was absurd, rampant hormones taking control of her thoughts, but who better to intertwine her life with than someone who was already aware of the creepy-scarys wandering the night?

-Or who better to murder than someone who could bring trouble to your world?-

She sighed, throwing herself back on the bed, hair still wet from the shower she'd just come from.

She ran fingers down the scars on her arm, the only signs she'd been hurt days ago. Opening and closing her fist a few times to marvel at the miracle of it, she let it fall back to her side, thinking back on all the things she'd found she was able to do.

Skimming through memory, her thoughts focused on the most recent event and the creature whose words suggested they'd come just for her, despite what this Hamal implied about them rarely coming near human populations. The fact that they were here was proof that he didn't know everything about them.

-*Maybe he doesn't know anything. Or maybe,* he *brought them here.*-

He brought them here? She couldn't ignore that they'd both shown up at the same time.

She closed her eyes. If he was here on some mission to harm her, what should she do? Should she leave town? Where would she go? How long before he found her again? And why would he have saved her from her most recent encounter with the strange and unreal?

-*You should have killed him.*-

At least Mike would be safe if she skipped town.

Alarm shot through her at the idea that this newcomer might use Mike to get to her. Would leaving help Mike, or merely force Hamal to go to him when he might have otherwise left him alone?

Her head ached, spinning with too many questions. As risky as it was, maybe her best play was to find this Hamal to see what information he had about what was going on.

***

She hadn't realized she'd fallen asleep until she woke. Chilled and uncomfortable, she was still at the edge of the bed, feet on the floor, naked form bare to the room.

Riddled with goosebumps, she crawled up the mattress. Digging under the covers until warmth stole over her, she revealed in the idea of more sleep, even as the sun attempted to breach the thick curtains. Enjoying the pull of unconsciousness, something kept her from falling over the edge.

Focusing on her senses, she scanned to see what it might be keeping her awake. There were no sounds.

Not now, but had a sound woken her?

A rattle from downstairs brought her fully awake.

When the smells of coffee and the sweetness of French toast wafted over her, she remembered Mike had promised breakfast this weekend. It was a thing he had started doing a couple of months ago. He'd come by and force-convince her to leave the house to attempt to get her to connect with the real world.

-Real world?-

Her inner-voice scoffed at the idea, and she agreed, but it made Mike feel better to think she was trying to make something of herself, whatever that might mean.

She rolled over, searching for the time.

Ten A.M.

Forcing herself from the warmth she'd just found, she stumbled, eyes half-closed, across the room to her closet. She pulled on yoga pants, sports bra, and a tank top before allowing her feet to propel her to the kitchen. The unusual smells of cooking from her kitchen drawing rumbles from her stomach.

"Morning 'Case!" His voice was chipper and she resisted the urge to wince. Instead, she managed a laugh from behind her foggy-brained stupor. He hadn't called her that in a long time. Headcase, or just 'Case, had been his nickname for her back during her teenage years when she'd been stupid enough to think she knew everything, arguing her opinion on every topic. So heated would she get during these conversations, swearing she wasn't mad though her every gesture and volume suggested otherwise, that the nickname had been born.

He handed over a mug of black coffee as she headed for the table set near the double sliding glass doors that were often open to let in the sounds of the woods. Now bathed in morning sunshine, she squinted as the rays washed over her skin.

"Late night?" His voice was light, but she knew he was fishing to see if she'd been behaving herself.

"Not so late." She blew into her mug to distract her face from his studious stare.

She was glad she'd gotten rid of the clothes she'd come home in. Covered in blood and brains and vomit, they were buried in a bag within a bag in the trashcan in the garage beneath other garbage. Even in the throes of exhaustion, she hadn't wanted Mike to ever see them.

His voice portrayed his disbelief, but he didn't press the half-truth. "Glad to hear it. I thought we could go out today."

He turned, holding two plates piled high with delicious breakfast carbs. She stood to grab the real maple syrup from the fridge, wishing it had been warmed, but not wanting to let the French toast cool to make it so.

"Go out where?" She forced her voice to remain bland.

He had dove into his breakfast without pouring syrup over the toast. "Just out." His mouth was full, but she understood him fine.

She poured syrup over one side of the stack in front of her, setting it down slowly as she considered her options. After what she'd put him through earlier in the week, she wasn't sure she could come up with a good enough excuse to say no. There wasn't much to do in their small town, and she was a little curious about what he had in mind.

"What's the weather doing today? We could go for a hike." She smiled as she said it, watching Mike's face to see how just how badly he would take this suggestion.

Her obsession with the outdoors was new, and Mike didn't exactly share in her enthusiasm for long excursions of physical activity, especially now that her endurance so outmatched his. The only time they'd tried it, it'd been a day full of him yelling for her to wait up, while she swallowed her annoyance at his slow progress.

He grunted noncommittally.

Ultimately, they decided to drive the hour and a half to the nearest town to be labeled a city and see what they could find to do. Dee appreciated that Mike was so worried about her that he would take one of his rare days off to shuttle her around in an attempt to entertain her. He didn't like that she just sat around all day, living off what her father had left. She didn't like that he worried, but she couldn't blame him for it, either.

Last year, when she'd returned home after being away for over four years, she'd taken all the steps necessary to get back into school, but never pulled the trigger. She was currently missing the second semester she would have been attending classes. School was a good idea, something that might help her figure out where her life should go, but something in her just couldn't follow through. Part of her thought it was a waste to go when she didn't know what it was for. Another part simply stalled on restarting her life, reveling in avoiding reality as long as she was allowed.

While all these points often came up on outings such as this, today was not one of them. Mike held his lectures in check, and Dee allowed herself to relax from the pressures of hiding. It was nice to reconnect with him as the friends they'd once been, rather than have him worrying about her.

A pang of guilt settled in her stomach. Maybe she should have stayed away and let him live his life, rather than force him to stay and watch over her. If she'd never returned here, would he have eventually moved on?

There'd been a girlfriend when he was in college, then another he'd been with when her father had died. She didn't know what happened to that one. It had never come up, and she never felt right asking, too afraid she had been the reason for his life halting in the town her father had always expected them to move on from.

Digging for the information she was too afraid to ask directly, she commented, "So, I haven't seen any girls around lately."

Mike was driving, staring out the windshield. "Nothing serious. Not a whole lot of eligible bachelorettes matriculating to no-wheres-ville."

She laughed. It had been one of the things her and her father had planned for; that she move to a city with more people and opportunities. Staying here was never in the cards, yet here they both were, one trapped by the memory of the very man who'd wanted more for both of them, the other caught by those trappings.

"You're traveling a lot though."

"Sure. Busy schedule. Not much time to take a breath and look at the sights, let alone date."

She felt worse. "Maybe it's time we relocate."

She was staring out the passenger window, not sure what her face would betray, not sure how she even felt about the suggestion that popped out of her mouth. Could she leave her father's house? She wouldn't necessarily need to sell it. Her inheritance would allow her to keep it and buy something else in a place she might be able to start an actual life. Mike brought in a pretty penny as controlling head in her father's company. There would be no worries about income.

"You think you're ready for that?" His voice was quiet, tone proving he had stayed only for her.

Her eyes closed. A tear fell down her cheek. "I can't wallow here forever."

"Where should we go?" Mike's voice was more cheerful, less guarded than his initial question. She tasted the excitement in his words. Her stomach dropped further.

She shrugged, taking a deep breath to wash the sadness from her voice, forcing a smile to reach her eyes as she turned to him. "Dad always pushed for New York or San Fransisco."

Eyes on the road, Mike said, "You were at NYU."

"Yeah, California is so far."

She remembered the conversations with her father Mike been involved with. Her father had been instrumental in guiding both of them towards their futures, knowing the small town was great for a quiet, protected childhood, but not so great when establishing oneself in a competitive job market. Dee had been a rare adolescent in absorbing her father's every suggestion, never seeming to mind his guiding hand; never rebelling to do her own thing.

After he'd passed, she'd struggled to find her way. She'd held on for a few months, always planning to return to school. In the end, she'd given in to the dismay that swarmed her. Running off to tour the country, she'd maintained just enough contact with Mike so he didn't worry too much.

She knew it'd been hard for him, especially when her weeks long trip turned into months that turned into years. What she heard in his voice whenever she called to check in that had her calling less and less. She'd been a coward.

-*You're still a coward.*-

She refused to imagine what it had been like for him when she'd disappeared. Through all that time, he had stayed here in the hopes that she'd one day reappear.

-*Good thing he did.*-

"Maybe California is the right answer this time around." His words brought her attention back to the conversation.

She nodded, thinking of Hamal, and whether he would find her on the opposite side of the country.

Pushing her fear of things unknown aside, she forced herself to remain engaged with Mike. "Let's schedule a house hunting trip."

A smile filled his face so bright Dee couldn't help but match it.

***

Hamal had watched the house all day. Nestled into the brush beneath the trees in Desiree's front yard, he arrived just in time to see her leave with Mike. When they hadn't returned after a few hours, he got cranky, wondering if she had it in her to flee. He hadn't read that in last night's body language, but she'd never left for such an extended period. She'd barely left the house, aside from her midnight jogs, so a day trip right after their meeting had him fidgeting with anxiety.

When Mike's car pulled into the driveway that evening, Desiree nestled in the passenger seat, his pinched muscles finally relaxed.

He dropped lower in the shadows as Dee perked around, eyes scanning the darkness in a way that was more perceptive than it should have been. Her eyes moved over where he hid, and his heart skipped a beat. Had she seen him?

If she had, she hadn't indicated it, calmly turning to follow Mike into the house.

Still isolated from his superiors about what he should do with her, he was sticking to his plan. He was sure the presence of Revenants-as-assassins was proof enough that one of the other Houses was after her. How Zibanitu and Porrima weren't all over this, he couldn't know, but he knew enough about their protocols to know that if they hadn't reached out, it was for good reason.

Wondering, for the zillionth time, who this girl was kept him excited rather than fearful.

Chapter Seven

Excited to have something to stimulate him after torturously waiting around with nothing to do for days, Hamal had to wonder if maybe she really did have a death wish. Would any other sane person be out, running through the night after being attacked on multiple occasions? Anyone else would have barred themselves inside to ensure the monsters couldn't break through the door to find them hiding under their beds.

It was another reason he was excited to engage her: not only to succeed in his mission but to figure out what made her tick. Her reaction on both nights to her attacks told of how afraid she'd been, but she'd faced both situations head on and was still out for more. That was the most telling of anything he'd seen so far.

His truck sat half on the road, half in the grass near where she'd been attacked that first night. As he had that night, he watched her jog her standard route through the camera feeds, looking up to watch her move past the truck when she drew close. But, instead of running by on her usual path through the town streets, she turned to run into the trees across the street from where he was parked, her speed surpassing any normal human's by the time the trees swallowed her from view.

This change in pattern was a development he hadn't been ready for. He scrambled out of his truck, grabbing his pack before hiking off into the brush, hoping he'd be able to track her even as he knew he'd never be able to keep up, cursing the lazy relaxation he'd fallen into.

As he pushed through the trees, a flare of nervousness poked at him. If she could see where she was going in this environment well enough to sprint through it, she would have easily seen him lurking in the shadows of her front yard. Was she leading him into a trap?

He ignored the unfamiliar feeling of nervousness that threatened his senses. While the idea that she'd seen him skulking about her front yard made him nervous, excitement overrode it. His blood thrilled at the possibility of a trap ahead. It had been so long since a situation had pushed his limits. He'd seen a glimmer of her speed. He'd seen her survive wrestling not one, but two, Revenants. Knowing she had no fight training, he was eager to see if he could take her. His exceptional training versus her brute strength could be an exciting match.

As he crept through the woods, he pulled his NVG's from his pack. Their use illuminated the dark world to a monotoned white hue. This augmented sight allowed him to pick up his pace, though he continued to focus on not snapping every branch underfoot to announce his presence to everything within one-hundred yards.

His attention snapped to the side when his ears picked up sounds other than the cacophony of frogs and crickets. There weren't any large night creatures he needed to worry about in this part of the country, so he wasn't concerned it was some terrifying predator out for its nightly kill, though if other Revenants were about, he might have a worse problem. He moved at a quicker pace, taking the risk that what he was hearing was Dee and not something he'd rather not run into.

The trees ahead erupted in loud thrashings as something humanoid darted by, followed closely by a second thing, their size not nearly as massive as the noise of their passing suggested. Based on the size and gait of the second form, he was sure he'd found Dee, glad she seemed to be chasing, rather than being chased.

No longer worried about how much noise he was making, he followed the pair. When the noise of their passage changed, he stopped fast, waiting for their changed direction to return them to him.

***

Moving into the trees was like slipping through a portal to a peculiar world where she had purpose.

She let the feeling wrap around her, refreshed by the empowerment that was a long-lost friend. So long she'd been harboring a self full of doubt, pushing questions behind shields of avoidance, that this odd sense of confidence was as welcome as it was strange.

If she'd given herself time to reflect, she might have realized much of this facade was brought on by the previous night's battle, her adrenaline high tricking her memory into viewing the event as an exciting adventure rather than a terrifying near-death encounter. But instead of contemplating this sudden shift in her reality, she ran.

What should have been evident from the start slowly filtered to the forefront of her mind: her eyesight was astonishing. Until meeting Hamal, she hadn't clued into it. Even on the brightest of nights, the trees sucked light to inky blackness. In the last moments of their conversation, she'd been able to see him fine as day, but it'd been obvious he hadn't seen her.

Then, a couple of nights ago he'd hovered just behind the treeline in front of her house, crouched in darkness that should have been enough to hide him from any searching eyes. His confident posture, portraying his full belief that there was no way for him to be seen, had made that fact clear.

She was still deciding what to make of catching him spying on her.

Oddly, it didn't incite dread, but rather a strange calm. Maybe acceptance of coming changes? Despite her subconscious still suggesting she kill him, she couldn't find it in herself to be afraid of him. He had helped her, hadn't he?

-*Too many questions. Just kill him. Then, no worries.*-

But what if he had answers? If she got rid of him, she had no way of tracing his path to find what he knew.

She let these thoughts pass to nothing as she succumbed to the thrill of the wilds around her. She pumped her legs harder, the snapping of leaves on her face a steady discomfort worth dealing with for the exhilaration of her power.

Even through this, something nagged at the back of her thoughts to finally wriggle its way to the forefront of her mind.

Stopping, she studied the strange tingling in the base of her spine, wondering at its cause. Was it the same feeling she'd had the other night?

It was too subtle for her to be confident in its similarity, but a warning was shouting its way to the surface of her consciousness, until the realization struck her like a slap to the face: *The creatures! You can sense when they're near!*

Unlike the other night, when the idea had still been a question, tonight it was so evident as to challenge how she hadn't been sure before.

Spinning, she caught the action of the thing just as it was about to launch at her. Dee pinned it in place with a weighted glare. Staring into its eyes, having ruined its surprise attack, she felt the power of the creature hum behind her eyes as it held its position, feral gaze gaping back at her.

They sized each other up, tasting in the air between them the level of threat each might pose to the other; anticipating how the other might react to a next move.

Fortunately for the creature, Dee's confidence didn't carry over to include knowledge of action. Staring back at the form whose edges blended with the foliage around it, Desiree was caught with how human this one looked. She wouldn't have noted this one as anything but human if not for the strange buzzing in her skull. In her head, it felt similar, but its appearance suggested it was something different than what had come for her thus far.

Time stretched as she waited, no idea how to press an offensive. Not forced to react to a rushing assault, Dee had no plan.

"What will you do, strange creature?" The hissing voice was low, almost whispered, each syllable stretched.

Dee gaped. *I'm the strange creature?*

The thing in the bushes sensed her hesitancy, the drop in confidence its voice had caused.

It sprang.

Even caught unaware, there was enough distance between them for Dee to react. Still, her combatant managed to wrack destruction across her shirt and skin with inhuman claws Dee hadn't noticed while studying its face.

Dee grit her teeth, more against the annoyance of her ineptitude than the pain that was kept at bay by chemicals flooding her system. Her eyes managed to stay on the creature as it rolled away, coming to its feet in one fluid motion, un-phased by her clumsy movements.

-You still have full function of your limbs. Point to you.-

The creature, eyes still focused on her with a furious intensity, spoke again. "You are untrained, even if you are strong. I was sent to test you, but I think instead, I will end you."

-That doesn't seem friendly.-

Barely contemplating its words, Dee was forced to backpedal from another attack. She flung herself to the side, just out of reach of claws threatening to cause more damage.

This wasn't at all what she'd expected when anticipating another fight. This was more than the snarling, reactionary beasts she'd been able to defend herself into winning against. This was a cognitive fighter, and Dee was in over her head.

-I think this time you really might die.-

Her panic crested beyond her body's capacity to understand.

Then, the fear fell away, overtaken by a numbing calm. The absolute truth that she was facing her death transformed a terrified state into a euphoric experience that brought clarity. This previously unknown lucidity wrapped a stillness around her that allowed her to *see*. A seeing that granted her knowledge to a purposeful path of action.

She was suddenly in motion, agile muscles bringing her body up and around, so she was taking the advancing creature by the arm, tugging and swinging so the body followed, spinning over itself to slam into the earth with a grunt of expelled air.

-Nicely done. See what focus will get you.-

It was a move Dee had learned years ago during a self-defense class. She'd barely been able to make it work then, even with a motionless partner helping her through the movements. They'd laughed at the idea of ever using it in a real-world application, especially for self-defense, but the move had lain in her memory where her focus latched onto it.

The Revenant's underestimation of her was the only reason it worked, and Dee knew it, even as she allowed the briefest of satisfaction to pass through her.

-How under-appreciated luck is. I wonder when yours will run out?-

The underhanded comment of her inner-cynic broke the spell. Time resumed its breakneck speed. Dee released a breath she felt she'd been holding since first locking eyes with her attacker. The Revenant, as stunned by its meeting with the ground as it was by Dee's ability to survive, stared upwards, eyes widening in a brief register of shock before transforming into spitting rage.

Dee stepped away, bracing for another attack, allowing the Revenant to flip from its back to hands and knees in an accomplishment that emphasized its inhuman agility. The pair stared each other down, Dee waiting for what would come, the other contemplating the odds of a successful attack.

Deciding against it, the attacker took off into the trees. Dee gave chase, thoughts of another night when she'd found herself unconscious in a cemetery outweighed by an instinct that insisted she follow the thing that could kill her.

-Maybe this will go better for us?-

She reminded herself that she'd survived that night.

Right on its heels, Dee was taken off guard when it abruptly pivoted. It kicked a leg against the thick trunk of a tree as leverage to spin around to reverse its defensive position to offense.

With just enough time to sidestep from its path, Dee moved behind a bigger tree. In another surprise move, instead of attack, it continued running in a straight line, back the way they'd just come.

A piece of Dee's mind was grateful for the change in direction. The way they'd been headed would have quickly put them out on the main road in town, opening the possibility she might be forced to explain what was going on to a random townsperson. Another piece of her mind wondered what in the hell the thing was doing.

-Not that it's likely you'll survive this night to have to worry about explaining yourself.-

She didn't argue, but if she let the creature go, she was sure it would be back another night. Heaven forbid it figured out where she lived. *Don't put off 'till tomorrow what you can do today*, her father's voice rang in her head.

The crazed gait of the creature laid a path of broken branches and trampled ferns ahead of her so Dee was forced to dodge and jump or risk turning an ankle. When a good-sized branch fell in time to hit her in the head, scraping against her face, she instinctively caught it against herself, ready to throw it in a fit of annoyance. Instead, she held it to her, realizing she had no weapon to help kill the thing she chased.

-Hadn't thought that far ahead, huh?-

She hadn't thought ahead at all. There hadn't been a whole lot of thinking going on as far as this entire crazy situation was concerned, but she was too stubborn to give up the chase now.

Gripping the branch as thick as her wrist and as long as her arm, she felt stupid for not having brought a weapon. The one she'd killed in the cemetery hadn't needed its head blown apart, but it had required a tool. She wasn't sure she was up to punching her fist through the things chest or ripping its head off with her bare hands. She wasn't even sure she could do either of those things. She hoped the branch was enough.

She cursed Hamal, part of her glad he hadn't shown up so she could pretend he wasn't some creep with an unknown agenda. His absence allowed her the delusion that his arrival had nothing to do with these things that were after her. The timing of their shared arrival to town was purely coincidence.

-Pretty slim argument.-

Hand clenched around her new weapon, she picked up a burst of speed, pouncing on the thing running full out in front of her.

***

Hamal came through the trees, frantically scanning the darkness for some visual that would bring him closer to his mark. The sounds he'd followed had gone quiet, so his mind went to the idea that he was too late to save Dee from whatever had found her.

Forcing this from his mind, he stumbled through a thick patch of bramble, stopping fast before tripping over a pair of legs stretched prone in the dark.

Concern that he'd just stumbled over Dee's dead body turned to relief when her voice brought his attention from the forest floor. "Seems to be more of these things around than you let on."

The strain in her voice emphasized the effort she was exerting to ensure the creature never got back up. Hamal looked back to the legs across his path, realizing they belonged to the Revenant that wasn't moving.

Hamal couldn't deny a small part of him was disappointed that he hadn't played the savior once again, while another felt an odd sense of pride that she hadn't needed his help.

He frowned at this latter point.

Stepping so he could see Dee's face, the scene came into focus. Hamal suppressed a grin. The girl was battling a Revenant already turning to husk. It would not be getting up, though Dee wasn't convinced. Her arms shook with the effort she was applying to the thick branch she'd managed to stick through the creature's chest, so much so, Hamal was sure she'd impaled it to the ground.

He scanned her form, noting the scratches she'd gained from this new encounter, while also noting there was too much blood staining her clothes to be explained as splatter from the damage she'd inflicted on her target. How many wounds had she suffered that were already healed?

Who was this girl? And were Zi and Porrima still unsure what was happening here?

Harder still to believe was that Hamal's meager human skills were all that stood between this anomaly of a girl and the things coming after her. Hamal could accept the idea that the information hadn't been available when he'd first been sent on this mission, but the continued silence was feeding a wary apprehension he wasn't used to dealing with.

These questions had him miss the opportunity to throw a sarcastic comment about her continued struggle with a corpse.

"This one was way smarter than the others. It had a full-on conversation with me. Then, right as I thought I had it, it turned on me. It friggin' tricked me."

Dee's statement pulled another layer of worry over him. A talking Revenant wasn't a Revenant at all, but something else. His mask of mischievous contempt slipped as he processed what this could mean, glad his goggles concealed his face from her questioning eyes.

Was whoever sending these things increasing the aptitude of the hunter? Should he expect an even more skilled assassin to show up next? Or was there more than one player after Dee?

Hamal's hands itched to pick up his phone. He'd never been cut off from a source to gather information, and he realized just how much he counted on the backup. He was good, but against increasingly powerful foes, he'd need to tag out. He wasn't arrogant enough to deny that.

Still, his decision to contact Dee was enough of a breach that he didn't want to complicate his position further by breaking this order of no communication.

Staring at the wilting corpse, he allowed himself the wasted second to wish he'd gotten here just a little earlier so he could have heard the words the creature had spoken. If it could talk, it could answer questions.

He remembered hearing of a thing like Dee's words suggested. Those that maintained their conscious minds, despite not being fully transitioned into the Soldiers the process was meant to create. Hamal had never been told what the transition rate was, but he imagined it couldn't be great. The question of him being turned had come up once, Zi's answer that he wouldn't risk such a highly prized asset to such a risky bet.

There were many things never directly questioned, and the hows of this process was one of them.

In his time with Zi, Hamal had gleaned, through conversations he was never supposed to have heard, that only three of the Masters had the ability to create Soldiers from humans, Zi being one of them. The process was risky, Revenants being one of a handful of possible outcomes if the transition went badly. Advanced Revenants, like what Dee was currently pressing into the earth (if they were called something else, he'd never heard it), were even more rare, with death being the most common overall outcome.

It wasn't often Hamal was at a loss. To say he was frustrated stated it mildly.

"This one isn't getting up again, is it?" Dee's question forced Hamal back to the moment.

With a smooth motion that belied the frustrated energy humming through him, Hamal drew his shotgun, pointing it at the creature's head, the weapon's passing movement ruffling Dee's hair, who threw herself away. "Whoa, whoa, whoa! Can I please get out of this without brains splattered all over me?"

Hamal smiled, a malicious glint of teeth that barely masked his desire to expel some pent-up energy. He paused, giving the dirt-and-blood smeared girl the extra second to move away before firing the weapon into the creature's face. It wouldn't have gotten up, but shooting its face off made him feel better.

Satisfied, he turned his attention to the girl who was brushing at her tight workout pants, unsuccessfully attempting to dislodge the dirt and grime she'd picked up from her fight. Leaves stuck to her like Velcro, pointing out of her hair like some poorly designed crown of thorns.

He chuckled, the sound bringing her gaze sharply to him, head angled down, so her eyes peered up from beneath lashes heavily shadowing her face. Even with the bright vision his goggles allowed, her eyes were pools of black. Another might have felt the hand of terror slide down their spine, but he'd seen too many scarier things. "C'mon. I'll give you a ride home."

When she frowned in response, he stepped forward, dropping the offered hand. "I know you have questions. So do I."

His smile didn't warm her to him. A glint in her eye shone with some unvoiced threat. A dare for him to try something against her?

He cocked an eyebrow to match the half-grin spread on his lips. "I bet I can even show you a few moves, so you won't get your ass kicked next time one of these things shows up."

The set of her shoulders squared. Adrenaline surged through him. Was she going to attack him?

He loosened his knees, readying himself.

When her shoulders sagged, it was obvious whatever fight she'd thought about putting up had fled, as had the opportunity for him to push his way into her world. This latter point was probably a good thing. Purposefully ignoring his directive not to make contact, he'd saved her life, a fact he was convinced would excuse indiscretion. But, as much as he'd crossed the line, there was limit to how badly he could screw this up. She'd just saved him from that.

Still, he was disappointed, not able to accept defeat. He forced a broader smile. "I'll show you that you can trust me. Then we'll get to showing you how to fight."

She searched his face. Maybe an answer to some internal question? Whatever it was, she didn't find it.

When she walked off into the woods he didn't try to stop her.

Despite this ending, he wasn't wholly disheartened.

Stumbling: Book One on The Fool's Path

Chapter Eight

Killing him probably was the best option. He'd been watching her, and not in that sexy, flattering kind of way. He'd been on her property, lurking in the shadows of the trees when Mike had dropped her off the other night. Adding in his repeated coincidental appearances, she was beginning to think it'd been him in the cemetery whose touch had brought her from unconsciousness.

-The first time he failed to facilitate your death.-

She closed her eyes tightly against this rationale she refused to believe. There was no reason for her to accept any of the things Hamal had said, but she still didn't think he was there as an agent against her.

She chuckled to herself, quieting the voice in her head for the first time in hours as she allowed her panicked anxiety to turn to ironic astonishment. Had it only been five days since the attack that had ended in the graveyard? Six? Her mind had trouble settling on this. It seemed like weeks had passed. It felt like she'd had more conversations with the mysteries stalker than two short repartees.

The SUV she'd run past tonight before heading off into the trees was his. She was sure of it. And hadn't she seen it on other nights? It explained how he'd found her so deeply in the woods on this most recent excursion. Even if he shared her same compulsion to jog late at night, he would have no reason to be hiking through the woods.

-Regardless, he's seen too much from you. You need to kill him.-

Even if he had been watching her this whole time, she wasn't killing him. She wasn't killing anyone. There were enough problems with her psyche that she wasn't sure what killing an actual human being would do to her. And she was sure, even if his presence was linked somehow with the things attacking her, that he wasn't working against her.

-Except he knows all about them. Except he's been watching you. Spying on you.-

Her eyes flashed to the windows. Anyone standing in the front yard, even if buried behind the layers of trees that fenced her property from the road, would easily see what she was doing. Not that there was ever anything of note to watch.

Gazing past her reflection in the glass, she wondered if she was staring right at him.

The idea startled her so she raced from the room towards the back of the house where the open kitchen ended in another windowed wall she had an easier time looking through, as no lights inside the house reflected back at her to impede her view. The exterior darkness was thick. Anything could be out there, waiting, biding its time.

Shivering, she turned away from the windows to make her way to her father's office; a place she rarely entered. It was one of few rooms in the house without windows.

As Dee crept softly over the threshold, her shoulders heaved relief that any prying eyes wouldn't be able to stare at her in this room. Her eyes swept the space, noting everything sat as it had on the day he died. It was kept dust free and polished, but not a thing was put away or removed. In all the time she was gone, Mike hadn't disturbed anything, and she'd never been inclined to, either.

Leaning back in the oversized leather chair, eyes closed, Dee embraced the memory of the dead to distract herself from thoughts of the living.

***

A thermal read of the yard indicated nothing around the house that might have spooked her into retreating. The look on her face just before she'd run from the kitchen suggested she'd been thinking too hard about all the things she didn't know. If only she'd let him in, he could answer so many questions. Just maybe, she could answer a few of his.

Hamal watched her move quickly to the office he'd never seen her enter, glad he'd decided to put up the camera in a room that had appeared unused when he'd initially scoped out the house. That it was a shrine to her father was obvious.

His working theory was that she had some mild amnesia. It explained why she didn't remember who had Initiated her. It explained why she didn't recognize the creatures who'd attacked her, and it explained how she didn't know how to use her gifts. Sure, there were holes in the theory, but most could be explained by the amnesia.

Running over arguments and counter-arguments further built up his excitement. He considered just walking up to her front door to force her to accept his explanation of what he was doing there. Sure, she could probably kick his ass. Sure, he was forbidden to do any such thing by his directive. But he'd already disobeyed, and he was committed to gaining her trust and teaching her to survive the next attacks until someone told him otherwise.

He reminded himself that he couldn't forget that she was dangerous to him. The thought briefly interrupted his planning. If she considered him a threat, would she consider killing him? Would trusting him be worth the risk? In a role reversal, he'd have already killed her. He relied on her naiveté to protect him from such a decision, but would he be wrong?

***

She'd narrowed the Hamal issue down to three possible scenarios. One: he was in cahoots with the creatures trying to kill her, so he was trying to kill her. Two: he was there to try and save her from being killed by the things attacking her. Three: he was sending these things after her so he could play white knight to get close to her.

Part of her leaned towards theory one, while the other part didn't agree. He'd seemed genuinely surprised on this last occasion when she'd explained to him about the thing talking to her. Sure, that wasn't enough to sell to a jury, but she didn't feel he was out to get her.

Theory two seemed the most probable, though why wouldn't he just tell her what was going on? It was insulting to her intelligence to think she'd believe the coincidence of it all.

-Is it, though?-

Theory three was the one she lingered on the longest. If not for showing up too late to be of any real help on two of three occasions, she might have been sold on this explanation. If she hadn't been able to handle herself, she'd have been dead. Twice. Pretty lousy planning for someone trying to set up a rescue.

-Unless they were never really going to kill you. Or, he really expected them to kill you, and we're back to the first theory.-

She frowned. Her only argument against this was the fact that she should have died that first night.

-Maybe he knows who you are. Maybe he knew you couldn't be killed. Maybe you can't die…-

Her breath caught in her throat at this latter idea. She'd never considered it, and rather than deal with the swell of emotion the concept brought from the pit of her chest, she tucked it away with all those other things she wouldn't face. Even her inner dialogue was quiet for once.

She sighed, letting her thoughts return to previous concerns. Even if she were wrong in all her theories, killing him would put her back to zero. She was tired of not knowing. Maybe it was time to stop avoiding the whole thing. Forced to search for answers she'd shunned, she wondered why she hadn't just faced them all to begin with.

Her nightmares reminded her why. On the other side of those fiery flames were answers she was too afraid to see. If she was directly responsible for the deaths of her friends… she didn't want to see that.

It was in this possibility that her brain had erected a wall against knowing.

Stumbling: Book One on The Fool's Path

Chapter Nine

-Seriously, you can't stay in for one night?-

She'd promised Mike she wouldn't go gallivanting all over town. She wasn't even sure gallivanting was something that could be done in a place this small. Either way, she wasn't confident she could resist the temptation to go out, despite her promise.

Pressing her forehead into the cold glass of the sliding doors that would lead from the kitchen to the backyard, she refocused this strange compulsion into an effort to figure out why she had it.

Before this new hobby hit her, she'd never even worked out, let alone felt the need to pound mile after mile of asphalt in marathon running sessions. The habit had started shortly after she'd returned home and, before now, she'd never questioned it.

She'd tried to keep her promise, going out during the day, or earlier in the evening. It was never the same. She felt intruded upon by the members of the town going about their varies tasks. It was as if the consciousness of the world encroached upon her solitude.

It made no logical sense, but it wasn't something she'd been able to stop. Even on those days when she'd run until she thought her legs would collapse beneath her, she'd been compelled to go back out once the sun had long set and the rest of humanity slept.

Sighing, she pressed her hands into the glass, interrogating another hard-to-decipher topic: the question of these creatures who hadn't given up in their obsession of taking her out.

-*Vampires?*-

She cringed at the word as if the term made everything crazier. Whatever they were called, they were real. All of this was really happening.

Revenants. That's what Hamal had called them, but her mind continued to think of them as the more fictionalized term.

-*A rose by any other name...*-

That they were after her had to be because of what she'd become. Unfortunately, that wasn't a story she could tell. She just couldn't remember. At first, she'd purposefully kept her thoughts from recalling any of it, but now, after digging through feelings she'd wanted nothing but to forget, the truth of what happened to her was nowhere to be found.

She shuddered, hands shaking from the stress of knowing someone, or something, was trying to kill her. So focused on the minute-to-minute of what was going on, any larger picture had been beyond her to consider. Would this behind-the-scenes puppet-master expect the answers to these questions? Would the facts that she couldn't recall help her or more quickly facilitate her death?

Struggling to breathe, she used the unyielding surface of the glass as an anchor to ensure her legs maintained their roots on the floor. Was this what a panic attack felt like?

-*You went out to fight them of your own volition last night, but tonight the thought of them is immobilizing you with fits of terror?*-

Last night it hadn't been so prevalent that someone was trying to kill her. Not on such a personal level. Last night there was only the knowledge that these strange things existed. Last night, her only goal was to ensure ignorant passers-by wouldn't get attacked.

This line of thinking calmed her mind. She couldn't succumb to cowardice at the expense of someone else. If there were more of them around, even if they were after her, could she live with herself if someone else was attacked?

-If you were worried about the safety of the town, you'd have started your patrol at a time that wouldn't give Mike a heart attack.-

Was she actually concerned about the safety of others, or was it a convenient argument she knew would supersede her promise to Mike without the need to feel guilty?

They're here to kill you. The echoing words were something different than the inner-voice whose sarcasm had become a standard commentary in her head. This was something else. This was the edge of clinical madness.

She perched in the nearest chair at the large dining table, sorting through her thoughts. Something similar to having her feelings hurt swelled to the front of her emotional upheaval. Someone wanted to kill her. Kill her. KILL Her. Kill. Her. How was she supposed to feel about that? How could she not take that personally?

Her head hurt. She was emotionally exhausted. So many thoughts had shut her body down.

Unfortunately, her body shutting down didn't give her a reprieve from the torrent of questions flooding her mind.

If they were targeting her now, whoever they might be, had they been targeting her all along? Was it her fault her friends were dead? Was it her they'd come after when the house had caught fire? Had the house been set on fire to kill her, but somehow she'd gotten out? And, why had they even been there at all?

There was still no recollection of details surrounding the house she'd witnessed in flames. She'd never seen it before it was on fire. She had no memory of the interior or meeting her friends there. Ray's beat up truck, the only transportation the friends had shared, had been in the driveway. It was the deciding factor in why she thought they'd all been there, though she hadn't stuck around to see what the police, or fire department, or anyone, discovered. Had the house ever been found? Were her friend's families still unsure what had ever happened to them? Were they all still lying as dust under the collapsed remains of the building?

Her breaths were heavy, tears streaming down her face, but still the thoughts came.

When she'd finally left the smoldering pile, it was to move blindly through trees and fields for days. No sleep. No food. But that had to be impossible so she passed this detail off as a side-effect of the shock she'd experienced.

She blinked fast, bringing herself back to the kitchen of her father's house.

With slow steps, she moved to the front of the house, pausing with her hand on the doorknob to consider her decision. After a moments hesitation, she stepped onto the porch. Her eyes searched the treeline. He was there, she knew it.

There was fifty yards between her and the first row of giant oaks, scattered with the thinner beech and pines that climbed fifty feet overhead. She could see well enough, despite the blackness of shadows beneath the trees. Hopping the banister, she moved through the yard, confidence, borne from faith in her decision, wrapped around her.

-*Don't be stupid.*-

She ignored the voice in her head.

"Hamal? I think it's time we talked." Her voice was conversational, not loud, but she knew he would hear. That he would respond was something she also did not doubt.

He stepped from the trees, smile covering his face as he looked her up and down, taking in the decisive attitude. "Thank god. The mosquitos in this place are ridiculous." A hand waving in the air around his face emphasized his point.

She ignored his attempt at humor. "You can teach me to fight?"

"I think it was my purpose in life to teach you to fight," he replied, smile gone.

She nodded, looking past him into the darkness beyond. "We can start tomorrow?"

His face was blank. "Tomorrow. Early."

Her eyes met his. "Not too early."

He stepped forward, tone lowered, all trace of joviality gone. "Let's be clear. I will train you, but this will not be some random extracurricular activity. This will be your life. You don't have time to treat this as a hobby. We will start *early*."

The change in his demeanor pushed through Dee's confidence. She forced herself to hold her ground and found she couldn't meet his eyes. What was she getting into? Fear asked her to renege on her proposal. But, she'd been scared before. At least this fear would help guide her through the others.

-Or it will kill you by surprise.-

Ignoring her inner cynic, she asked, "What do you mean, I don't have time?"

She blinked fast under his penetrating glare before a smile covered whatever he'd excavated from her expression. In spite of the smile, his eyes bore down on her with an intensity that made her squirm. "You know they'll keep coming. And they'll keep getting stronger."

She dropped her chin in the slightest nod. Hamal matched the gesture, looking past her to the grand house. "You know, if I stay here, I'll be able to keep an eye on things. We'll have more time to train."

Dee was unable to keep the dismay off her face. She'd had the same idea, but hearing it from him made it seem like a spectacularly bad one.

-You think?-

He flashed a winning smile, the scar on his face dancing with the movement, drawing Dee's eye, so his earlier intensity was wiped clean. "You think about it. I'll be back in the morning."

Moving to walk away, he stopped short, turning back to her with a serious look on his face. "You stay in tonight. You stay in every night I'm not with you."

She nodded, wondering at the fluttering of butterflies his words uncaged from her stomach.

When he was no longer in sight, her inner voice chastised, *You let him tell you what to do?*

She frowned. She had, but wasn't that what she'd just signed up for?

She made her way back to the house, wondering what she was supposed to do now that she couldn't run.

Chapter Ten

Back at her house the next morning, Hamal's spirits soared. Not even thoughts of what might happen to him when Zi found out he'd disobeyed a direct order could take away his excitement at finding out firsthand what this girl was capable of.

When no one came to the door at his insistent knocking, his excitement turned to annoyance. No way was she going to change her mind and stand him up. No way she was going to give him the slip and take off in the meager few hours he'd allowed himself to sleep. Talk about a reputation buster.

Easily bypassing the lock on the door for the second time, he was through the house and up the stairs, barely looking around on his way. Extensive reconnaissance had given him a perfect awareness of the house's layout, so he knew her bedroom was at the far end of the hall, taking up almost the entire east wing of the upstairs.

Surprised by the locked door of her bedroom, the deterrent held for only a second before he slammed through it. Not expecting someone to be just inside the door, he found himself flipped to his back.

Staring at the ceiling, he laughed, a genuine, full-throated sound. It'd been a long time since he was taken so completely by surprise. Apparently, she'd heard him racing up the stairs. She wasn't just some stupid girl, as he continued to forget.

"Christ, Hamal! I almost killed you."

He rolled his head to look at her. "I doubt it. But nice job taking my feet. I never saw it coming."

An oversized t-shirt was all that covered her. Unable to peel his eyes from so much naked skin, he took in the line of her leg that ran to where the edge of the shirt barely covered what lay—

"Alright! Get out! Let me get dressed!"

He rolled away, tearing his eyes from her. "Be out front in two minutes! I can't believe you made me wake you up."

"You never said how early."

He laughed at the shyness now lacing her words, allowing his eyes to travel back in the room as she moved away towards the closet, not ashamed to follow her movements as she pulled panties on, then leggings, stripping the shirt off to reveal flawless skin against a femininely-muscular back.

He quietly said, "Next time, I'll be more specific about what early means."

"Good idea," she mumbled.

When she turned, shirt barely over her head, she gasped, jumping back. "Gah! Hamal! You are trying to give me a heart-attack! I thought you were in the hall! You always such a creeper?"

"Creeper, huh?" He was smiling again.

"Yeah. Creeper." She'd stopped walking forward, her face alternating between anger and embarrassment.

He turned. "I won't break into your room if you don't oversleep."

Seeing her like this was not the way to start their working relationship. He did not need to think of her as a piece of ass. Unfortunately, his imagination had been fed, and he'd need more than a few nights away to forget.

Two hours later, he was reassessing that.

She was doing everything in her power to hide her gifts, and he was furious. He wasn't here to train some random girl self-defense. He was here to prepare a fantastic anomaly how to survive against things equally extraordinary. There wasn't enough time for them to dance around her secrets.

"You know I've been watching you. Why do you think I don't know you're stronger than me? Faster? Quicker? Stop. Dicking. AROUND!"

His words stopped her short, and there was no difficulty interpreting the look of hatred she gave him. He didn't know what she'd expected, and didn't care. She could hate him all she wanted as long as she learned to protect herself from whatever else might get sent after her.

Hamal watched her battle with her rage, watched it boil towards the surface. He smiled, a trademark expression that was far from cheerful. "There it is. That's good. That's what I need to see. Be mad! Don't just accept what's being thrown at you."

Not letting her stew in her hate, he rushed in with a flurry of punches she managed to dodge by being forced to increase her speed.

"There she is." He stopped his assault to give her a complimentary nod.

Her eyes narrowed.

"Look, I'm here to help you, and that includes helping you from yourself. I get why you hide what you can do, but that time is over. If you don't practice with all your skills now, you'll be off-balance in a real fight."

She continued to study his face, panting from the quick bout of activity.

He continued. "If I were you, I wouldn't trust me either, but we don't have time for that. I need you to take a leap here."

A startled laugh burst from her mouth.

The corner of his mouth turned up in a smile.

His next words washed any feeling of humor from both of them. "There might be Soldiers after you right now. I can not help you against them.

They will put me down with a flick of their finger. You, though, we might be able to get trained up to survive them."

Dee's eyebrows rose at this exclamation. "Who are you?"

He cocked his head as if not understanding the question.

"Why would you risk so much for me?"

He shrugged.

She gave an overdramatic sigh.

His next words came slowly, carefully, as he succumbed to her frustration, "I was sent to watch you. I think there's still time to save you."

She stared into his face, clearly waiting for further explanation, but he wouldn't tell her more. Couldn't. He'd already stepped too far beyond what he'd been ordered to do here.

She frowned. "Why were you sent to watch me?"

He matched her expression, knowing he didn't contain the bitterness he felt. "Honestly, I'm not sure, though after seeing you in action I have a theory."

Again, she waited for more that never came. She sighed again, her frustration clear, pulling another sardonic smile from her teacher. "Any chance you might share your theory with me?"

Ignoring her question, he moved to a fighting position.

She paused, and he was grateful she let go of the thought to wait him out.

Overall, it had been a good first day.

Dee lay in the grass, eyes closed. When he'd finally called an end to their training session, she'd slumped to the ground in exhaustion. Jogging was great exercise, but it was nothing compared to what he'd put her through. She'd definitely sleep good tonight.

The thought pulled his eyes to her, remembering this morning, her form barely covered in a t-shirt—

He shook his head, pulling his eyes away to block the path his thoughts were taking him. If the Rishi's wanted her, there would be no room for him, and they most definitely would want her. There were going to be a few fights over whose House acquired this one. There was too much potential in her for her to be overlooked. She'd be like a shiny new toy. Allowing a personal indulgence here, now, while he had her to himself, would only lead to a mess later.

Besides, she was his job. She was the mission. That was all. Overstepping these lines would only sully a reputation he'd worked his entire life to build amongst a group that would always be stronger, faster, and just plain better than him.

Breaking the calm quiet that had settled over them, her words surprised him. "I'm not sure what I can do."

He met her gaze, waiting for more.

Her eyes moved past him to stare at the clear sky. "I'm fast, and strong, and quick. I've never learned to fight. I'd never even been in a fight until the other night."

"You killed a couple of those Revenants by yourself," he answered in a matter-of-fact tone.

As soon as the words were out he knew he'd said too much.

Her face brightened, then her eyes narrowed. "You were there in the cemetery."

He shrugged admission, managing to keep his cool against the suspicion in her eyes.

Her eyes closed again before opening slowly to study his face. "You were worried I'd died." She sat up.

He frowned. "Let's not get all mushy. If I'd lost you, my reputation would be shit."

She dropped her chin in a nod. "Right. Yeah." She cleared her throat. "I did kill a couple. But that had more to do with luck than anything."

He laughed, a friendly sound. "Well said, but not everything can be given to luck's meddling hands. There's something in you that refused to be bested. That's what I saw. That's why I'm doing this."

Before she could get to questions he couldn't answer, he stepped towards the house. "Alright, I think it's time to eat."

She jumped to her feet, a burst of energy flowing from her in a manner he couldn't help but find endearing. Something had been released from her while they'd trained. It'd been a unique experience for him to witness her anger turn slowly to joy. This joy she found in their training was something he was almost jealous of. The girl who needed to feign arrogance to pretend confidence hadn't surfaced since that moment. In its place was the mold of a confident warrior he was excited to charge.

Still, it was only the first day. Only time would tell if the mold was stable enough not to break under the pressure of holding its contents. It was good she enjoyed training, but he knew the realities of why they were doing it was still separate her mind. That would be the hardest thing to sell, and it was the point he was most afraid he wouldn't have time to explain.

"What's a good place to order in from around here?"

Her face fell. "Just pizza."

Did she think he was going to take her to dinner?

"You want to shower?" Her voice held no trace of the disappointment he'd seen on her face.

He kept his face neutral. "That would be great."

She showed him the giant bathroom on the first floor after grabbing some clothes that looked like they would fit him. He grinned at her when she handed the pile to him. "Lots of guys leaving things behind?"

"Don't you wish I'd talk to you about my sex life," she snapped, her face flushed with embarrassment.

His grin turned to laughter. "I know you don't have a sex life."

He laughed when her face turned crimson and she fled the hallway.

Chapter Eleven

He looked around, taking in the luxury of the room that put many of the hotels he'd stayed in to shame. It was, by far, much more elegant than the seedy motel he'd been forced to stay in that was the only lodging in this nowhere town. Glad the girl had finally agreed to have him stay with her was quite the understatement.

After showing him the room and where to find towels and toothbrushes, she'd left him to himself. Since his earlier comment about her sex-life, her self-conscious nature was back in play.

He shook his head, loathing that one.

It was why he'd never had any interest in finding a long-term woman. Most women were too unsure of themselves; too needing of finding self through another's reflection. The ones that weren't like that had no patience for long bouts of separation his lifestyle would force, a fact he respected enough not to waste their time with. He'd never had trouble finding one-night-stands to satisfy his hunger and was too busy to be lonely.

Still, he couldn't keep his mind from conjuring the image of her standing over him in nothing but a shirt that had barely concealed her.

***

Dee was pacing back and forth behind her locked door, an action she knew wouldn't stop Hamal if he wanted to get in. Still, it made her feel a little better.

Now what?

-Now what, indeed.-

She should sleep.

Somehow, over pizza, she'd been convinced to let him stay.

-Death-wish, much?-

She didn't think her life was in danger with him here, but her inner-voice continued to try to convince her she should kill him rather than wait to see what he could teach her.

-If you think you're safe with him in the house, what's with the rut you're carving in the floor?-

She huffed at the point. It was the second-guessing that had her pacing. Thinking it was safe to let him stay an hour ago was turning into a mess of what-ifs in her head.

He'd said something about Soldiers and a something-else that might be sent after her. Another something that would try to kill her?

There'd already been four attempts on her life in... how many days had it been since she'd passed out in the cemetery?

-Does that matter?-

Probably not, but she felt figuring out the particulars might slow the crazed thoughts threatening to bash through the dam she'd erected to keep them from overloading her mind. She squeezed her eyes shut in concentration, counting backward slowly.

Seven days. Today was the seventh day since the cemetery.

She took a breath of relief as if working out this detail was a monumental victory.

One week. A week she'd been hiding from her best friend, hoping he wouldn't notice any changes in her. Luckily, he'd been away on business.

Her walk back and forth across the room continued, the path increasing in frenzy as her mind ran with exponential possibilities for her future.

-Freaking out will not help.-

Her footsteps stopped. Her eyes closed. Her body was still for the first time in long hours.

This stillness only allowed her mind to concentrate on illusions of how her panic wished she would react. In her mind's eye, ranting words screamed through the house so the rafters shook and outbursts of violence wrecked her bedroom to heaps of shattered furniture. The visualization ended with her jumping through the glass of the window and rolling to her feet on the yard before sprinting away through the woods to never be heard from again.

She opened her eyes, refusing to break down.

Instead, she moved from the room, even as she knew she should be forcing sleep on herself. To think rest would come was a fantasy she knew better than to indulge. Instead, she was taking her advice to meet things head-on.

***

"Bottom line is, I don't know why these things are after you."

Her frown was deep. "Why are *you* here?"

"I told you, I was sent to watch you. Figure out what you were."

"What I was?"

"What you are."

"What I am?"

"That's annoying."

"Annoying?" She let out a breath of laughter, and with it some of the intensity she hadn't meant to be pushing on Hamal with her questions. Neither had she meant to repeat everything he was saying. "What do you mean *what I am?*"

"I think you know what I mean."

She paused, letting the answer pass. "Who sent you?"

"I can't tell you that."

Dee watched his face, startled that he'd straight up tell her he couldn't tell her. She wasn't sure if that was better than him lying.

-*Not* better *than him lying?*-

"Why can't you tell me?"

"Some secrets aren't mine to tell."

She nodded, not liking his refusal to answer, but respecting the reason for it.

-*If the reason is actually true, and not some bull to further trap you.*-

Storming down here with little thought to what she would actually say, she found herself struggling to come up with coherent questions. She figured it would be too much to ask that he just tell her everything he knew.

Before she could come up with something direct to ask, he said, "Essentially, I'm an assassin."

She held his gaze, waiting for a sign that he was making fun of her. When she decided he wouldn't say more on his own, she broke the silence. "An assassin?"

"An assassin."

"How does one become an assassin exactly."

He chuckled, turning to grab a shirt. The movement brought her attention to what should have been obvious the second he opened the door to her knock: his naked torso.

How she hadn't noticed he wasn't wearing a shirt seemed impossible when the fact slammed her in the face. Struggling not to stare when he turned back to her, caught not just by his physique, but by the tribal-ram tattoo that covered his chest, reaching from shoulder to shoulder, down both biceps, and to his navel.

-*Cool.*-

The front-door to the house opening distracted both of them. Hamal had a gun out, sweeping Dee behind him, before she reacted.

"Dee? Whose car is out front?" Mike's voice drifted up the stairs, footsteps telling he was moving towards the back of the house, which meant he was going for the kitchen. It was the only time Dee'd ever been annoyed by the casual relationship the pair had. Mike knew her well enough to think she would be sleeping at this time of night, as well as know that a hot drink made every visit better.

Dee moved from the room before Hamal could tell her to wait, flying down the stairs. She almost ran into her friend who was making his way back from the kitchen to check why he hadn't heard her call back to him. "Mike! Hi! I thought you were out of town."

"Took a late flight rather than wait for the morning one." He studied her for a moment before lifting his eyes to the stairs she'd just bounded from, then back to her, a smile blossoming across his face. "There's someone here."

Dee tried not to look panicked. "There is."

"Is this someone a gentlemen caller?" His voice dropped to a teasing whisper, and he made as if to step around her. She moved in front of him, eyes wide in horror that he might go up and see Hamal.

"Not like you mean."

He stopped, raising an eyebrow as he looked at her. "Oh? How did I mean?"

His eyes glinted with humor, and she dropped her dismay. She even managed a smile, all while continuing to silently ask that Hamal stay upstairs. "He's in the guest room."

Mike's eyebrows rose, his eyes returning to look up the stairs. "Hmm. I'm not sure if that makes me more comfortable. I think I'd rather you had some sleazy one-night-stand than have some random stranger bunking in your house for the night."

"How do you know its a random stranger?"

He cocked his head with a look that said he knew she knew why he would know that.

She raised her eyebrows in defiance, forcing him to verbalize his answer.

His face turned serious, voice dropping further to ensure Dee's mysterious tenant couldn't overhear. "I'm excited to see you've spoken to another human being that wasn't a server at a restaurant, but I worry."

Dee smiled, matching his whisper. "I know. And I appreciate it. But you don't need to."

Mike looked over her head, and she knew Hamal had just come down the stairs behind her. She spun, throwing Hamal a look that expressed her dislike that he'd shown his face, before turning back to Mike to introduce the two, fake smile plastered across her features.

Hamal, managing not to come off with his usual intimidating arrogance, moved forward to shake Mike's hand with a smile that expressed real warmth at meeting Dee's only friend. "Mike, great to meet you. It's real great that Dee's letting me stay here for a couple nights."

-Real great?-

Dee listened carefully to the change in timber and cadence of Hamal's voice, wondering if this weren't telling of his roots, or just another scary detail about the supposed assassin; that he would change his face as the moment needed. How had he been manipulating her with the masks he chose to show her?

She watched the encounter between the men with studious eyes.

-I told you to kill him.-

Mike pumped Hamal's hand. "Nice to meet you as well. What brings you to our little slice of nowhere?"

Hamal's smile remained. "Just some relaxing travel. This town is definitely relaxing."

Mike laughed at this, turning away to move back into the kitchen. Hamal trailed after him with Dee staring daggers into the back of his head.

The smell of grounds making their way into the press drew both Dee and Hamal farther into the kitchen, despite the fact it'd been bedtime a few moments before.

Mike continued the conversation as he made coffee. "Relaxing, it is. Sleepy, even. How'd you run into Desiree?"

Dee threw him a look of pleading, relaxing as he answered. "Apparently, we share a love of late-night exercise."

Dee took a seat closest to the sliding doors so she could stare into the darkness. She felt Mike's heavy gaze at the mention of late-night jogs. The very jogs she'd promised to discontinue.

She pretended not to notice, forcing herself not to flinch from his next words. "I see. Strange habit."

Hamal shrugged while Dee ignored Mike's pointed look.

She was surprised when Hamal continued explaining. "Yeah, but it tended to be the only time I could consistently find to fit it in. Now, it's just a habit I haven't bothered to drop."

Mike grunted in pseudo-understanding, pouring the freshly made coffee into three mugs, one which he brought to Dee. Another he set in front of himself while the third remained on the counter. Mike gestured with a head nod. "Milk in the fridge. Sugar just above the coffee, if you need it."

Hamal rescued his mug from the counter and took a seat at the far end of the large wooden table opposite Dee and Mike.

Looking out the window, Dee didn't catch whatever look Hamal must have made that had Mike explaining the large table. "Dee's father owned a large construction and real estate firm. There were always groups of people over for dinner, often staying in the house for a few nights while working on various jobs."

Hamal nodded, surprising Dee again when he continued engaging Mike. "You grew up here, too?"

Mike shook his head. "I didn't grow up here, but I've spent most of the last ten years here. Dee's like a sister to me."

Dee, still staring out the window, felt Hamal's eyes on her. She'd taken her steaming coffee from the table and was blowing on the hot liquid as she avoided being brought into the conversation.

-Why is this a good idea? Letting these two talk? Mike doesn't know what Hamal knows, and Hamal doesn't know what Mike knows. Keeping it that way seems like a great idea. Though if you just kill Hamal, there'd be no worrying about it.-

Dee continued to blow on the coffee held close to her face.

-You could at least tell Mike to get out of here. You're going to start saying too much if you get any more tired. Filter shuts off, remember?-

She sipped her coffee. Still too hot.

-Kill Hamal, then take a vacation. Somewhere like the Amazon.-

It wasn't how she'd wanted any of this to go down. Not that she'd had much time to think about it, but she knew that if she had, having Mike meet Hamal wouldn't have come up. That it was happening propelled Dee into a position where she felt more like an observer of her life, rather than a participant.

Part of her, most of her, was okay with this, as it allowed her to sit back and watch in a detached manner. A small part of her, the part that was eager to find out what Hamal could enlighten her of, was stymied by Mike's presence. So, as a passively waiting being, she stared out the window, sifting through the words spoken, and unspoken, in the kitchen behind her.

She sipped her coffee again.

"Dee, you'll be alright? I can stay..."

Mike's words brought her attention back to the kitchen. Holding in a sigh, she swiveled around to face the man talking to her. "I'll be fine." Her eyes shifted quickly to Hamal, then back to Mike before dropping to her coffee, taking another sip to give her something to focus on besides the two pairs of eyes asking more than she was willing to provide.

Mike nodded, pausing for a moment before getting up to rinse his mug then put it in the dishwasher. "I'll call you later. Be good, 'Case."

Dee nodded, meeting his eyes while forcing a smile to reach her eyes. "Sleep tight."

Mike grinned at Dee before shooting Hamal a warning look as he left the kitchen.

Dee waited until she could no longer hear Mike's car, a much longer time than Hamal, who was content to wait her out. When Mike's presence had completely cleared her senses, she turned her attention to the stranger she'd allowed in her house. Part of her wanted to be mad that he'd come downstairs to intrude on her life, but she had invited him here. Also was the matter of how long he would stay if she questioned everything he did.

-Don't do that. Don't give him power over you.-

She knew the truth of this but was too curious to finally find some answers that she ignored the advice. Instead, she bit back her comments of how he'd handled Mike's entrance, concentrating instead on their conversation that had been interrupted.

She took a deep breath to settle her nerves. "You were telling me how one becomes an assassin."

A smile pierced Hamal's neutral mask. "No, you were asking. I hadn't been telling you anything."

Dee annoyance at this answer flooded her face before she could catch it. With another breath, she forced her face to neutral. "I suppose that's fair."

"Is it?"

He was goading her and she knew it, but she wasn't sure how far to push.

-He came to you, remember?-

That was true.

"You told me you were an assassin. I didn't ask that."

"You don't believe me?"

Her mouth twitched towards a smile. "Not really. Why would an assassin be sent to gather information?"

Hamal matched her grin. "I wondered the exact same thing. I don't think my being an assassin has anything to do with why I got this job."

Dee raised her eyebrows in question, but Hamal didn't elaborate.

She was bone tired, the energy she had earlier to force this conversation now evaporated. Looking at another full day tomorrow, today rather, brought a new wave of exhaustion over her. "Alright, how about sleep now. We can play twenty questions later."

Hamal shrugged, sipping his coffee like he was there at her sufferance, though she knew that wasn't true. It was merely the face he was showing.

-Killing him is still an option.-

Her mind was oddly blank as she wondered what she had gotten herself into.

"You sleep. I've got some things to take care of, but I'll see you again in the morning." Hamal's words surprised her.

She didn't try to keep the look of distrust off her face. "'Some things to take care of'?"

"You're repeating."

"I'm not repeating. I'm questioning."

"Questioning?"

She glared across the table, head balanced on hands propped up with elbows on the table.

He laughed, standing to put his mug in the sink. "Don't make me wake you again."

Chapter Twelve

He looked around, taking in the luxury of the room that put many of the hotels he'd stayed in to shame. It was, by far, much more elegant than the seedy motel he'd been forced to stay in that was the only lodging in this nowhere town. Glad the girl had finally agreed to have him stay with her was quite the understatement.

After showing him the room and where to find towels and toothbrushes, she'd left him to himself. Since his earlier comment about her sex-life, her self-conscious nature was back in play.

He shook his head, loathing that one.

It was why he'd never had any interest in finding a long-term woman. Most women were too unsure of themselves; too needing of finding self through another's reflection. The ones that weren't like that had no patience for long bouts of separation his lifestyle would force, a fact he respected enough not to waste their time with. He'd never had trouble finding one-night-stands to satisfy his hunger and was too busy to be lonely.

Still, he couldn't keep his mind from conjuring the image of her standing over him in nothing but a shirt that had barely concealed her.

***

Dee was pacing back and forth behind her locked door, an action she knew wouldn't stop Hamal if he wanted to get in. Still, it made her feel a little better.

Now what?

-*Now what, indeed.* -

She should sleep.

Somehow, over pizza, she'd been convinced to let him stay.

-*Death-wish, much?* -

She didn't think her life was in danger with him here, but her inner-voice continued to try to convince her she should kill him rather than wait to see what he could teach her.

-*If you think you're safe with him in the house, what's with the rut you're carving in the floor?* -

She huffed at the point. It was the second-guessing that had her pacing. Thinking it was safe to let him stay an hour ago was turning into a mess of what-ifs in her head.

He'd said something about Soldiers and a something-else that might be sent after her. Another something that would try to kill her?

There'd already been four attempts on her life in… how many days had it been since she'd passed out in the cemetery?

-*Does that matter?* -

Probably not, but she felt figuring out the particulars might slow the crazed thoughts threatening to bash through the dam she'd erected to keep them from overloading her mind. She squeezed her eyes shut in concentration, counting backward slowly.

Seven days. Today was the seventh day since the cemetery.

She took a breath of relief as if working out this detail was a monumental victory.

One week. A week she'd been hiding from her best friend, hoping he wouldn't notice any changes in her. Luckily, he'd been away on business.

Her walk back and forth across the room continued, the path increasing in frenzy as her mind ran with exponential possibilities for her future.

-Freaking out will not help.-

Her footsteps stopped. Her eyes closed. Her body was still for the first time in long hours.

This stillness only allowed her mind to concentrate on illusions of how her panic wished she would react. In her mind's eye, ranting words screamed through the house so the rafters shook and outbursts of violence wrecked her bedroom to heaps of shattered furniture. The visualization ended with her jumping through the glass of the window and rolling to her feet on the yard before sprinting away through the woods to never be heard from again.

She opened her eyes, refusing to break down.

Instead, she moved from the room, even as she knew she should be forcing sleep on herself. To think rest would come was a fantasy she knew better than to indulge. Instead, she was taking her advice to meet things head-on.

***

"Bottom line is, I don't know why these things are after you."

Her frown was deep. "Why are *you* here?"

"I told you, I was sent to watch you. Figure out what you were."

"What I was?"

"What you are."

"What I am?"

"That's annoying."

"Annoying?" She let out a breath of laughter, and with it some of the intensity she hadn't meant to be pushing on Hamal with her questions. Neither had she meant to repeat everything he was saying. "What do you mean *what I am?*"

"I think you know what I mean."

She paused, letting the answer pass. "Who sent you?"

"I can't tell you that."

Dee watched his face, startled that he'd straight up tell her he couldn't tell her. She wasn't sure if that was better than him lying.

-*Not* better *than him lying?*-

"Why can't you tell me?"

"Some secrets aren't mine to tell."

She nodded, not liking his refusal to answer, but respecting the reason for it.

-*If the reason is actually true, and not some bull to further trap you.*-

Storming down here with little thought to what she would actually say, she found herself struggling to come up with coherent questions. She figured it would be too much to ask that he just tell her everything he knew.

Before she could come up with something direct to ask, he said, "Essentially, I'm an assassin."

She held his gaze, waiting for a sign that he was making fun of her. When she decided he wouldn't say more on his own, she broke the silence. "An assassin?"

"An assassin."

"How does one become an assassin exactly."

He chuckled, turning to grab a shirt. The movement brought her attention to what should have been obvious the second he opened the door to her knock: his naked torso.

How she hadn't noticed he wasn't wearing a shirt seemed impossible when the fact slammed her in the face. Struggling not to stare when he turned back to her, caught not just by his physique, but by the tribal-ram tattoo that covered his chest, reaching from shoulder to shoulder, down both biceps, and to his navel.

-*Cool.*-

The front-door to the house opening distracted both of them. Hamal had a gun out, sweeping Dee behind him, before she reacted.

"Dee? Whose car is out front?" Mike's voice drifted up the stairs, footsteps telling he was moving towards the back of the house, which meant he was going for the kitchen. It was the only time Dee'd ever been annoyed by the casual relationship the pair had. Mike knew her well enough to think she would be sleeping at this time of night, as well as know that a hot drink made every visit better.

Dee moved from the room before Hamal could tell her to wait, flying down the stairs. She almost ran into her friend who was making his way back from the kitchen to check why he hadn't heard her call back to him. "Mike! Hi! I thought you were out of town."

"Took a late flight rather than wait for the morning one." He studied her for a moment before lifting his eyes to the stairs she'd just bounded from, then back to her, a smile blossoming across his face. "There's someone here."

Dee tried not to look panicked. "There is."

"Is this someone a gentlemen caller?" His voice dropped to a teasing whisper, and he made as if to step around her. She moved in front of him, eyes wide in horror that he might go up and see Hamal.

"Not like you mean."

He stopped, raising an eyebrow as he looked at her. "Oh? How did I mean?"

His eyes glinted with humor, and she dropped her dismay. She even managed a smile, all while continuing to silently ask that Hamal stay upstairs. "He's in the guest room."

Mike's eyebrows rose, his eyes returning to look up the stairs. "Hmm. I'm not sure if that makes me more comfortable. I think I'd rather you had some sleazy one-night-stand than have some random stranger bunking in your house for the night."

"How do you know its a random stranger?"

He cocked his head with a look that said he knew she knew why he would know that.

She raised her eyebrows in defiance, forcing him to verbalize his answer.

His face turned serious, voice dropping further to ensure Dee's mysterious tenant couldn't overhear. "I'm excited to see you've spoken to another human being that wasn't a server at a restaurant, but I worry."

Dee smiled, matching his whisper. "I know. And I appreciate it. But you don't need to."

Mike looked over her head, and she knew Hamal had just come down the stairs behind her. She spun, throwing Hamal a look that expressed her dislike that he'd shown his face, before turning back to Mike to introduce the two, fake smile plastered across her features.

Hamal, managing not to come off with his usual intimidating arrogance, moved forward to shake Mike's hand with a smile that expressed real warmth at meeting Dee's only friend. "Mike, great to meet you. It's real great that Dee's letting me stay here for a couple nights."

-*Real great?*-

Dee listened carefully to the change in timber and cadence of Hamal's voice, wondering if this weren't telling of his roots, or just another scary detail about the supposed assassin; that he would change his face as the moment needed. How had he been manipulating her with the masks he chose to show her?

She watched the encounter between the men with studious eyes.

-*I told you to kill him.*-

Mike pumped Hamal's hand. "Nice to meet you as well. What brings you to our little slice of nowhere?"

Hamal's smile remained. "Just some relaxing travel. This town is definitely relaxing."

Mike laughed at this, turning away to move back into the kitchen. Hamal trailed after him with Dee staring daggers into the back of his head.

The smell of grounds making their way into the press drew both Dee and Hamal farther into the kitchen, despite the fact it'd been bedtime a few moments before.

Mike continued the conversation as he made coffee. "Relaxing, it is. Sleepy, even. How'd you run into Desiree?"

Dee threw him a look of pleading, relaxing as he answered. "Apparently, we share a love of late-night exercise."

Dee took a seat closest to the sliding doors so she could stare into the darkness. She felt Mike's heavy gaze at the mention of late-night jogs. The very jogs she'd promised to discontinue.

She pretended not to notice, forcing herself not to flinch from his next words. "I see. Strange habit."

Hamal shrugged while Dee ignored Mike's pointed look.

She was surprised when Hamal continued explaining. "Yeah, but it tended to be the only time I could consistently find to fit it in. Now, it's just a habit I haven't bothered to drop."

Mike grunted in pseudo-understanding, pouring the freshly made coffee into three mugs, one which he brought to Dee. Another he set in front of himself while the third remained on the counter. Mike gestured with a head nod. "Milk in the fridge. Sugar just above the coffee, if you need it."

Hamal rescued his mug from the counter and took a seat at the far end of the large wooden table opposite Dee and Mike.

Looking out the window, Dee didn't catch whatever look Hamal must have made that had Mike explaining the large table. "Dee's father owned a large construction and real estate firm. There were always groups of people over for dinner, often staying in the house for a few nights while working on various jobs."

Hamal nodded, surprising Dee again when he continued engaging Mike. "You grew up here, too?"

Mike shook his head. "I didn't grow up here, but I've spent most of the last ten years here. Dee's like a sister to me."

Dee, still staring out the window, felt Hamal's eyes on her. She'd taken her steaming coffee from the table and was blowing on the hot liquid as she avoided being brought into the conversation.

-Why is this a good idea? Letting these two talk? Mike doesn't know what Hamal knows, and Hamal doesn't know what Mike knows. Keeping it that way seems like a great idea. Though if you just kill Hamal, there'd be no worrying about it.-

Dee continued to blow on the coffee held close to her face.

-You could at least tell Mike to get out of here. You're going to start saying too much if you get any more tired. Filter shuts off, remember?-

She sipped her coffee. Still too hot.

-Kill Hamal, then take a vacation. Somewhere like the Amazon.-

It wasn't how she'd wanted any of this to go down. Not that she'd had much time to think about it, but she knew that if she had, having Mike meet Hamal wouldn't have come up. That it was happening propelled Dee into a position where she felt more like an observer of her life, rather than a participant.

Part of her, most of her, was okay with this, as it allowed her to sit back and watch in a detached manner. A small part of her, the part that was eager to find out what Hamal could enlighten her of, was stymied by Mike's presence. So, as a passively waiting being, she stared out the window, sifting through the words spoken, and unspoken, in the kitchen behind her.

She sipped her coffee again.

"Dee, you'll be alright? I can stay..."

Mike's words brought her attention back to the kitchen. Holding in a sigh, she swiveled around to face the man talking to her. "I'll be fine." Her eyes shifted quickly to Hamal, then back to Mike before dropping to her coffee, taking another sip to give her something to focus on besides the two pairs of eyes asking more than she was willing to provide.

Mike nodded, pausing for a moment before getting up to rinse his mug then put it in the dishwasher. "I'll call you later. Be good, 'Case."

Dee nodded, meeting his eyes while forcing a smile to reach her eyes. "Sleep tight."

Mike grinned at Dee before shooting Hamal a warning look as he left the kitchen.

Dee waited until she could no longer hear Mike's car, a much longer time than Hamal, who was content to wait her out. When Mike's presence had completely cleared her senses, she turned her attention to the stranger she'd allowed in her house. Part of her wanted to be mad that he'd come downstairs to intrude on her life, but she had invited him here. Also was the matter of how long he would stay if she questioned everything he did.

-Don't do that. Don't give him power over you.-

She knew the truth of this but was too curious to finally find some answers that she ignored the advice. Instead, she bit back her comments of how he'd handled Mike's entrance, concentrating instead on their conversation that had been interrupted.

She took a deep breath to settle her nerves. "You were telling me how one becomes an assassin."

A smile pierced Hamal's neutral mask. "No, you were asking. I hadn't been telling you anything."

Dee annoyance at this answer flooded her face before she could catch it. With another breath, she forced her face to neutral. "I suppose that's fair."

"Is it?"

He was goading her and she knew it, but she wasn't sure how far to push.

-He came to you, remember?-

That was true.

"You told me you were an assassin. I didn't ask that."

"You don't believe me?"

Her mouth twitched towards a smile. "Not really. Why would an assassin be sent to gather information?"

Hamal matched her grin. "I wondered the exact same thing. I don't think my being an assassin has anything to do with why I got this job."

Dee raised her eyebrows in question, but Hamal didn't elaborate.

She was bone tired, the energy she had earlier to force this conversation now evaporated. Looking at another full day tomorrow, today rather, brought a new wave of exhaustion over her. "Alright, how about sleep now. We can play twenty questions later."

Hamal shrugged, sipping his coffee like he was there at her sufferance, though she knew that wasn't true. It was merely the face he was showing.

-Killing him is still an option.-

Her mind was oddly blank as she wondered what she had gotten herself into.

"You sleep. I've got some things to take care of, but I'll see you again in the morning." Hamal's words surprised her.

She didn't try to keep the look of distrust off her face. "'Some things to take care of'?"

"You're repeating."

"I'm not repeating. I'm questioning."

"Questioning?"

She glared across the table, head balanced on hands propped up with elbows on the table.

He laughed, standing to put his mug in the sink. "Don't make me wake you again."

Chapter Thirteen

Hamal pushed her hard. With so many training hours, and his vigilant oversight, he gave Dee no time for anything else. Other than a few calls to Mike, her life was wake, train, eat, train, sleep. Over and over for a month, Dee struggled to remember what life had been like before this tyrannical mentor had moved into her house.

Hamal had no trouble finding time for extracurriculars. Most nights saw him slipping out after they'd gone to bed. Dee knew well enough what he was up to by the smell of the women wafting off him when he returned. An odd sense to have heightened, and an awkward way to realize it, the recognition of what he was doing with his time left her bitter that he could go out but she was forbidden to leave.

-Right, 'cause you're in no way jealous.-

Just like he never explained to her where he'd been, she didn't tell him she knew. It was the perfect reminder that she keep her eye on the ball. When her thoughts slipped to the idea that she was never going to meet someone else who had a handle on a supernatural world that wasn't supposed to exist; whenever she felt herself slipping to the idea that he might be the ideal partner for her, she remembered his trolloping.

-He probably thinks you're a freak. You're just his pet project.-

Standing in the kitchen, coffee in her hands steaming her face, she stared absently at a point in the room. She'd gotten up early to train but Hamal wasn't even there.

-You should have killed him.-

He'd spent another night away, making it the third night this week. The second week after he'd moved in, he'd gone out once. The next week, twice. These last two weeks had seen him gone more than he was there.

Face set in stoic nonchalance, she moved to the front of the house, curling herself onto the porch swing to wait for his arrival.

-Right, this is you not caring.-

It was illogical, and dangerous, for her to be jealous. She knew it. Her brain knew it, but other parts of her had been lonely...

She pulled out the long knife Hamal had gifted her, turning it in her hands, watching how the sun glinted off the blade, wondering why a knife, and not a gun, would be the thing he gave to her.

He'd called it Damascus steel, explaining the eight-inch blade's dark and light patterns were formed in the process of melting the different metals together. She thought the designs were reminiscent of flowing water, the ivory handle elegant in its simplicity and her fingers traced the patterns lightly.

There were no serrated edges as she imagined a long hunting knife should have, the curved edge of the blade sharp enough that she didn't touch it. Not again. The straight side of the knife beveled towards the sharp edge and it was here her fingers caressed.

Hamal's SUV rolling up the driveway pulled her attention. She had little trouble masking her face with the same contemptuous humor he was so good at, her body language relaxed, almost catlike in its curled position on the bench seat.

Until now, she'd been concerned with ensuring Hamal would stay. Not asking too many questions. Not doing anything that might scare him. In short, she'd been on pins and needles.

This morning, all that had vanished, buried beneath her annoyance.

His eyes didn't rise to meet hers until he was climbing the porch steps. That he was brandishing gourmet coffee and bagels meant he'd traveled over an hour to procure breakfast. If there'd been any question about where he'd been, this fact answered it.

Dee smiled, a look she hoped portrayed contempt for where he'd been as well as a confident aloofness that it didn't matter. Maybe a little bit, she hoped to scare him.

*

"I brought treats." He kept his voice friendly, a mask to guard against what he saw reflected in her eye. The attitude she was throwing him hit him with a sharp pain he didn't understand. He refused to believe he felt regretful.

She flowed off the bench, movements more feline than human. He'd only seen her move like that this in their training sessions. Those moments when she forgot to hide a part of herself, but this was something more.

A twang of fear rolled over his shoulders.

Who was this girl? Even after the weeks he'd been there, that thing he sensed hiding beneath the surface remained elusive. Was the girl standing in front of him now a glimmer of what that thing was?

As she moved closer, his breath held. She seemed taller; larger. Something more powerful than any Soldier. Maybe training her hadn't been the best idea.

"I like treats."

Her voice shook him from the paralysis that had come over him. The mocking arrogance she'd shown only a second before had vanished under the smile she now wore.

She took the tray of coffees and bag of bagels from him into the house.

His eyes lingered, caught on the mug she'd left on the floor boards of the deck, but his concentration was on where she'd brushed him as she'd passed. Electrified by the passing contact, he was afraid to move after her just yet.

Was there a subtle threat in her posturing? Had it turned to flirting?

Since the first morning he'd returned from the arms of his conquest of the week, she'd never let slip that he was anything more than a teacher to her. It was another part of what forced him away. That thing about wanting what you can't have? It was real. More and more often he had to give himself the pep talk about why she was off-limits. Why any involvement the two might succumb to could only end badly. More likely for him than her.

Badly was a word he kept himself away from when dealing with Rishi business.

The threat he'd seen in her was worse than this hypothetical bad. He knew he couldn't take her if she made up her mind to get rid of him. The thought had crossed his mind that she might decide he was too dangerous to live. That was before he'd moved in. Now...

Now, he'd just be more careful.

He followed her path to the kitchen. She'd settled with a cup of his procured coffee, still warm despite the long drive from where he'd picked it up. He stared at the remaining cup in its holder, set on the table next to the bagels she'd set near a tray of butter. Had he really brought her breakfast, like they were a couple or something?

He shook his head, eyes flickering to her to see if she'd caught his reaction before moving to the coffee. She wasn't paying him any attention, her gaze out the window consistent with her usual mien. There was no trace of whatever had overcome her outside.

He was trying to avoid the fact that the girl who'd met him on the porch had excited him. That hint of something wild, untempered, underneath the veneer of an unlearned damsel. There had been the girl who would be fit to survive the Rishis games.

Energized by this new sense of who Dee was becoming, Hamal left his coffee untouched to make his way upstairs to a shower where he washed off the remnants of last nights foray. Letting the water pelt over his face, squeezing his eyes against what was forbidden, he struggled to find his center.

It was only when he allowed anger to overwhelm him that he broke from the forbidden. Anger that he couldn't control his feelings. Anger that he'd been put in this situation. Anger that he wasn't strong enough to do what might be necessary to keep Dee safe.

Anger that he couldn't take what he wanted.

Finally, he turned off the shower, stepping out with thoughts focused on what needed to be done. Today would be another hard day. It was what was demanded.

He'd finally heard from home-base. Porrima, a Rishi who'd given up control of her own House a millennia ago to assist Zibanitu in maintaining order, had contacted him. Her dislike for him was no secret. Even as a boy he'd known to avoid her.

It had been her who'd approached him about this mission. The last person he'd ever expected to see at his door, she'd wielded an open laptop without saying a word. Zibanitu's face waiting patiently on the screen was the only reason he'd let her in. To have her perched rigidly on his sofa, face a mask of discontent for all Zi was telling him, had made it difficult to concentrate.

Short and chubby with mousy brown hair, her pinched face forever told how superior she was over everyone. If not for Zi's personally asking him to take this job, Hamal would have been elated to tell her to shove it.

Her self-important tone on the phone this morning had ruined any cheer that he was getting details about what was going on. When he heard what she had to say, everything was worse.

There would be Revenants in the area, most likely sent to test if Dee was something more than she seemed.

Hamal had laughed, unable to speak, stomach and face hurting from the outburst. Giving in to the humor of it had stayed his rage. Laughter might be forgiven. His temper wouldn't have been.

Porrima had been angry enough with his laughter that she'd hung up on him. He could handle that. When she called back, most likely at the insistence of Zi, she allowed Hamal to explain the reason for his response.

She was less happy when she learned how old their intel was, then threatened his life when she found out he'd made contact with the girl. Silence settled over the line when he explained how he'd been training her to protect herself for weeks.

As dangerous a game as he was playing, Hamal couldn't help but grin that he'd rendered the Rishi speechless.

When she found her voice, Porrima explained how she would use this opportunity as leverage to see him extradited from the House.

He hadn't been worried.

Not *that* worried.

The third call surprised him. This time she explained, in a voice tight with displeasure, that Zi approved of Hamal's decision to get involved with the girl. Of course, she didn't expect continued competent choices, especially considering his reputation with human women.

He'd laughed at her, again. She'd hung up on him, again and hadn't been in contact since. This was more than fine with him. He'd already forgotten her threats. What he hadn't forgotten was how old their intel was. A sense of foreboding had settled over him. If Hamal was on his own, they were screwed.

He moved down the stairs, thoughts shuffling through the little he'd learned since taking this mission, forced to continue to speculate on what was going on. He'd been running this mission on conjecture from the beginning, always with the idea that eventually he'd have answers.

Whoever had been sending tests at Dee had to be deciding their next move. He didn't believe she was in the clear, regardless of these quiet weeks that suggested just that. Still, he saw the prudence in laying low. Any movement, whether bringing Dee to Zibanitu or sending Soldiers here to protect her, might draw attention. This attention could force someone's hand that might otherwise remain quiet.

Given the Rishis vast network of spies and information gathering, few secrets stayed so for long. It was why Hamal continued to be grateful that a swarm hadn't descended. Once that happened, Zi would be forced to decide whether to bring her in or take her out.

It was another thought that sent a curious sensation through him. His feet paused as he hit the first floor. He was far from capable as her only protector if Soldiers started showing up. He was Zibanitu's pet human, allowed here because his presence couldn't cause a diplomatic riot.

Zibanitu's pet human. The words rang through Hamal's head in Porrima's annoying, matter-of-fact tone. The phrase no longer annoyed him as it had in his youth. Zibanitu was the reason he knew all he did, was capable of all he was and allowed the life he never regretted. Even if this mission ended as his last, there was nothing he'd choose differently.

When he entered the kitchen, his head was settled.

Dee was bouncing on her toes, staring out the tall wall of windows into the backyard. She turned to him as he grabbed the coffee he'd left on the counter.

Her eyes widened in surprise. "You're going to make me wait longer? Let's go. Let's go."

Her words were light, but the energy leaking off her told of her need to get moving.

So far, she'd obeyed his decree to stay inside, despite him not following his own orders. He was surprised she'd followed his rule. She'd never listened to Mike.

"It's not that late. I figured you'd still be in bed."

She raised her eyebrow at his deflection. "Well, I'm *not* still in bed."

She looked into the backyard. "How about I get out there and loosen up while you let the rest of whatever stink that is fade off you."

He stood up straighter, but she was out the back door, tumbling nimbly through the grass before he could mouth off a comeback.

Pressing his lips together at her comment, the thought occurred to him that sending an attack while he was gone all night was the perfect opportunity for whatever might come next. His selfish need had superseded the question about whether or not she'd be safe to protect herself.

That his first reaction was embarrassment quickly turned to guilt pissed him off, so the anger he thought he'd mastered left him seething.

Who he was mad at, he wouldn't admit to anyone.

Stumbling: Book One on The Fool's Path

Chapter Fourteen

Dee's muscles were plenty warm by the time Hamal made his way outside. She stood as close to the treeline as she could be without actually being in the trees. The slow movements of the kata Hamal had shown her had progressed to the quicker, tightened motions that made the exercise strenuous enough that she had a light sheen of sweat coating her body.

She felt his eyes on her as he walked across the yard.

As usual, she deciphered nothing of what he might be thinking from his body language. His face, always impossible to read behind a mask of arrogant mocking, did nothing to help her either. Did he know she knew he was studying her? Not that he wasn't doing it every moment they were training, but there was something different about this.

-He was sent here to watch you. He admitted this to you, but you're wondering why he's studying you?-

That he'd never explained all his motives for helping her wasn't a point she'd forgotten. Sometimes it slipped her mind, snapping back when she found herself doing, or saying, something to him only friends might do.

They weren't friends. It was something she repeated to herself, along with remembering the fact that this detail might just keep her alive when whatever game he was playing finally made its way to the light.

Still, it was hard keeping him at a distance. His relaxed manner, quick wit, and enveloping confidence enfolded her to him, even as he taught her to protect herself against creatures she still struggled to wrap her mind around.

She pulled her attention back to the trees in front of her, letting their comforting wall give her a sense of protectiveness.

-In your own backyard you need protection, yet in the darkest hours of the night, you're okay jogging around town?-

She admitted to herself there wasn't much logic in the nuances of her paranoia. Who could see her in the backyard of the house set far from the road, circled by woods? Her subconscious didn't care, which was why she always moved closer to the treeline when she could. If Hamal had come outside first, they'd be in the center of the large clearing that was her backyard.

As his approach neared, she stopped her warm-up to turn her full attention to him. Meeting his eye made her self-conscious, so she turned away before the blush could consume her face. To hide the movement, she swung her arms back and forth across her body to stretch and keep her muscles loose.

She wasn't even sure what she'd been thinking that would have caused her to blush.

Taking a long, cylindrical bag from its position draped across his back, Hamal pulled two long, slightly curved swords. Dee wanted to call them katanas but didn't know enough about bladed weapons to say so out-loud. Whatever they were, their presence sparked new excitement that she'd be learning something different today.

The weapons glinted in the sun. "The only way to be sure they're really dead is for them to lose their heads. Super sharp, bladed weapons is the only way to guarantee that."

Dee's eyes were all for the glint of the light reflecting off the silver metal. "We haven't decapitated anything so far."

"True, but the things you've seen will seem like toddlers to what might be coming."

Dee took the blade Hamal handed her. Concentrating on its blunt edges, she turned it in her hand, keeping the terrified scream sounding in her brain at Hamal's words quarantined. "I thought you weren't supposed to bring a knife to a gunfight."

"Who said anything about a gunfight?"

She shrugged, concentration focused on the way the grip felt in her hand, pulled by the weight of the metal as it trailed away from her. "You've mentioned Soldiers. You said you wouldn't be able to protect me from them. I guess I just assumed they used guns."

"They do, actually."

Dee sighed, dropping her attention from her new toy. "So, I ask again, why bring a knife to a gunfight?"

Hamal actually laughed. "Well, this is a sword, not a knife, and, you should bring as many weapons as you can to every fight. At least, that's what I say. I also say, don't get in a fight with things that can kill you with a bullet but won't die the same way. Your chances of getting close enough to use the beheading trick are usually not good." He shrugged. "Sometimes you have no choice."

Thinking of another point, Dee frowned. "I've been learning hand-to-hand defense to protect myself from things that don't fight hand-to-hand?"

"None of the Revenants had weapons. That's who you were learning to defend against."

"But now I might need to fight these Soldiers?"

"Possibly."

"Jesus."

"No."

Dee blinked fast. "Was that a joke?"

His face was unreadable. "Was it funny?"

She ignored him, thinking about how she'd almost been toast when coming against the 'B'-team of the supernatural hierarchy. Now, she was learning these other guys, these Soldiers, the guys whose only purpose was to fight other supernatural supers like themselves, might be coming after her, too?

Her eyes darted around the yard, heart rate spiking at the thought that these things might be on her at any time.

Hamal noticed her panicked look. How could he not? "Don't get soft on me, Dee. We've made a lot of progress. This is nothing to worry about."

Her eyebrows rose in disbelief, though the comment did what it was intended: broke her from her spiral down fear's path. "Nothing to worry about, huh?"

Hamal expressed a vague non-answer, moving away so he could begin his own warm up.

Dee continued her questions, matching his pace as he jogged around the perimeter of the yard. "They can only kill each other with blades, but they all carry guns?"

"Yeah, they're usually decked out in all the newest, coolest toys."

"But, they can't kill each other with bullets?" She re-asked the question to focus her thoughts from panic.

"The bullets might not kill them, but have you ever been shot? Not pleasant. They feel pain. Injuries still debilitate. They just, probably, won't die from them."

Dee envisioned spray from an automatic weapon keeping some super soldier wielding a sword at bay. Hamal's words seeped further, and she shot her eyes to his face. "Probably?"

He shrugged. "Sometimes a freak thing happens. It's rare, but it's happened that a Soldier has died from bullet wounds. Not all Soldiers—come out—the same."

"Come out?"

He shrugged again, and she wasn't sure if he didn't have more of an answer because he didn't know, or if he wasn't willing to tell.

She closed her eyes, trusting her body to follow Hamal's rhythm around the yard without tripping while she settled her thoughts. Her eyes popped open. "The Revenants can't use guns, can they?"

She wasn't looking forward to the possibility of being shot at. Her healing abilities were outstanding, but she didn't want to find out if a bullet would kill her.

"Well—" Hamal hesitated, forcing Dee's attention to observe his face. Here was a rare instance when she was sure he weighing what he was willing to tell her.

After a moments pause, he decided to answer. The shock of it almost had her missing what he was saying.

"There are a few, let's call them levels, of Revenants. The one you got in the cemetery was a Level One. These talking ones—well, honestly, I'm not sure what they are. The talking ones don't typically show signs of heightened strength, not without other problems..." he trailed off, eyes going distant for a second before he pulled himself back. "Just trust me. There are a few that would be able to carry a gun and use it adequately, but I can't believe they'd be sent here."

"Use it adequately?"

"Able to shoot you. Adequately. Shoot you. To death."

Somehow, Dee found it in herself to chuckle. "I feel like it's a terrifying thing that these things are running around capable of handling weapons *adequately*. No police force or government agency has ever figured out these things are out there?" If her comment had been enough to give away her disbelief in his story, her tone more than made up for it.

It was Hamal's turn to chuckle, a glint in his eyes that sucked the breath from her. "Who says they haven't?"

The comment stopped Dee's push for him to tell her the truth, hearing the possibility in his words of secret agencies tasked to deal with the hidden problem of monsters among them. Her attention turned from his face to stare at the trees beyond.

He'd been hiding information from her, she'd known that, but this spin opened a line of possibilities she'd never considered. It was information that validated his secrets.

-Is that what you're getting out of this? His right not to tell you things?-

Her attention returned to his face. "Are you working with an agency like that?"

"No." There was nothing to read in the answer. Nothing registered on his face or in his voice that might suggest he was lying or had more to offer that he was refusing to give her.

She huffed. "Whatever. You were going to show me how to cut people's heads off or something."

*

Dee's learning curve with the weapon excited them both. Once he explained that the movements were the same from the hand-to-hand forms, there was no stopping her. He'd learned weapons first; hand-to-hand being the last phase of his training.

The point was to kill things, and these tools enhanced that. Forced to fight without a weapon meant you were having an epically bad day. He hadn't started Dee with a sword because as much as he acknowledged he was disobeying his orders, he hadn't wanted to put himself in a position where he might have armed the very thing that might need killing. Now that he'd gotten the okay for what he was doing, it was time to level the playing field.

Backpedaling faster this his legs could keep up, Hamal fell. Lashing out with his weapon, hoping to catch her with an unexpected attack as a last resort even in the moment of his failure, she managed, with a speed he'd not yet seen from her, to deflect the attack. Her eyes, too intent on her prey to let up, showed how far she'd drifted into the zone of the fight. A ripple of fear slid over him. Not for what might happen here, but for what she would be if he continued to push her. What she could be if they continued to force her towards the thing she would need to be to survive them. Or, if those others got her, what she might be when they molded her to their desires.

Landing on his back, breath bursting from his body wiped all thought from his head.

Dee followed, falling on top of him.

*

A part of her brain registered that she'd gained the upper hand, pushing Hamal back as he fought to maintain his defense. When he tripped, a sound that might have been glee sounded in her brain but wasn't enough to bring her from the flow. Hamal had mentioned this place where one's body moved perfectly of its own volition without the mind getting in the way. It was terrific. Her body chased the feeling, unwilling to let it go.

He struck out at her, a move that should have taken her by surprise, but her flow would not be redirected. Parrying the move, she found herself falling with Hamal, barely catching herself before the front of her head smashed into his face.

-*Flow, huh?*-

Breathless, Dee smiled in pride that she'd taken Hamal down, searching his expression for recognition of her achievement. What she saw in his eyes hit her like a slap.

It wasn't pride in the skills he'd taught her. It wasn't even annoyance that she'd won in so clumsy a manner.

What beamed back at her was pure lust.

*

This was the very thing Hamal had been avoiding. Thoughts he was able to distract himself from were thrown in his face in a heap he couldn't just flip off. Her body pressing against him reminded him of the glimpse he'd gotten of her naked form under her oversized t-shirt on the first morning he'd arrived. Not to mention the camera's he'd hidden all over this house that showed she rarely wore clothes while moving about her dreary existence.

They were sights that haunted his nights. They were sights that made it tricky for him to remain in this role of aloof tutor. Her eyes, blue spheres that drew him in, pierced his own, so the only thing he could manage was complete stillness while he waited for her to remove herself from him.

Only, she wasn't moving. She was going to kiss him. The idea threw a smattering of emotions through him that moved quickly from panic to indifference. Who cared if their relationship got sexual? He wouldn't be with her much longer anyway, so what was the big deal?

It was Hamal who made the decision, lifting his head from the ground to find her lips with his. She never hesitated, their first touch sparking the desire they'd been repressing to a blazing need. Taking her head in his hands, his kisses turned forceful as he claimed her. Her weight pushed further into him when she moved her hands from holding herself off of him to press over his own framing her face.

In a sudden move, he flipped them, so he was pressing into her, their mouths never disconnecting, bodies moving together as they reacted to their host's desires.

Then, he was standing, breathless. He stared down at her for a brief second before turning to stride purposefully into the house.

*

Dee listened to him rush away, following his path in her mind. She heard him move through the house, then out the front door.

She continued to lay in the grass, eyes never straying from their stare into the pale blue sky, even after his SUV, screaming down the road, was no longer heard.

-*That was stupid.*-

That was stupid.

-*So much for your*—-

Shut it.

She rolled slowly to her feet, relishing the endorphins even as she waited for them to subside. She hoped the memory wouldn't betray her the next time such a situation arose.

-*Don't let there be a next time.*-

Sage advice.

She had been avoiding it, but here it had happened anyway when they'd both least expected it.

Chapter Fifteen

"Playtime's over! Get your shit together. Go again!"

-Well, at least things didn't get weird.-

This was more than weirdness. She wasn't sure what it was, exactly, but it wasn't that.

-You're sure, sure?-

Something had happened in the few hours he'd been gone. When she'd asked, he'd just gone on and on about how if she wanted to survive there needed to be less talking, less worrying about everyone's feelings, and more sweat dripping.

Yes, dripping sweat was essential to the cause of her not dying.

-Definitely sounds like weirdness from the kiss.-

She ignored the voice in her head. It wasn't that. At least, it wasn't *only* that. Hamal was worried. No, he was scared.

The thought terrified her.

They'd been training relentlessly for over an hour. She was surprised his voice hadn't gone hoarse with so much battering of her ego. If her confidence hadn't hit an all-time high with the introduction of the sword, she might be fighting off tears. Still, despite his exceptionally harsh treatment, he was teaching her things that could help her survive the insanity that was now her life.

"Why are you stopping!"

Dee's answer was quiet, eyes staring towards the front of the house. "Mike's pulling up the driveway."

Hamal threw a disgusted look towards the house. "Of course he is."

A frustrated snap of his wrist sent his sword piercing the ground and his steps actually stomped towards the house like a three-year old's tantrum. The glass door vibrated in its frame as it was slammed shut behind him. Dee flinched at the sound.

Leaving worry over Hamal's reaction for another time, Dee walked around the house to meet Mike. She refused to let him see her stress, forcing cheerfulness into her voice. "Hey, Stranger. Early day?"

His gaze took in her sweaty, grass-stained clothes, but he kept his questions to himself. "Something like that. I'm actually on my way out of town. Have lunch with me before I go?"

Dee stole a glance at the house, seeing if she could catch Hamal's watchful eye on her. "I'm sure that can be arranged. Have time for me to shower?"

He looked her up and down. "I will make time."

She laughed, slapping his arm playfully as she turned to the house, Mike following in her wake. His gaze lingered on Hamal's SUV still parked in her driveway. "Roommate working out?"

"He's teaching me some things."

She'd avoided talking about Hamal the few times Mike had brought it up. She knew he was dying to know what the deal was, but she wasn't a good enough lier to alleviate his questions. So, she didn't talk about it.

"Gardening?" He motioned to the dirt and grass stains covering her clothes.

She laughed. "No, some self-defense stuff."

He went rigid.

-The next time someones asks if you're gardening, you. Say. Yes!-

Mike's voice was quiet. "You're being safe? Not running around in the middle of the night?"

"No, Hamal keeps me in at night." Her face turned crimson at the realization of what she'd said, and she whirled around. "Not like that. We're not— "

Mike was laughing. "Relax, 'Case! I'm not your dad. I'd be ecstatic if you were having sex."

Her face blazed. "Wow! Awkward much?"

He laughed again. "We're friends. I can say that."

She laughed too. "Yeah, I guess you can."

Mike made a beeline for the kitchen as Dee went upstairs to start a shower, surprised Hamal wasn't waiting for them as they came in. He wasn't in his room, either.

With only a slight pause and a shake of her head, she continued to her room and the momentary bliss of a shower.

***

Impulsivity he'd had since childhood had been tempered by the implicitly understood fact that he would always be outmanned. Add that to the fact that few even bothered to look at him as much more than a pet, Hamal had quickly learned to hold his opinions to himself. That he hadn't stifled his reaction earlier with the girl was a bad thing. It was an impulse he'd expressly forbidden himself to give in to.

This case was messing with him. Out of the loop, out of sight of his betters, and out of contact with those who persisted in guiding him, he'd made his own decisions. Many, based on emotion. He could admit that. Impulsive, emotional decisions. Still, they were choices he didn't necessarily regret even when set against the fact that they would probably cause him a lot of grief in the future.

They were already causing him a lot of grief.

He walked, marching through the woods intent on finding something.

From the newest intel he'd received, he figured they had another day before Han's Soldier showed up. Or, someone was already here, checking on them; spying on them.

It's what his phone call with Porrima had told him. It's what had him acting crazy. It's what had him afraid.

The snide bitch had relayed the information as if telling him what she had for lunch. Zibanitu's hard line of neutrality wouldn't allow him to interfere directly with the girl they still didn't know enough about to warrant the risk.

Hamal kicked at the bramble as he walked. Wasn't the fact that Sabik Han was sending someone enough of a reason to get involved? As far as Hamal knew, no one had heard from Han's House in centuries. Hamal only knew of him from stories whispered in secret, the name not even allowed in Porrima's presence.

He was scary. Capital 'S' scary.

Zibanitu worked hard to maintain peace between the Houses whose millennia-old feuds could easily destroy pockets of the human world that had risen around the ashes of their culture's demise. Hamal appreciated the effort. As a member of the human race, he didn't want to see it destroyed because of ancient disagreements that should have been lost to time.

Not that he'd spent much time with his kind over the course of his life, but he still felt enough of a connection that he didn't want them swept up in the dangerous underground world he'd grown up in.

The peace Zi had shouldered through thousands of lifetimes was priority enough that even Hamal's death, the pet human, wouldn't shake him from his decision. Hamal's end would mean nothing when weighed against this bigger picture. Dee's would mean nothing.

Even after discovering the fantastic anomaly that she was, Zi wouldn't sway from breaking his own arbitrary rules. Hamal was sure there was nothing that ever would. It was probably the reason the Rishi among Rishis had been able to hold on as long as he had.

Who else could boast perseverance like that?

Hanging tightly to his anger kept the fear at bay. Hamal was no match for the Soldiers, their heightened strength and speed combined with unmatched training would put even Dee to shame. There was no way Hamal could keep Dee safe if one of them were on their way to her. That it was one of Sabik Han's only meant the likelihood of survival was even less.

Even so, he never once thought he should leave her. It hadn't been suggested that he do so, nor had Porrima offered any helpful advice. That they were working on it didn't instill confidence. They'd been working on it since before he'd arrived.

This was the first time he'd ever considered the fact that they weren't omnipotent.

He scowled, then again when he thought of Dee off with Mike having lunch. Lunch? Didn't she understand the danger she was in?

He stopped, the quiet of the forest pressing around him.

No, she didn't understand. Sure, she was scared. There were even moments when that fear threatened to turn into all-consuming terror, but she didn't really realize what was going on. How could she? He'd been so worried about not overwhelming her, added to the gag order he had on most topics, he hadn't been able to relay exactly how tough the Rishis, and their armies, were.

He hadn't been able to explain what they were. He assumed she'd understand when she finally saw it all herself. Unfortunately, it looked like the only time she'd be able to see it would be the same time it was killing her.

Fishing his phone from his pocket, he made a call, hoping he wasn't sealing his own death warrant.

Chapter Sixteen

She gave herself a moment to tilt her head back; to breath in the humid air of late summer; to watch the stars twinkle from so far away before she looked towards the trees. A lifetime ago her existence had consisted of lounging around the house waiting for the sun to go down so she could lose herself in the running. A lifetime ago, her life hadn't been in constant danger.

-A lifetime ago you were bored to tears.-

There was something peculiar about tonight's exercise; something that settled a somber calm over her. Maybe it was in the way Hamal had explained she would pick their path. Or the manner in which he'd brought so many new gadgets for a seemingly simple exercise. Or maybe it was just because he'd been acting strange all day.

Whatever it was, this wasn't like the last time he'd taken her out. That had clearly been a learning experience. This was something else, and Dee wasn't sure what to make of it.

-You can still just kill him.-

Dee ignored the voice's distrust. It was an irrelevant position at this point. She'd decided to put her faith in Hamal to train her and was too far on that path to back out now. It didn't make sense that he would go through all this trouble if he did have some nefarious plan.

-Because you don't see it doesn't mean it's not there.-

She was calm. A wall built around the things that couldn't be changed.

She met Hamal's eyes briefly before moving towards the trees, putting her hands to the straps of her new backpack, as he'd done to his own. Both had triple-checked the draw speed of their weapons, feeling in their core that there would be need of them. There was something in the air that told Dee this night would be unlike any other.

-Maybe it's telling you to stay inside.-

She moved away from town, directing their path towards the thick woods that ran South and a little West for miles without break. She kept her mind open, listening for any hint of an impression that something was out there.

Hamal was close on her heels. She imagined she felt his anxiety. The thought that there was something he hadn't told her begged to be asked.

-Like that would be a surprise.-

"What is it?" He'd noticed her slow their pace.

Her head panned back and forth as she peered into the shadows, posture hunched slightly, knees ready to spring. Something wasn't right.

"Something's not right."

Dee's sweat pooled between her shoulder blades where her pack pressed against her. She wanted nothing more than to strip out of the immobilizing load.

The air pressed around her.

-Don't tell him. He already knows too much about what you can do.-

Dee sighed, a release of frustration at the need to keep secrets that might mean their deaths. Would Hamal even be able to help her decipher what she felt if she did tell him? Was there even time?

There was a not-so-subtle difference in the one she sensed near; something off from the other Revenants she'd tracked. If she hadn't known better, she would have said the thing she felt wasn't a Revenant at all.

-*Great. Are we about to meet a whole new creepy-scary?*-

"Hamal, what else could be out here?"

He moved up next to her. "What do you mean?"

"I mean, what else could be out here. You said there were different levels of Revenants. Could they be out here?"

He opened his mouth to answer, but closed it without saying what he was thinking. His goggled face moved to stare into hers. "You know when they're around? You can—*feel*—them, or something."

The look on her face was answer enough.

His next words surprised her. "I think pulling your weapons might be a good idea."

She did as she was told. As he slid his shotgun to his back, replacing it with the rifle he carried, Dee pulled the long knife he'd gifted her in her left hand, the 9mm H&K she liked in her right. Despite him insisting she needed a smaller weapon to aim more accurately if she planned on using a one-handed grip, it was the one she'd decided on. The smaller Walther was snug at her back.

Hamal had been splurging to increase her arsenal.

He took a breath. "Alright, where to?"

-*You really suck at keeping secrets.*-

There was nothing to be done about it now.

That he was nervous made her almost pass out from fright. It took a few seconds and a lot of inner-coaching, for her to convince her feet to move forward. Once they did, she fell into a zone that took over her senses as she allowed herself to be pulled along by instincts, quietly leading the way through the trees as if she'd been doing it her whole life.

*

Hamal's slower pace had him quickly falling behind. If she heard his whispering for her to slow down, she ignored it. Torn between his fear of not being there to help her and the worry that he'd give away their position by being too loud, he hurried after her as fast as he could while remaining quiet.

Moving silently through the woods was an exercise in futility. Everywhere he placed his feet, noise followed, so he was forced to move painfully slowly. He was a city boy; his targets typically taken out in much more urban landscapes.

When Dee came back into view, she was crouched behind a tree, as still as a cat about to pounce on its prey. His nerves frayed, he took a breath to ensure his words wouldn't come out in a yelling blitz as he moved next to her. "The point of the exercise is to have the teacher near-by so he can teach."

She nodded, but he sensed she wasn't paying attention. He took another breath to berate her attitude, cut off when she motioned ahead with her chin. "It's almost to us."

Hamal peered through the white-phosphorous world, waiting to see what it was they'd been tracking. Or had it been hunting them?

As if in answer to his thoughts, Dee spoke again. "It knows we're here, but I don't think it can see as well as I can."

Hamal glanced at Dee, this time worried for an entirely different reason. It was like she'd shed some mask of the girl he'd been training and revealed the warrior underneath: cold, calculating, and unwaveringly focused. He shivered at the confident energy radiating off of her; at the matter-of-fact tone to her voice.

And what did she mean she thought she could see better than whatever was out there?

In a burst of speed beyond what he'd ever seen from her, she was attacking.

She was half-way to her target before he saw who it was.

He shouted a warning that fell on deaf ears.

The finely crafted gold snake symbol of the Ophiuchus' House hung around the perpetrator's neck to his waist. The few similar items Hamal had glimpsed, only in pictures, hadn't been this grand. Whoever this was, was at the top of the food chain.

Standing smoothly, Hamal anchored his shoulder to the tree they'd just crouched behind. He trained his weapon forward, real fear for Desiree washing his senses in a dampening fog. Not even Zibanitu's men would face off against one of Han's men without ensuring they had favorable numbers. Dee had no chance of winning and Hamal had no chance of successfully helping.

But he wouldn't just stand by and do nothing.

He slid through the trees, so his position didn't have Dee in his line of fire.

*

Dee's focus was sure, her plan clear. There was no place in her mind where doubt distracted her from felling this foe, though later she would marvel at the fact.

When none of her shots landed, the face of her prey smiled in delight, his laughter ringing around her.

Dropping her pistol, she moved her hand to pull her sword, at the last moment seeing his own hidden against his leg. Shifting the knife to her strong-hand, she left her sword sheathed in the possibility she might surprise him with it later. She launched herself into the air, aiming to pass over him, twirling, so her eyes never left her opponent. She sliced out with her knife and felt the blade grab cloth, then skin, before his movement took him away from the blade's bite.

She landed with bent knees, transitioning directly into a lunging second attack.

But he was ready. He easily parried this second attack, barely acknowledging where her knife had found his shoulder. His expression told her that he'd allowed her to finish her acrobatics rather than ending her in the air when he could have.

Dee launched herself to the side, rolling behind the trees for cover.

From her left, she heard the tap-tap-tap of Hamal's rifle fire, which spun the Soldier away from her with a growl. "Hamal! I'll get to you!" His voice dropped, so he seemed to be talking to himself, though his tone carried to the pair stalking him. "Stupid human has no reason to be here."

His tone was conversational, words directed at Hamal. "Smart of Zibanitu to send you though. No one plays politics better than Zi. Too bad The Ophiuchus cares nothing for his rules."

Only a part of Dee's attention was on this little speech as she stalked towards him. Deciding on offense, Dee came at the Soldier with sword drawn.

He whirled to her, his blade easily defending.

Then, he ran.

Dee followed, adrenaline pounding through her.

The Ophiuchus' man turned abruptly, but Dee was ready. He missed a step, forced to backpedal against Dee's flurry of strikes.

Despite his failed attack, a smile crept across his concentrated features.

Distracting them both, a rustle charged through the trees.

They broke apart to look at what was coming, both ready to face this new foe. Dee sensed Hamal in the trees behind her, telling her whatever was coming wasn't him.

Recognizing the newest threat, Dee's opponent abandoned his mission.

Dee halted at Hamal's command, letting the stranger disappear into the trees.

Chapter Seventeen

Hamal was explaining the evening's events to the bronze-skinned newcomer, while Dee pretended not to freak out. That this stranger was here on Hamal's request had her seething. Hamal's quick explanation, centered around the idea that he'd wanted to show Dee the reality of what she was up against in a controlled environment, hadn't pacified her.

-Controlled, my ass... what was with that other guy?-

That *other guy* was Barnard. Sent by The Ophiuchus, an enemy to all the Houses, no one was sure how he'd gotten word of Desiree's existence.

The stranger standing in her kitchen was Atkins, a Soldier from another House. Not one of Zi's.

-Fortuitous that they arrived on the same night.-

Atkins studied Dee for a moment before returning his attention to Hamal. "I don't think a secret has ever been so well kept. If you hadn't called, we still wouldn't have any idea this drama was unfolding."

Dee kept quiet, afraid her anger would erupt in a violent outburst if she allowed herself to speak. That and the press of power radiating from Atkins was unlike anything she'd felt so far, scaring her in a way not even Barnard's presence had. There'd been no question in her mind she could take that one, as misleading as it might have been. With Atkins, her only impulse was to run.

Atkins continued to speak to Hamal. "Amalthea's first questions dug up the hint that Zosma's been looking into some girl who might possess skills akin to our Soldiers. This is probably what tipped The Ophiuchus off. Whatever other answers that may have been uncovered were after I left to come here."

Hamal was nodding at Atkins' while glancing at Dee. She hoped her casual posture, eyes staring into the coming dawn as if she wasn't paying attention to the conversation behind her, was enough to hide the fact that she wanted nothing more than to kick them out of the house. She wondered if they would leave if she asked. Things had escalated from bad to nasty. Nasty enough that Hamal had gone into full protector mode.

He hadn't let her out of her sight, even with the death glares she'd been sending him.

There would be no getting rid of them.

She knew Hamal's next words were for her benefit. "It was Zosma who knew enough to test her? Sending the Revenants? The Ophiuchus wouldn't waste the time. He'd have just come and taken her."

He paused and when he resumed talking through the questions, his voice was quieter.. "How did he find out when no one else had caught on?"

"Zibanitu caught on," Atkins replied.

When no one filled the gap in conversation, Dee turned, repressed energy expelling her voice too loudly. "So, this Zosma, why would he want to test me?"

Hamal and Atkins shared a look that Dee couldn't decipher.

Her eyes narrowed. "Will there ever be a time when I can know what's going on?"

Hamal chocked on a laugh, managing chagrin when Dee threw him a venomous look. "Sorry. It's not funny, but you still don't understand who these things are or what their attention might mean for you."

Atkins raised an eyebrow.

"Sorry, Atkins, but you know what I'm saying."

Dee looked at Atkins, wondering what Hamal had apologized for, unless—Atkins was one of the things Hamal was referring to.

She froze, awed curiosity mixed with fear rendering her inert. Until now, the things sent after her had remained separate from whoever, or whatever, was dispatching them. Now, finding herself next to one of those *things* that might be controlling from behind the curtain, she wasn't sure what to do.

The two had continued talking. Atkins' calm grating against Dee's nerves enough that it pulled her attention back to what was being said. "...no one will want her in his hands. They'll come together to protect her from him. Assuming they don't consider her a threat."

"I'm right here," she barked.

Atkins looked at her with his weighted stare and she realized what it was about him that scared her. His gaze was anchored with an ageless wisdom she'd never encountered; a calm center that spoke of carefully contained violence.

She found herself holding her breath while his gaze was on her, only letting it out when it moved away.

"I'm sure my Mistress will take her, but we'll need backup to transport her. Barnard won't simply tuck tail and run."

Hamal's voice was distracted. "I didn't think he was Soldier."

Atkins' had turned to peer out the windows, staring into the brightening sky painting the trees from black to green. "He's not."

Dee's stomach dropped. Atkins wasn't a Master? Barnard wasn't a Soldier? She wasn't even sure how to prepare herself for what the Rishi's might be like.

So her mind didn't get lost down the path to despair, she focused on Atkins feature by feature.

His auburn hair fell past well-muscled shoulders. He was taller than Hamal's six-foot by at least four inches, towering like some ancient statue given life. His upper body was covered only by a leather vest that reminded her of some primitive tribal clothing. Cris-crossing his chest under this outer layer were straps that held bladed weapons of all sizes.

Trailing her eyes back to his face, she realized he'd been watching her study him. She blushed.

Whether from her embarrassment of being caught staring, or because of how he scared her, she rushed out of the kitchen, words tumbling out of her mouth before she'd considered what she was saying. "I'm going to pack some things."

-*Yeah? Were going with them.?-*

As if she could say no.

*

Hamal was astonished when she didn't put up a fight, though after her run-in with Barnard maybe she'd figured there was no other option. He stared at her retreating form, forcing himself from following to keep her in sight. Instead, he listened as her steps faded up the stairs.

"She's not what I thought she'd be." Atkins' quiet voice brought Hamal back from his wandering thoughts.

Hamal chuckled. "I'm surprised you gave it any thought at all."

A trace of a smile showed itself, equivalent to a hearty laugh for the ancient Soldier. "If she is what is rumored, it has been millennia in coming. Long have my people tried to do this very thing. How she managed to go so long under everyone's radar is a story I'm very curious to hear."

"What do you think she is?"

Atkins' contemplative stare was Hamal's only answer.

Hamal had to admit it didn't seem such a bad thing, whatever had been done to her. He would have sacrificed much to gain what she'd received. But, if she'd been created differently, if she were something *other*, things would get messy fast. A mess that might be enough to break the truce Zibanitu had maintained for so many centuries.

Hamal's eyes met Atkins, holding the Soldier's typical benign expression.

The suddenness of sprinting steps from upstairs turned their attention.

Dee's blurred shape disappeared towards the front of the house. She was out the door before Hamal had reacted, Atkins right behind her.

Hamal called out, but neither paid him any attention.

*

Though he could have stopped her, Atkins was curious to see what had incited such a reaction. He stayed behind, not distracting her forward attention, watching her pull a pistol in her left hand, and a fine eight-inch knife in the other. Whatever had called to her, it was not something she found friendly.

After following her through the trees, across the road, and through more trees, he understood what was going on. She'd caught one of their scents, remembering that Hamal had mentioned this was a trick of hers.

Unfortunately, the scent she'd caught was not of an enemy.

Atkins opened his mouth to explain, but it was too late. Dee had fired the 9mm rounds while picking up a burst of speed.

Daniel and Dimitri, Soldiers sent from Zibanitu's House, jumped and dodged the attack, their voices, first Dimitri's then Daniel's, rising over the burst of gunfire in the night air. "Damn. Wait! Stop! We're—" Her last shot landed, spinning Daniel around, though he managed to keep his feet. He roared to the sky, "Ahhhh! That hurts, you crazy bitch! We're here—"

He turned back around just in time to meet Dee's downward sword arc with his wrists.

Atkins breathed relief that the Soldier had bothered to wear his gear. The vambraces were standard issue, as the sword was the scariest weapon to face for a creature who could only die by bladed weapons.

Dimitri, hesitating, stood motionless through the engagement. Casting a glance at Atkins, he looked relieved that the elder Soldier reached the fight just in time to interfere with Dee's follow-up blow. Atkins pulled her sword from her in a move that defied physics and stepped between Dee and the newcomers, his free hand pushing into Daniel's chest, so he stumbled backward, still cursing his injury to the night.

*

"Relax, everyone, please." Atkins' voice was level, lacking the volume the stress of the situation might have invoked from another, but his words were obeyed without hesitation.

Dee, breathing hard, stepped back a few paces. Standing in the middle of the woods with a trio of supernatural creatures, she wondered if running out like a crazy person had been the best idea.

-We need to work on your impulse control.-

"Daniel. Dimitri. We haven't had time to brief her." Atkins' calm voice further settled the group's nerves.

-Brief? They've been brief alright. Vague even.-

The Soldiers nodded. Dimitri glanced around Atkins to throw Dee a sheepish look. "Sorry. We would have waited until you were in the loop, but we were told there's a severe time crunch."

-That's why the walk through the woods and not a car ride up the driveway?-

Daniel, his hand prodding his shoulder where her bullet had hit him, was less forgiving. He hissed, turning annoyed eyes to Dee's face. "How'd you even know we were here?"

Dee didn't answer. Her eyes drifted back the way they'd come when Hamal's scuffling reached her ears. He was still minutes from reaching them, and she wondered if she should go help him along. The sun had risen, but not much light breached the trees.

The Soldiers stood patiently, awaiting orders, a complete switch from the hollering they'd just been engaged in.

Atkins seemed confident Dee wouldn't continue to try to kill the newcomers. "Dee, my apologies for the manner this is all being sprung on you. I imagine everything will be fully explained, in its time. Right now, we need to get you out of here before the Ophiuchus' people come in force."

Dee, who'd only been half listening as she tracked Hamal's progress towards them, snapped her head around. "There might be more on the way?"

Atkins answered plainly. "Barnard will have called in reinforcements. They won't be afraid to fight for you, especially now that we're here to close their window of opportunity."

"How does Sabik Han even know she's here?"

Dimitri's words were mumbled but Atkins answered as if the question weren't rhetorical. "I imagine the same way your Master knows."

Dee looked between the three Soldiers. "I thought The Ophiuchus guy sent Barnard."

Daniel let out a sound that might have been a choked laugh. Dee's eyes flickered quickly to him, then back to Atkins, nerves too far gone to care of she was being laughed at.

Atkins answered, ignoring Daniel's laughter. "Sabik Han is The Ophiuchus, a title given him when he unmade the world."

-*Unmade the world?*-

"Who're these guys?" She stared at the pair of new arrivals, one light-haired where the other was dark, both over six feet tall and covered in tactical gear. She eyed the coverings on their arms that had allowed Daniel to so easily block her sword, wondering where she might get a pair of her own.

"Dimitri and Daniel are the forward guards." Light then dark.

-*Two guys?*-

"Just two guys?"

Atkins' nodded, ignoring the implied question. He set off at a walk, that was a jog for Dee's shorter stride, back towards the house.

Hamal met them fifty-feet back. He said nothing, only pausing to meet Atkins' eye, then run his gaze over Dee to assess if there were any injuries, before matching his pace with the group.

Daniel smiled upon seeing Hamal. "Well, well. No wonder this was kept quiet for so long."

Hamal humphed.

Dimitri's face revealed nothing.

-*Nice to know they're all on the same page.*-

Dee hated agreeing with her sarcastic inner voice. It was like no one knew what was going on; everyone stepping on everyone else's toes.

Thoughts of Mike flooded her mind, and she turned to Hamal, eyes emoting fear. "They won't involve Mike, will they?"

Hamal kept his gaze ahead, deliberately not meeting her look. "They shouldn't."

"Shouldn't? Like, shouldn't: they won't, or shouldn't: I can't tell you he's in danger because you'll freak out?"

Daniel answered, "They'll only involve him if it's absolutely necessary. He's safe today."

How did he even know who she was talking about?

She whirled on the newcomer, forcing the others to crowd her. They wouldn't put their hands on her if they didn't have to, knowing it might encourage her anger, but neither did they want her to attack the newest member of their group for a second time.

"What do you even know about it?! I would hand myself over without a thought if they threatened to do anything to Mike."

Daniel glanced past her and Hamal to Atkins. "She's sparky." His eyes met hers. "I like her."

Her eyes narrowed, and she took a step forward, stopping when she pushed against Hamal. As fun as it might be to fight them all, the headache pounding behind her eyes told her now was not the time.

Frustrated, she was surprised when Hamal spoke. Something Dee couldn't place permeated his tone. "Careful, Daniel."

Daniel's eyebrows rose, eyes turning to meet Hamal's with a look of both surprise and respect. He chuckled. "Well, well. Curiouser and curiouser." He returned his gaze to Dee, but it was Dimitri who spoke to her, head gesturing towards Hamal. "Don't settle for this one. You haven't even begun to see what's out there. Zibanitu's charity case could never keep up with you. You're one of us."

Daniel opened his mouth to say more, but Dimitri's hand on his shoulder stopped him. He held Dee's eye for a moment, before stepping through the group to stride confidently towards the house.

Dee turned to watch the pair walk away, unsure what she'd seen in Daniel's gaze. Something like humor, but also anger, and... lust?

She shook her head to fling it all away.

Chapter Eighteen

Dee was in the backseat, sandwiched between Dimitri and Daniel. Slamming the door against his objection to the seating arrangements, Daniel had stared Hamal down through the window as if daring him to object.

Hamal hadn't risen to the bait. Taking the passenger seat to allow Atkins to drive, he should have been ecstatic. His mission was about to end. Once they dropped Dee off at Amalthea's, he would never have to worry about her again. He'd never have to think of her. He should be relieved, but instead, he felt—pensive?

It had started an hour ago when Dimitri convinced Dee to arm wrestle. It was an absurd request that she'd refused. When the Soldier hadn't let it go, egged on by Daniel, she'd finally agreed just to shut them up. Even Hamal hadn't believed she could win. These guys could, literally, dodge bullets. Daniel had healed the wound to his shoulder so quickly it was like it'd never happened. Arm wrestling seemed irrelevant after that.

But she'd won.

She beat both Dimitri and Daniel.

They hadn't let her out of their sight since, and despite their very purpose there being to ensure her safety, there was something different about the way they watched her after her display of strength.

Hamal wasn't sure why this bothered him so much.

Atkins had expressed the futility of the wasted time but hadn't pressed the issue. Not had he seemed put off by the way the pair latched on to their charge. So, Hamal had stayed in the corner, keeping himself aloof as the Soldiers acclimated to their assignment, digesting the flutter of unfamiliar feelings.

Hamal's eyes narrowed in their stare out the windshield, remembering the moment when Daniel had jumped up, excited rather than indignant that he'd lost the Neanderthal battle, hugging a bewildered Dee. What did he care if Daniel liked her? Or Dimitri? The Soldiers wouldn't be around long either. They'd be joining Hamal back with Zibanitu.

Except that might not be true.

Amalthea had allowed Atkins to come when Hamal had broken the rules and called the Soldier. She then agreed to open her doors to them where Zi couldn't. As the self-proclaimed head of all the Houses, Zibanitu would be forced to explain Dee's existence and strange attributes. Keeping her from his House would allow him to feign ignorance. That Hamal was human, so not technically one of them, was a loophole that had allowed him to be here without worry that Zi would have to answer questions.

Amalthea, in turn, was allowed to call on Zibanitu for help in the form of a few Soldiers, since she was unable to create any of her own. A couple of Soldiers given on loan wasn't something Zi would be compelled to explain. That he'd only sent two of his youngest highlighted how cautiously he was treating this situation. Theoretically, two Soldiers could be on loan for an indefinite period without turning heads.

Both Dimitri and Daniel, born human, had survived the stressful change to superhuman. Zibanitu had never allowed the conversation that Hamal attempt this transition, and until today, Hamal had never thought to push it. Hamal had always considered himself lucky in this regard, enjoying the freedom his aloofness gave him. Now, sensing the pulse of the three behind him, noting how much like them Dee was and how quickly she'd fit into the world he only fringed, he wondered if his time had come.

Four dark SUV's, identical to the one they were in, were pulled over at the entrance to the upcoming rest stop. Dee leaned forward between the front seats. "Who are they?"

Hamal turned his head to answer, surprised to find her so close. His hand clenched the door to battle the feelings swarming in him.

Before he could answer, Dimitri leaned up between them. "It's the cavalry!"

The Soldier's eyes shone with good humor, and Dee smiled with him. She sat back as Atkins slowed their vehicle to let two of the caravan pull ahead of them, the other two following. Without stopping, they all merged back onto the highway as if they'd been traveling together all along.

Dee asked, "Are they all Soldiers?"

Daniel answered, "Probably. There might be a medic or two, but I'm not sure if they'd care about anything but firepower—"

"Daniel." The one word from Atkins stopped Daniel's speech. Dimitri made a sound that was followed by a chuckle from Dee.

Dimitri faked a whining tone. "You guys are always so serious."

"Only about serious things." Atkins' eyes never left the road.

***

Thinking back, she couldn't be sure if it was the sound of impacting cars, or the jostle of her body as it was thrown from the vehicle, that woke her. When her crazed motion came to a sudden halt, she struggled to remember how to even open her eyes.

The *tap-tap-tap* of suppressed semi-automatic fire pulled her from the brink of unconsciousness, though her eyes remained closed. Through the pandemonium of sound, she heard her name shouted, focusing on it as a tether to pull her fully awake.

Eyes snapping open, cheek pressed to the asphalt, her first clear vision was of the caved-in roof of one of the SUVs close to her face. She tentatively pulled her arms from her sides to press palms into the ground.

"Dee! Wait! Stay down!"

She complied, not sure whose voice she was obeying, not even sure if she could have found the strength to push herself up anyway. A hand on her back told her someone had come up beside her. "You alright?"

She managed a groan, which elicited a laugh from whoever was near. The sound told her it was Dimitri. She was surprised how deep her relief was that he was okay, her thoughts quickly turning to the others. If she was in this bad of shape, how would Hamal be?

"Good. I'm—" A burst of weapons fire cut him off, the thundering noise of his return assault deafening. In the sudden wash of silence, he spoke in a rush, "Okay, I'm going to keep shooting at the bad guys. You run into the trees there. I think Hamal made it. I saw Metis with him." He glanced down to make sure Dee was listening. "I know, I can't believe she let him out of her sight either."

Not having a clue who, or what, he was talking about, Dee managed to sit herself up, strength coming back in exponential returns. She felt her body knitting itself together, prompting another groan. This process was not exactly painful, but painful was the only word she had for it.

-*Time to expand your vocabulary.*-

The Soldier recognized her confused expression. "You don't know what I'm talking about. Why would you?" He laughed, a strange sound juxtaposed against the raging of battle around her. He was crouched, firing over the overturned SUV Dee had been happily napping in not so long ago.

Dee ducked her head against the loud popping exploding through her eardrums, the echoes of the reports making it impossible to figure out where they were coming from.

A part of her brain recognized that she should be dead. The damage to the truck suggested it, and her body lying on the pavement reinforced the idea. A second flipped vehicle was near enough that she wondered if it had rolled over her.

-*Yup, you should definitely not be alive.*-

Sensory overload was pushing her to panic, so she continued to analyze these data points in a detached way to maintain the eerie calm she was currently experiencing. If she was forced to engage with her surroundings, she just might lose it.

"Ready?" Daniel slid in beside them, the scraping sound of his clothes against the asphalt pulling Dee's attention.

-Let's not lose it just yet.-

She rose to a crouch next to him, balancing on the balls of her feet, adrenaline pulling her further from her daze as her blood finished repairing her injuries.

Trying to block out the loudness of wild bursts of gunfire followed by indecipherable yells from Soldiers, she focused on Daniel, nodding that she was ready. What she was ready for, she wasn't entirely sure.

Through the shattered windows of the totaled truck in front of her, she mapped the place Dimitri had pointed for her to go. She didn't see anyone there, but having no better plan, she trusted he knew what he was talking about.

-There's that trust *word again.-*

"Didn't I say you were one of us?" Daniel laughed, firing a burst behind her as Dimitri fired to the side. He let the clip fall to be replaced by a fresh one while yelling, "Go go go!"

The first *GO* already had her on her way, stumbling the first two steps before her body remembered its dexterity. In two breathes, she was in the brush.

*

Amalthea watched the chaos on multiple screens spread across the long wall.

While the Rishi prided herself on an estate full of bright, airy rooms filled with plants and flowers, this room she'd had purposefully built beneath the others in sterile grays and whites. No view to the outside world was near except from secondary sources that might beam the information onto one of the slew of monitors that sat around the room. The wall she now stared at, twenty feet of 3D capable viewing, was linked to the Soldiers she'd sent after the girl.

Each Soldier's visual display showed the fight from their point-of-view, along with the skewed feeds from the dash-mounted cameras inside the vehicles, most tilted at ninety or one-hundred eighty degrees, as well as a satellite feed Phecda had managed to commandeer.

Processing all the information wasn't enough to calm her. Watching had never been her thing.

She spoke into her headset, a direct link to Ainn, who'd she'd put in charge of the retrieval, "Twenty minutes until pick-up."

"Roger."

There were eighteen of the Rishi's people on site, plus Hamal and Desiree, at the time of the ambush. She hadn't seen the hit, but the aftermath marked the events she'd missed. Her people were in trouble, and all she could do was pace back and forth in front of the screens, listening to the chaos.

Would the others reach them in time?

*

"You really are tougher than you look." Hamal's voice came from further in the brush. She turned to find him supported by the most unnaturally attractive man she had ever seen. She tried to focus on her mentor, glad he wasn't dead, though not unscathed, but her eyes continued to return to the other man's face.

"What happened?" She was surprised at the calmness of her voice.

The beautiful man answered, effortlessly supporting Hamal's weight with no sign of difficulty. "The Ophiuchus sent his troops. We knew he would. We'd hoped to make it back to the estate before he caught up to us." His demeanor was different than the other Soldiers she'd met; his energy something else, as Atkins' had first seemed. Whatever this new variation might be, he felt powerful enough to be just as scary.

Dimitri had said it was Metis who had helped clear Hamal from the wreckage. Dee assumed that's who she was looking at.

She studied Metis' face, his skin the same bronzed tone as Atkins, hoping to find something there that might explain the difference she felt in him. His beauty lay in the flawless skin that almost glowed, as well as eyes that shone with an inner light she'd never imagined was more than hyperbole.

A shout pierced the din of chaos behind her, bringing her attention back to the dire situation they were in.

She turned, using a tree as cover as she peered out towards the fighting. "Are we winning?"

This time Hamal answered, his voice breathy and forced. "Hard to tell, but with Atkins and Vali out there, I wouldn't bet against us."

"Vali?"

Her questions were interrupted when a spray of bullets flew nearby. Metis deposited Hamal on the ground. Hamal grimaced against a thick tree, eyes closed, breathes ragged. Metis moved towards the fighting, pausing near Dee to study the battlefield.

Dee moved away from Metis towards where he'd left Hamal. She stooped down to him, wincing at the struggles his lungs were having. She didn't have to know much about his injuries to assess they needed to get him out of there. His leg was broken, and by the shortness of his breaths, she guessed a few ribs, too.

She patted his arm awkwardly, not sure what else to do.

Metis pulled a pair of long knives, or short swords, and jumped into the fray. Dee imagined she could hear his weapons cut the air as he slashed and stabbed at their attackers.

Returning her attention to Hamal, she found he'd fallen to unconsciousness. She knew there was nothing she could do to help him. Feeling utterly useless, she stood. Her motion to pull her weapons reminded her that they'd been taken and put in the trunk of Hamal's SUV.

Just dig in here. No reason to go out there. They can handle themselves.

-But it would be so much fun if we did.-

They definitely could handle themselves, but still, her feet had brought her closer to the road so she could better see the conflict on the street.

Three of the five trucks she'd been traveling with had flipped, blocking both lanes of traffic. The SUV she'd been in the most damaged. A pair of mammoth trucks explained how the caravan had been flipped, tossed and crushed. On the far side of the road, she saw where these vehicles must have lain in wait. A construction site cleared of trees was big enough to have hidden the ambush from those not looking for it.

At least, she imagined that's how it went.

Gunfire surrounded her, the echoes of the blasts ricocheting through the trees, so it was impossible to tell how many there were, or which direction the reports were coming from. Remembering what Hamal had explained about why they used guns and that the weapons probably wouldn't kill any of them, gave her a modicum of comfort. The real fighting wouldn't begin until the gunfire stopped.

Sighing loudly, she looked out over the carnage of vehicles littering the road, tracking the best route to where her weapons were hidden.

Someone leaped over the truck she was eyeing, turning quickly to fire at whoever was giving chase. Not sure who the Soldier was, Dee realized she'd never be able to distinguish between those on her side and those trying to take her. Except for Daniel, Dimitri, Atkins, and Metis, she didn't know the faces of who fought for her. Apparently, tactical gear didn't come in *good guy* and *bad guy* colors.

*

From the satellite feed, Amalthea saw the girl who'd incited this storm peek her head from the tree cover.

She whispered to the girl on the screen, "Stay put. We're here to keep you safe. Don't make our job harder."

*

She was convincing herself it was worth the risk to make a move for her weapons, body still crouched out of sight, when a voice called out to her. Dee's eyes panned the chaos for who it was.

His dark clothing blended in with the shadows of twilight quickly pressing on them.

Barnard.

From fifty feet down the road, his back pressed against a vehicle that had managed to stay upright, he met her eyes. Something in his gaze held Dee's.

She hadn't noticed his beard when they'd battled in the woods. It seemed an obvious thing not to see. She could understand why his striking cheekbones wouldn't have registered, or that his piercing eyes were an almost unnatural shade of amber, both characteristics that should have labeled him handsome but somehow didn't.

Barnard extended a hand as if she could just take it like a child to be led away. It was a gesture of welcome, of safety.

-*Don't be nuts.*-

But how would it be more nuts than what she was already doing? Maybe going with Barnard would stop the fighting. Maybe Barnard was the good guy. If he'd gotten to Dee before Hamal, would this situation be reversed? How could she know whether she was picking the side that was in her best interest?

*

Barnard. It wasn't a surprise to see him there. He was the one Han had sent to meet Dee near her house.

Still, Amalthea was astonished to see Han's right-hand so near danger. Barnard was never one to throw himself into battle. He served an advisory role to the Ophiuchus, who was not known to take much counsel. She wondered, not for the first time, about the nature of their arrangement that kept the servant relevant.

Used to not getting answers to the hard questions, she watched the Messenger's hand come out in a gesture that spoke his desire for the girl to go with him. If Desiree decided to go along, there was no one near to stop her.

In quick staccato, Amalthea prompted the computer, "DORTHY, ping the nearest operative to Desiree."

Immediately, the electronic voice replied, "I have pinged Operative Ellie."

Barely a second passed. "Ellie here, Rishi."

"Ellie, Barnard is on site and currently engaging the contact. He's—"

"I see them."

Startled at being cut off, she settled her feelings quickly as she watched the female Soldier's camera move stealthily through the engagement to intercept her target.

*

A barrage of bullets turned Dee's attention. Dimitri sprinted towards her, his super speed blurring his steps until he was crouched next to her.

"Deja vu?" His voice was conversational, but his glance asked what the hell she was doing.

"I thought I might be able to help."

Daniel was suddenly on her other side, studying her as if seeing her for the first time. "Since it's you they're after, I think laying low is the best idea. Wouldn't want them to sneak up on you and steal you away while we were trying not to die."

He was right. They were both right. She'd known it, but she'd wanted to get away from the sound of Hamal's injuries.

-So, you'd rather get shot at?-

Daniel sent a barrage of gunfire towards the center of the chaos.

Dimitri spoke between bursts of fire. "We've got reinforcements on the way to pick you up. Atkins and Vali are doing just fine taking Han's forces out while the rest of us keep them inside the funhouse of wrecked cars. Everything will be fine."

*

Amalthea sighed in relief when Dimitri and Daniel distracted the private interaction between Desiree and their enemy. From Ellie's camera, Amalthea watched Barnard come into view, but she lost visual when the camera swung around to meet an engagement from a trio of Han's men. Ellie fired a couple of quick bursts, diving behind cover and low crawling to a new position.

Amalthea searched the other feeds, looking for Desiree from another's point-of-view. It was good news that she didn't find the girl quickly. It meant she was far enough away from the battle to be out of sight of those engaged. Still, she couldn't help a twinge of nerves that it also meant the girl could be taken right from under their noses.

Ellie's feed showed that she'd finally flanked Han's trio. Atkins and Vali, whirling beings of violence, helped the Soldier take them out.

Amalthea breathed relief before returning her attention to the satellite images that were the only source for Desiree's location.

The girl now stood flanked by Zibanitu's Soldiers.

Barnard had vanished.

*

Dee looked to where Barnard had stood. He was gone, along with his offer to take her out of there. Returning her attention to her more direct surroundings, noting how carefully Dimitri and Daniel were protecting her, she wondered how exactly she had planned on helping them.

-I think your plan stopped at retrieving your weapons from the back of the SUV.-

Her gaze returned to the truck laying on its hood, its crunched body making her wonder if she'd even be able to open the back if she made it there. "My weapons are in the back."

"Okay?" Daniel was searching the wreckage through the scope of his rifle.

Sliding from the cover of the trees, Dee stayed crouched, preparing to beeline for the spot in the center of the wreckage. Daniel's arm on hers spun her back to cover. "Whoa there. Your weapons can be replaced. I'm not letting you go out there."

Dee huffed, eyes moving behind Daniel to rest on Hamal hunched against the tree. She focused, desperate to see some movement that told her he was still alive, but there was too much background sound for her to get a good read.

The noise was getting to her, grinding on her nerves so much she wished she'd stayed unconscious. Its intensity forced a sense of vertigo through her, and she stumbled forward. Her hand flung out to catch herself, landing on Daniel's shoulder.

"Is she hit?" Dimitri's voice behind her was panicked while Daniel's hands frantically groped her to deduce if she was hurt.

When he relaxed his hold on her to reassure his mate she was okay, she pulled away, sprinting towards the crashed SUV and her weapons.

-Yes! Let's get down and dirty!-

Both Dimitri and Daniel lost a critical second as they stared uncomprehendingly after her before following, guns blazing a path of cover for the girl who seemed to have lost her mind.

Slamming into the crushed vehicle jolted some of her sense to the forefront of her brain, but it was too late to take back her decision. Daniel slammed into the truck next to her while Dimitri crouched away from the vehicle to cover their back. Daniel's fire over their cover barraged her brain, so she squeezed her eyes closed.

Breathing deeply to help force the sounds away she searched for just a nanosecond of calm.

A nanosecond was all she got.

*

Amalthea's eyes remained on Dee. She couldn't tear her eyes from Zibanitu's pair keeping close watch over her, even as the others kept enemies away.

Only the trio coming from the girl's home hadn't been equipped with surveillance and communications gear. Dimitri and Daniel had never had the opportunity, and Atkins had left too quickly for them to think this far ahead.

If they'd been able to comm-up, the Rishi would have been able to warn the pair they were being closed in on.

She rushed to ping Ainn, already knowing there wouldn't be time.

*

Daniel was kicked backward. Dee turned to help, but a second assaulter rounded their cover, weapon peppering Daniel, while more gunfire told her the same was happening to Dimitri behind her.

She may have screamed.

Jumping the one assaulting Daniel, Dee spear-tackled him at the waist. She used the momentum to swing around and throw Daniel's assailant to the ground, burying her elbow in his face. His arms came up to stop her assault, bringing the tactical knife strapped to his forearm to her hand.

She broke it free from the snap that held it in place and buried it in his neck, wrenching it across in an attempt to sever his head from his body, actions born from pure adrenalized instinct.

The knife wasn't long enough for a clean cut, nor was she in the right position to cleave through both muscle and bone, but he was sufficiently incapacitated that she could turn to the others.

Leaping to her feet, facing where Daniel had fallen, knife in hand, she ducked instinctively when another burst of weapon fire went off, nearer than before. She kicked with all her might into the ribs of a second attacker now straddling Daniel, long blade poised to strike a killing blow. The Soldier flew, spinning, down the road to bounce roughly against one of the overturned SUV's.

She turned to those engaging Dimitri. She managed to disarm and disable one but was too late to stop the lethality of the other assault on her bodyguard.

*

Amalthea stared at the screen, mouth open in astonishment. These were The Ophiuchus's soldiers. Even against her best, they were nothing to be trifled with, and this girl had just taken out three of them.

"Rishi?" Ainn had been waiting for orders, confused when her open comm remained silent.

"Get to the girl. She's in the center of the wreckage. Dimitri and Daniel are down. She's a sitting duck."

"Understood."

*

Dimitri was still breathing, but not doing well.

The same could be said for Daniel.

Bullet holes peppered their torsos. Daniel's neck looked like the guy Dee had just left, though ripped apart by bullets rather than a blade. How munition weapons might kill the hard-to-kill was now clear to Dee.

But they weren't dead.

-Yet.-

Dimitri was unconscious, but Daniel's panicked eyes flashed to her as she dropped to his side. She took his hand, an instinctive reaction to bring him comfort even as she was loath to touch him and cause him more pain.

"Daniel?" She whispered. It carried all the questions she'd never asked, all the sympathy she'd ever felt, and all the hope that they'd all be alright.

He closed his eyes, his expression now vacant. Dee was afraid she'd witnessed his last breath. Tears welled in her eyes as a fierce rage took her breath.

Looking around for someone who could help, she watched the enemy Soldier she'd kicked get up, glaring at her as he held his ribs. She knew she'd broken them, but his healing factor would be knitting them back together. That was unacceptable.

Daniel's sword lay in its sheath half underneath him. Dee retrieved it, moving towards the enemy Soldier, the naked blade resting loosely in her hand, fear washed from her mind.

"We're here to take you with us," the Soldier was saying, but Dee was beyond hearing. Barely registering his words, their sounds muted by the rush of blood through her system, she stalked closer. The murderer's eyes went wide, seeing his death in her face.

He pushed his hands in front of him. "Wait! I won't hurt you. We were told to bring you unharmed. You no longer have to be deceived by the others."

His words came in a rushed babble, but Dee did not hear. She leaped at the Soldier who didn't defend himself. Whether out of strict obedience to orders or because he didn't believe she would kill him, she didn't pause to consider.

A quick twirl gave enough force to cleanly cut through the pleading Soldier's neck. His head dropped from his body, eyes staring in surprise as it was tossed through the air. Barely giving him a second look, she turned back to the Soldier whose head she'd mostly cut off with his own knife.

There was nothing to worry about from him. A statuesque Soldier who hadn't been there a moment ago, a Soldier Dee assumed was on her side, stood over his torso, having finished the job Dee had started.

Dee paused, intimidated by the newcomer, but Daniel's throaty cough brought her attention back to him. The newcomer stepped to Daniel's side but maintained a watchful eye on their surroundings as Dee fell to her knees next to her injured guard.

She barely looked up when another soldier knelt opposite Daniel's body. This one was petite as the other was giant. Long auburn hair spilled down her back when she ripped off her combat helmet.

*

"DORTHY, how are we with local law enforcement?"

The computerized voice responded after barely a second's pause, "We've intercepted all calls to emergency services. The road continues to stay closed to potential witnesses."

Amalthea's voice was sharp. "Who called it in then?"

"Noise of a firefight like this will travel. This isn't as remote a location as the direct surroundings may suggest." It wasn't the computer who answered.

Amalthea turned to greet the woman coming into the room, welcoming her presence with a smile. "Phecda. I thought you'd left."

The taller woman stepped next to Amalthea, eyes scanning the monitors behind neat glasses designed for aesthetic, rather than practical, use. None of the Rishis had ever suffered trivialities of mortality such as fading eyesight.

The rest of the Rishi's appearance matched this clean look. Expensive business suit tailored perfectly to her trim form, hair carefully managed in a sensible pony-tail, tasteful make-up highlighting her features perfectly but not overtly. Phecda was ever practical.

"I couldn't miss the excitement of what my intel spawned."

Amalthea's smile deepened. Though it was often buried, she knew this one had a heart buried beneath her many layers. "Find anything else?"

Phecda's lips turned up.

Amalthea chuckled. She'd never been good at playing Phecda's game. The game. Amalthea communicated too directly to effectively play at subtly. Phecda dealt in information, and it wasn't good business to give away her commodity for free, even to a friend.

What she'd done for Amalthea would cost, but Amalthea was sure it would be worth it.

"Atkins and Zi's guys went in without gear?" Phecda's smile vanished, eyes ingesting the information on the wall in front of her.

Amalthea nodded. "We hadn't thought to send gear. Things happened too fast."

Phecda frowned. "Still, the other cars would have been stocked with backups they could've used." Her frown deepened. "Vali has tactical command?"

"Vali's too interested in his personal body-count to ever have tactical command."

Phecda nodded. Amalthea wasn't known for military strategy. There'd been few times in the whole of their history that Amalthea'd been directly involved in any fighting, zero where her House had been in a point position. Amalthea knew it was why Phecda was here. The curiosity of watching Amalthea direct a tactical mission was an opportunity that may never arise again.

"Ainn has command."

Phecda scanned the screens, noting stress levels from the biometric feeds, combat styles of individual Soldiers, anything that might prove useful later. She said nothing more. Amalthea knew it was just her habit to gather information.

*

The female Soldier was pouring powder into the holes littering Daniel's body while he squeezed his eyes shut, struggling to breathe. Dee watched helplessly as guilt ate at her. If not for her, none of them would be getting shot at, and Dimitri and Daniel wouldn't be dying on some backroad in the middle of gods-knew-where.

Dee squeezed his hand.

His neck wounds were closing on their own, the introduction of the powder speeding the process. Dee wondered what it was but wouldn't interrupt the medics tasks. She watched as it seemed to soak and clot the blood, quickly turning his bleeding wounds to pinkish marks across his body.

The woman handed a thick wad of gauze to Dee. "Here. Hold this in his neck. Press hard."

"*In* the wound?" Dee looked down, stifling her urge to throw up. The girl nodded, continuing her triage. Another had been working on Dimitri, and Dee's gaze went to him, wondering how he was hanging on.

She put the gauze to Daniel's neck, gasping when his eyes flew open in pain.

"It hurts, but its better than him dying," the medic said with out looking up from her work.

Dee pressed on the neck wound, closing her own eyes so she wouldn't have to see Daniel's expression of agony.

*

"Did we get everyone out?"

Ainn's voice paused. "We lost Tau. Injuries were sustained all around."

Each Soldier was monitored closely when they were in the field, but there was always the possibility of equipment failure. Ainn's confirmation only validated what was displayed in front of them.

Amalthea's voice was sad. "You all fought well. We were strong. Against the best, we succeeded in our mission."

"Thank you, Rishi." Ainn's comm channel closed.

Phecda watched Amalthea's face, judging the truth of the feeling saturating her response. What she saw there convinced her of its validity. Affection had always been a part of Amalthea's personality, but after so long, Phecda was surprised to see it still held a place so close to the surface.

Too many of them had forgotten who they were, now hiding behind masks they'd perfected over so much time she wondered how many remembered their roots.

The Keeper of Secrets made a mental note not to stay away so long. Personal visits could be useful for other kinds of intel.

"How many of Han's are down?" Phecda stepped back to Amalthea's side after checking over the equipment she'd loaned to get the satellite surveillance up and running.

Amalthea repeated the question so the V.I. would respond, "DORTHY? How many enemy units are down?"

"My estimation is eight, Rishi," the computerized voice was loud in the quiet aftermath of the chaos.

"It seemed we were able to get Dee out too easily." Amalthea's voice was quiet, contemplative. She was proud of her people but understood the prowess of their enemy. She hadn't expected success with such minimal casualties.

The computer continued its assessment. "The enemy seemed unwilling to risk harm to the target. They only engaged at a distance, enabling your units to keep them away. The reinforcing caravan was able to pick up the first team with little difficulty."

Phecda nodded. "They didn't push their perimeter. They weren't expecting so many to be protecting her."

"A mistake I'm sure Han won't make again."

"Han," Phecda whispered the name as if speaking it for the first time. It'd been so long since the name attached to The Ophiuchus' title had been uttered so brazenly.

"That is his name." Amalthea's voice was laced with annoyance.

Phecda nodded, tilting her head as she filed this information away with the others. Had enough time passed that old wounds could heal? Was the human platitude *time heals all* relevant even for them?

Looking back at the monitors showing vehicles leaving the battle zone with the asset secured, Phecda contemplated what other things this new revelation might breed among the Houses, and how she might anticipate them so her market would be full when the time came.

Chapter Nineteen

"Hamal did an outstanding job. You weren't there. She was downright scary."

"I don't know what girl you saw, but that one up there is as frightened and clueless as any I've ever come across."

Amalthea listened to the conversation distantly, never pausing in pruning the rose bushes that ran the length of the low wall surrounding her garden patio. They needed their time to sort things out before she would come in with the final word. And, she wasn't embarrassed to admit, she was interested in hearing about the strange girl from those who had seen her in action.

Zibanitu's unwillingness to commit himself to direct involvement had offered Amalthea this chance. That, and the fact that Phecda had been close at hand when she'd received her information that The Ophiuchus was planning a military strike.

Even with that information, they'd all been unaware of Barnard's visit to Dee until Atkins had called in the tip, already too late to be of use. It was fortuitous that Hamal had broken orders by calling on Atkins, which was the only thing that had saved the human's life, and maybe even Dee's. Assuming Hamal survived his injuries, Zibanitu might forgive the transgression his pet had made when he'd called on another House for aid.

Sending her own people had been a risk the likes of which she hadn't taken in recent memory. Amalthea had no way to replace her numbers if they fell. Only through favors and goodwill had she managed to amass the small army that made up her House. Tau's fall would be felt for decades. Maybe longer.

Daniel, though still alive, didn't seem to be healing. Although stable, he was in bad shape and mystifying her medical staff. There were questions about whether The Ophiuchus (Han, she scolded herself) had found some poison that somehow slowed the healing process. That Daniel had survived his wounds at all suggested not, but Amalthea was already battling the rumors. Thankfully, none sitting here had brought it up. Her temper would have ignited like Vesuvius if they had.

Time had taught her, rather ungracefully, the benefit of prudence, so she stilled her turmoil. The next forty-eight hours were crucial, both in what they did about the girl and how they reacted to Sabik Han's strike. The likelihood that Han would attack her estate was low, but this probability depended on how badly he wanted the strange girl. The girl who, until yesterday, far fewer had known existed.

Hoping the others didn't catch wind of what was going on, Zi agreed with Amalthea that they lay low. The more who got involved, the messier things would be for everyone. Zibanitu's compound was more secure than her estate, but that wouldn't matter if they couldn't get her there safely. They'd already seen what could happen, and the distance to get her to Zi's was much more significant than getting her here had been.

It also afforded Zibanitu more time to decide how he would formally address the issue. Having the girl stay here meant he had no one to answer to. Han's attack might have forced his hand, so he was glad not to have to take responsibility just yet.

Amalthea's thoughts drifted back a few hours to when the caravan, full of amped up Soldiers, had arrived, along with one of her own dead, and three of Zi's severely injured. A team had met the incoming group, opening doors even before the trucks had come to a full stop to bring the wounded to the on-site hospital. Those uninjured had stood guard, every cell on high alert in case another assault pressed them on their home turf.

Dee had sat on the far side of the Humvee she'd shared with Atkins and a driver, facing away from the thickest of the commotion, seeming oblivious to the frenzied movement around her. Any attempt to remove her from the vehicle was met with no response. Not wanting to risk frightening her even more, they'd let her be.

Amalthea had come to greet her guest. The Rishi had watched quietly as the remaining medic looked up in frustration that she couldn't get the girl to respond, let alone leave the truck. Amalthea met the medic's gaze and shook her head, allowing the medic to back off to attend other duties.

The sudden silence hadn't brought the girl from her trance either.

Amalthea had remained on the opposite side of the girl, able to see directly through the truck to where she sat in the back seat. All the doors were open, the driver impatiently waiting steps away so he could pull the truck out of sight.

It was Amalthea's turn to try to convince the girl to come with her. Voice pitched to motherly kindness she coaxed, "It'd be best if we could get you inside."

She remembered this girl's fighting prowess from the video feeds so was loath to push too hard and risk inciting defensive wrath. But, if the girl were in shock, they'd need to get her inside right away.

"Desiree? Is it okay if I sit with you?" Amalthea took the nonresponse as a yes. Climbing into the back seat, she sat with her shoulders squared to the front, even as she kept Dee in her periphery.

She hadn't bothered to really look at the girl when the fighting was taking place, so Amalthea used this time to examine her guest who continued to stare unseeing into the surroundings. If she hadn't seen her with her own eyes, Amalthea's skepticism would have been high, along with her anger that she'd risked so many of her own to save this one not even rumor had spoken of.

She replayed the scene in her head: Dee moving quickly, too fast for any pure-blooded human, to meet the threat that had taken out Dimitri and Daniel.

Was she a rogue Soldier? It wasn't common, but there were stories...

And if she were a Soldier, her skills were already catching up to those few who'd been alive since the beginning.

Hamal's mentorship was evident in her movements, the slight variations of the style of Zibanitu's House tailored for his less physical skill. Hamal had learned much in his years among them but could never match the enhancements of the Initiated. Yet, in this case, he'd been the only one who could have started this adventure with this strange girl.

She smiled despite herself, wondering how much foresight Zibanitu conjured, or if his over-preparedness only suggested prescience. Had he known all along who this girl was? Had he held the information close to his chest for the rest of them to flesh out on their own? Had he only interceded when someone made a move?

Silent minutes passed.

Amalthea extended her hand. "It's time to go inside."

Dee didn't move and Amalthea was afraid they'd have to force her out of the truck, a move that would do nothing good for building trust. Just as that seemed to be the last option, Dee asked, "Who are you?"

The girl's quiet voice held a trace of that strength Amalthea had witnessed from the field. The Rishi smiled, glad the girl would be walking from the truck of her own volition. "I'm Amalthea. I am the Rishi of this House."

Dee's head turned towards her, face tilted slightly, eyes focused far away. "Rishi?"

Amalthea gave a faint nod. As the words were processed, Dee went rigid, breath catching in her throat.

Maybe she wouldn't be leaving the truck on her own two feet.

That the girl understood the title meant Hamal had taken more than one liberty with his mission. Amalthea held her anger in check for a more appropriate time.

Atkins moved towards them, stopping in front of the SUV so he could meet his Master's eyes through the windshield, ensuring he wasn't stepping on her toes before he moved around to Dee's side of the vehicle. Amalthea wasn't sure what he thought he could do but allowed him his experiment. She was loath to have to resort to violent means to extradite the girl from the vehicle.

Coming around to Dee's door, he knelt so his head was level with her thighs. Dee's eyes followed him, head now dropped to look at the Soldier.

"We're safe here." His voice was a whisper. The rigidity that Amalthea had brought out of her faded until slowly she allowed Atkins to help her from the truck.

Atkins escorted her through the large estate, leading her over the acres of front yard before entering the towering house that sprawled in a half circle away from the front. Their arms remained entwined, as if he were escorting her to a school dance, as he followed the girls Amalthea had instructed to ensure Dee got everything she needed.

Desiree had been upstairs, in a suite on the other side of the house, ever since.

The Rishi's thoughts snapped back to the present. She returned her shears to their place before taking her seat with the others. Metis made to rise, but a gesture from her assured him she didn't need anything.

She held his eye for a moment, exceedingly grateful he hadn't been harmed. There were only a few times in their long history that he'd defied her, and going with the team to rescue this girl was one of them. The decision had shocked her, but it said much about the curiosity this girl brought to them all.

The others quieted as she sat, her attention on the thin file that had been Hamal's in front of her. Her eyes scanned the meager contents before closing it. Desiree Galen. How had anyone caught on to the idea that she should be watched? Not even Phecda had had a clue.

Amalthea smiled kindly, meeting each of their eyes before speaking. "What have we done about the possibility of him attacking us here?"

"Our perimeter monitoring system is being extended as we speak. Phecda has promised eyes on any known locations where he might send troops from. Everyone is up, securing the estate, but—"

Amalthea nodded. "But we are too few."

The speaker nodded gravely, sitting back as their Master's attention turned to Metis. "Nothing still from the prisoners?"

"When the threat of death is all we have and they know we won't kill them, interrogation has no power."

It was as she'd expected. Only the young soldiers were susceptible to interrogation. When your memories stretch back over centuries, time holds an entirely different significance. Lengthy torture sessions became more harmful to the interrogator than the prisoner, so it was impossible to get data from those who weren't already of a mind to give it away.

It was just as well. She'd rather her people stay away from the horrible things that happened in the throes of attempting to break ones will.

"I have a meeting scheduled with the Air God. We'll see if he can help us fortify."

"Will he be angry we lost Dimitri?"

Amalthea took a breath, holding it for a moment before releasing it slowly. Dimitri hadn't survived. Daniel was critical. These were points she wasn't looking forward to relaying, especially as she'd only lost one of her own. Still, it couldn't be avoided.

"He won't be mad enough to risk the safety of the girl."

Chapter Twenty

Dee hadn't slept long. Nightmares of gunfire kept her sleep light and unrestful. Jolted from slumber for the last time by a dream filled with explosions and decapitated heads, she stopped trying. Instead, she stared into the darkness, blinking away the fading images of horror and anxiety.

Maybe the nightmare had been the last couple of months. Maybe, she'd finally woken up.

The room around her was still, the quiet so deep a part of her latched onto this thought. The chaos and panic that had been her life were replaced by a sense of peace she hadn't known in years. Snuggling further into bed, she closed her eyes, her brain quiet, relishing the serenity.

But her body wouldn't let her stay in bed forever. No longer able to ignore the call to the bathroom, Dee forced her feet to the floor.

Her toes curled against the unfamiliar feeling of the smooth surface, her steps unsure as she moved towards a white door cracked open ahead of her. Being in this strange place knocked any allowance her brain was giving her that she was no longer in danger. An alarm was rising from the depths of her psyche, pushing the tranquil calm under a tide of fear.

Her inner-voice was uncharacteristically quiet, though she felt its contempt at her attempt to forget the last twenty-four hours.

Reaching past the door, she found the light switch to this other room and flicked it on. She flinched from the light until she acclimated to the soft glow of the lamps.

Hanging onto the doorframe, she blinked blurry sight around the room that was as big as the one she'd just come from. A sunk-in-tub she could almost swim laps in was at the far end, polished porcelain shining brightly against the darker tile of the surrounding walls. Hanging plants flowed from the ceiling above it, a few fronds almost reaching the floor. The left wall was taken up by a glass box that was the most immense shower she'd ever seen. Potted trees rimmed the glass and she imagined that bathing inside the cage would feel like showering under a waterfall of the Amazon Jungle.

With a smile, she stepped into the room.

She turned to the mirrored wall on her right and her smile fell. Her image reflected back at her, hovering over a double sink nestled into a floating counter, showed a face patchy with healing bruises. One side of her face was healing a wound that had left the skin removed from cheek to jaw. Both eyes were the yellow-green tinge of healing bruises. She couldn't imagine how awful she'd looked a few hours ago.

-*You look awful now.*-

With a gasped breath, she fell forward into the counter, catching herself on straight arms, head falling against her chest with closed eyes as the entirety of the last twenty-four hours overcame her.

Dimitri and Daniel showing up in the woods near the house.

Her attacking them.

The ambush on the road.

Dimitri.

Daniel.

...Hamal.

Where they alive?

Rishi.

The word shot through her, shattering all other thought, snapping her eyes open. This strange word was the title for whoever was after her. For the one who'd sent Hamal to watch her. For the Master of this place where she now stood.

She took slow breaths.

-We should have killed Hamal.-

She couldn't help a bark of laughter. The event that had started everything could be argued as that moment when he'd walked into her world, though, really, he'd only been a symptom of the more significant problem. A problem still being defined.

-Sure, but killing him would have alleviated the need for a gun battle on some back road. How do they cover that up, anyway?-

The question only supported the idea that these Masters, these Rishis, were powerful on a level she'd never considered, able to act outside of a system Dee had thought controlled everything.

Avoiding looking at herself in the mirror, she turned, leaning her back against the counter, eyes panning the room, this time for something she could arm herself with.

Finding nothing, she returned to the dark bedroom.

The curtains pulled against the picture window allowed no light to pass, attaching a sense of timelessness to the room, so she wasn't sure if the day had given to night, or back to day, or if she was in a place where the sun even shone.

Her brain asked her to move across the room to check but her legs refused.

What was she doing? What was happening?

-You think Hamal was teaching you how to fight these things for fun?-

She hadn't thought about it, to be honest. Even as she'd known Hamal was training her for this very scenario, her brain had managed to ignore the fact that bigger things were going on. Here these bigger things were, no longer too obscure to ignore.

She was in the house of a Rishi.

A shiver came over her, then another as she remembered sinking a blade into the Soldiers who'd attacked Dimitri and Daniel.

Dimitri. Daniel. Hamal. She remembered she still didn't know if they had made it.

-*You* have *been mostly unconscious.*-

She shuffled to a second door, one she hoped would let her escape this room. As she turned the doorknob, a young girl, no more than twelve years old, entered, staring up at Dee in surprise.

They looked at each other for a moment before the girl bowed her head, soft voice explaining that the mistress had asked she not leave the suite.

-*Mistress? Suite?*-

"So, I'm a prisoner?"

Startled, the girl stammered, "I don't think so, just, they weren't sure you were feeling well."

Dee's voice was stern. "I'm feeling great. I want to check on Hamal and Daniel and Dimitri."

The girl's shoulders relaxed. "Hamal will be fine. He isn't quite ready to move yet." Her tone softened. "Daniel... they're still not sure what will happen with him."

Dee's shoulders fell. Unsure why she felt such protection over the Soldier she barely knew, she peered at the girl staring at the floor as if reading her face might procure more information.

-*Guilt. That's all it is. Misplaced emotions. You don't care about any of them.*-

She ignored the voice, whose callous words tore through her heart. She didn't really think that, did she?

-*If you kill this one, you can leave.*-

"What about Dimitri?"

The girl's silence was answer enough.

Dee's steps took her falling back to the bed. Sobs found their way from her throat. She covered her mouth with her hands as if she could stop the torrent of grief. She'd barely known him. He'd barely known her, but still, he'd fought to protect her. He'd died doing that very thing.

Eyes pressed together, she fought against the swell of emotion; fought against the stiff reality of what she was involved in; fought against a despair that threatened to render her mind unable to deal with it all.

The need to move, to get out, pushed her to her feet so she was making for the door at top speed so fast the girl could voice no objection. She threw open the door, moving into the large living area beyond, barely noting the lavish living space she'd been assigned.

She was at the exit in a flash, the double mahogany doors much more robust than those that had separated her from the bedroom. Expecting the doors to be locked, she was excited when they opened, a breath of tension releasing that she wasn't a prisoner.

Flinging both doors inward so they rapped loudly against the wall, she stepped into a vast hall. With a passing glance she noted plants decorating every spare inch of space. Across from the doors was a chaise lounge Atkins stood from.

His calm gaze took in her mood. "We thought you might not take an order to relax without questions."

Dee stared at the warrior, remembering it had been he who'd escorted her here when they'd arrived. She hadn't been afraid of him then like she was now.

She took a breath, hoping her voice wouldn't waver. "Dimitri didn't make it."

The warrior had the courtesy to look mournful. "He did not. He fought bravely."

"And Daniel? Hamal?" Anger was growing inside her, focusing on the only being here she might vent it on.

"Hamal is in fine condition. Daniel," his voice dropped, and he seemed reluctant to add anything. "We don't know what will happen with Daniel."

Her hands balled into fists at her side as she realized the futility of engaging the being in front of her who was easily twice her size, and probably double that in skill.

-*Or maybe you're just a coward.*-

She scowled, turning her attention from Atkins to look up and down the hall. "I was told I'm not a prisoner."

"That's true."

"Can I walk around?"

"Yes, but not yet."

She frowned, her eyes locking on his momentarily, before snapping away from the intimidating weight of his stare.

"Hamal? Can I see him?"

"I'm sure this will be the first place he visits when he's allowed to get out of bed." Atkins took a step towards her. She got the impression she was being herded back to the room. She took a breath, holding it as a wall against her intimidation.

His tone dropped, soothing, "There is nothing to fear here, but we are concerned for your safety. It is why we ask you to stay in your rooms. It is easier for us to secure you this way."

"Secure me?"

Atkins nodded, taking another step towards her.

Dee looked up and down the hall again, knowing there was no way to defy the Soldier but stalling all the same, as if some idea would come to here that would allow her to change his mind. Atkins' eyes never strayed from her. She was sure he would stand there, unmoving, until the end of time, if she remained there as well.

Resigned to this, she sighed, accepting her fate. "So, I just hang out here then?"

He made no move or gesture, nor did any expression brush his face, but Dee knew his answer was affirmative.

Feeling defeated, she turned back to step into the room that was her prison, regardless of what they called it.

-At least no one's tackled you yet.-

It was true, she seemed safe, but at what cost? Being sequestered wasn't the same as being safe, was it?

-Is it time for philosophy then; freedom versus safety?-

Ignoring the voice, she wondered just how secure she was. Was she not being housed by the very thing she should be running from?

-A little late for that.-

Doors still open behind her, she turned, questions about her security and who they were securing her from dying on her lips. Atkins remained standing in the center of the hall. He was one of them. How could she trust anything any of them told her? Maybe she should have gone with Barnard.

-Point-of-fact: Barnard is also one of them.-

Atkins spoke quietly. "Why should you trust us? That is not something I can answer. It is not something anyone can ever answer. Had you gone with Barnard, he would not have been able to answer it any better, nor his master. You are in the unique position of being at the mercy of those you can't know if you should trust or not. You have only the guidance of Hamal to reflect on, another who you may have trusted unwisely. Only time will show if you made any correct decision. But remember, if you find your position here a mark for gratification, it was Hamal who made it so."

Dee stared at his feet, caught by his voice that suggested calm wisdom she'd never experienced from anyone, wondering if he had read her mind. She wanted to like him. To trust him. Hamal trusted him enough to betray his orders to ask for help from the Soldier.

-We. Don't. Trust. Hamal.-

Was that true?

Her inner voice's declaration forced a sense of isolated self-preservation through her. She stood straighter under the knowledge that she might be on her own, needing to rely on all she'd been taught to get her out of there.

Whatever Atkins saw in her in that moment made him more alert.

Noting the Soldiers subtle change had her lose whatever it was that had fluttered through her so the moment passed.

Dee turned, shutting herself in the suite. Leaning her head back against the thick wood of the door, she closed her eyes. Leaving this place wouldn't solve anything. She'd be running forever if she started now, or until they were bored of her.

-Or killed you.-

They wouldn't get bored without extensive analyses, which running would only prolong. When she thought of it like that, the overzealous protection seemed entirely benign.

-At least you're not a lab rat in some dank dungeon... yet.-

Ultimately, she was at their whim. Facing Atkins in the hall was one thing. She might stand a chance against one warrior unwilling to kill her, but she wasn't strong enough to take them all on.

-Sounds a lot like being imprisoned.-

She didn't disagree, but it was irrelevant.

She opened her eyes to the room, finding the girl watching her.

Taking a step from the door, Dee spoke to her. "So, what is there to do around here?"

The girl, fearful eyes turning to excitement, was quick to reply. "Maybe you're hungry?"

Dee smiled at the quick speech pattern of the child. "What do I call you?"

The girl blushed, eyes dropping to her feet. "I'm called Paige."

"Paige. Nice to meet you." Dee's eyes traveled around the room, this time more slowly, taking it in.

Plants covered the room, lining the floor and hanging from the ceiling in front of the wall of windows opposite the door. Others, dispersed throughout the elegantly decorated seating and waiting areas, clustered together on the white-marble floor that reflected the green of the plants back to the room, so it glowed with a refreshing light.

"Wow. This place is beautiful."

Paige smiled.

Dee moved to the windows that showed a sweeping expanse of manicured lawns, decorated with flower gardens and mazes of greenery that stretched to forest at the horizon. Dee couldn't even begin to guess at the amount of acreage she was overlooking, never doubting that all she saw was in the Rishi's jurisdiction.

"Where are we?" she asked.

"This is Amaltheum."

"Amaltheum?" Dee said the word slowly, recalling the Rishi she'd met at her arrival. "Amalthea lives in Amaltheum?"

Her inner-voice chuckled for them both, but the girl was unaware of the mocking Dee gave the title.

Dee held the humor from her tone. "Where is Amaltheum? Are we still on the East Coast?"

When the girl didn't answer, Dee turned to find her looking confused.

"You don't understand what I'm asking?" Dee's voice was gentle even as shock laced her words.

The girl shook her head, wringing her hands.

Dee shrugged, smiling to show the girl there was nothing to worry about, filing away the odd information. "I think I will eat. Would you join me?"

Paige looked horrified and insisted it wasn't appropriate. Finally, Dee let the matter drop, but only because the girl seemed so uncomfortable.

Paige smiled, relieved and moved towards the bedroom door. "I'll draw a bath. There are clothes for you as well. Food will be ready when you're finished."

Laughing to herself that asking for food had been interpreted as bathtime, Dee realized she did need to clean up.

Paige was wise beyond her years.

Stumbling: Book One on The Fool's Path

Chapter Twenty-One

Hamal was grateful for the highest-tech medical care in the world, but his injuries were still taking too long to heal. Not only that, Amalthea refused to allow him to get out of bed, though he was more than fine enough to walk, even if he needed crutches to do so.

He was worried about Dee.

He was concerned about his worry about Dee.

He knew this worry was the only reason the forced bedrest had him agitated, but the knowledge didn't alleviate it.

Coming across Barnard in the woods had brought a fear to his veins he'd never felt before: fear for another's well-being.

Hamal closed his eyes against the memory of that night, thinking instead of his upcoming trip home that would allow him to leave this mess for the Rishis to figure out. His involvement had long outplayed itself. His part had ended as soon as Dimitri and Daniel had walked on the scene.

He took as deep breath as his lungs would allow, ignoring the sharp pain, holding it for a couple of seconds, before releasing it slowly, calming himself as he'd been taught to do. Days. Days and he would be back at Zi's, his life able to resume its normalcy.

She'd asked about him. They made sure he was aware of this fact, and he was curious why they would make such a point to tell him. They'd have placated her by saying she would be able to see him when he was well enough. He wondered if it would happen before he was shipped out.

Amalthea strolled into the room, trailed by Metis, Atkins, and Ainn, each nodding a greeting that he returned. He searched for signs of how dire matters were in the world beyond this room. Not surprising, there was nothing to read from their expressions.

The Rishi moved to his side, grasping his shoulder in a motherly gesture only she could get away with. He smiled to mask the annoyance he felt. Here was the interrogation he'd been waiting for.

"Hamal, they tell me you're recovering wonderfully. How do you feel?"

"Wonderful."

Ignoring his dry humor, or maybe missing it all together, Amalthea left his side to claim one of the chairs that had been brought in behind the interrogators. Atkins shot Hamal a look of warning.

Rather than wait for the questioning to begin, Hamal took the initiative, speaking directly to Amalthea. "I should thank you for giving me time to rest before bringing in the Inquisition."

Ainn smiled, turning her face to Atkins to hide it from Amalthea and Metis, who were less than pleased by Hamal's attitude. Atkins wasn't amused either, sighing silently that his friend would take such liberties with his Mistress. Hamal was allowed much leeway in his own House, but here, with all that was going on, the leash would be much tighter.

"The Inquisition? I'm sure you wouldn't compare us to that farce if you'd been there." Amalthea kept her voice pleasantly conversational, though the flash in her eyes couldn't be mistaken. "And I'm absolutely sure you don't want to give us any ideas about how to handle your lack of respect."

Hamal's eyes swept the four seated in a semi-circle near his bedside. "Maybe not, but I still can't help thinking I'm about to have all sorts of information extricated from my being."

"A bit dramatic, no?" Hamal was surprised to hear Metis speak. Ever at Amalthea's side, his reputation was only as a silent observer, as if his supernatural good looks were all the threat necessary. If he'd ever been anything but a pretty face, Hamal had never heard the story.

Hamal shrugged. "We shall see, yes?"

Metis' eyes tightened but otherwise didn't respond.

Amalthea's voice remained patient. "We'd like you to tell us about your time with Dee."

Hamal closed his eyes, setting his head back on his pillow. After a moment, he turned his head to look at Amalthea. "You know I can't say anything until it's cleared by Zibanitu."

The answer was expected; none flustered in the least that he not readily give them information.

The Rishi spoke again. "Tell us what happened after you were ambushed on the road three days ago."

Had it been three days?

Hamal chuckled. "What happened after two huge fucking trucks hit us? I can tell you that. My right side was crushed, then we were all flipping. Dee got ejected somehow. I'm still trying to figure out how that happened. At the time, I was sure she was dead." His voice broke so he paused, taking a few breathes before continuing. "I was sure the truck was going to roll right over her. I still think it did. Atkins wasn't in the car anymore either, but I figured he'd just climbed out while the car was flipping." Hamal's eyes met Atkins'. "You're like a superhero, man."

Atkins gave the barest of nods.

Hamal continued. "Gunfire started from the treeline. I assume from the direction the trucks came from, but I couldn't see, and the damn echo made it impossible to pinpoint where. The screeching of trucks crunching across the asphalt was a little distracting. As were my lungs being punctured. Then, I was being carried through the brush by Metis."

He gave Metis a nod, thanks he hadn't been able to provide until now.

"Did you see any of the fighting?" Amalthea's question turned his attention.

Hamal shook his head. "I heard the gun-fire. Dee made it to me, but after Metis left us, she took off back towards the fighting."

The Rishi leaned forward, genuinely curious about how the human might answer. "Why would she do that?"

"I taught her to fight. She must have thought she could help."

"You heard about the ones she took out on her own?" He hadn't and he knew Amalthea knew that. Any information that would have made it to him in this isolated room would only do so because she willed it. She'd asked the question to judge his reaction.

Used to dealing with this kind of subtle underhandedness from Porrima, and having mastered the art of containing his emotions because of it, his face betrayed nothing. Dee had learned quickly, but her after-the-fact reactions to the stress of combat had continued to worry him. It was much of the reason he wanted to see her as soon as possible. She was probably sitting alone in some room freaking herself out.

He ignored Amalthea's studious gaze.

Ainn, who'd commanded the escort team that had gotten ambushed, explained the story. "Dimitri and Daniel were guarding her. Four of the Ophiuchus' Soldiers attacked. They were both down. Dee retaliated. Protected them. She's the only reason they weren't KIA."

Hamal allowed some surprise to show through with this news. "They were both hurt?"

Ainn nodded. "Daniel's just regained consciousness. He'll be alright. Dimitri didn't make it."

Hamal's head fell back to his pillow, his chest constricting under the realization of how close Dee had come to seeing her last day.

He picked his head back up. "Dee took out the ones that took Dimitri and Daniel out? Alone? She's alright, though?"

The words were out before he caught his error. They'd interpret too much of his feelings through his questions.

Taking another breath, he lay his head back on the pillow, closing his eyes to give himself a moment of feigned weakness to collect himself. His injuries were severe enough that it would be expected. Silently, he chastised himself for caring.

"Dee's fine. She received no wounds from battle." Atkins' blunt response brought Hamal's eyes to him. Though the closest thing the Soldier had to a friend, Hamal was no such thing in this situation. Atkins was a commander of Amalthea's forces, here to play his role in debriefing the outsider.

As grateful as Hamal was for the information, it did little to relieve his anxiety. What did he mean, no wounds from battle? Had something else happened, or was he merely answering the question as it was asked?

Hamal forced himself to express only benign calm. He wasn't sure why Amalthea's people would care what he felt about her. Except, he was never sure what mattered to the Rishis; never sure what information was being stored away for later use as ammunition in manipulating others for their own purpose.

He focused on the facts of Dee taking out the Ophiuchus' Soldiers. Of all the units to meet in combat, The Ophiuchus' were the most feared.

He allowed a sense of pride that it had been his training that had put her in the position to do this.

Ainn continued the questioning. "You trained her?"

Hamal nodded, not looking at any of them, instead, staring at the ceiling, head still resting on his pillow.

"Had she had any training before yours?"

"None. That's what she told me, anyway."

"You don't believe that to be true?"

"I believe her. She's not a good liar."

"How long had you been training her?"

Hamal met Ainn's eye, then Amalthea's. "No disrespect, Rishi, but I'll need Zibanitu's approval before I can talk to you. I'm sure I've already said more than he'd appreciate."

Amalthea looked at him for a moment, visibly judging how far she might push him and what ramifications the pushing might have on her. Dimitri was already dead, having died under her roof. Until very recently, Daniel's state of health was unsure. Zibanitu would not be pleased, even as he would appreciate her help in circumventing whatever Han had planned. Badgering his pet human might not be the smartest thing at this point, at least not until the human had had a chance to be debriefed by his own Master.

She stood, and the others followed. "Thank you, Hamal. We'll let you see Dee as soon as you can be out of bed."

"You won't let her here to see me?" The words fell from his mouth before he could stop them.

Ignored, he was left alone in his prison.

Chapter Twenty-Two

For four days Dee stayed in her rooms, sleeping, eating, resting, before sleeping some more, stewing in all the unknowns. Her mind raced to put together the limited information she had. Staring out the window was her main hobby, but even the beatific view didn't help her pull what she didn't know from thin air.

Hamal still wasn't out of bed.

Daniel was doing much better, but she wasn't allowed to see him either.

Finally, on the morning of the fifth day, while Dee stood in the center of the large room, slowly repeating the katas Hamal had showed her, her body sick of the lack of physical activity, Amalthea sent word: Dee would continue her training here. Dee was grateful, if for no other reason than to be allowed out of her rooms.

She thought Hamal had been a harsh master, but she wasn't prepared for the pair Amalthea set on her.

On a quiet, secluded patch of yard on Amalthea's immense estate, Ellie and Ainn worked her mercilessly. Their speed and power easily surpassed her own, so she was in a position she'd never faced before. With Hamal, she'd continuously pulled her punches and slowed her movements, but with these two, those habits were only getting her into trouble.

"Get up! Let's go again."

Dee pushed herself upright, eating dirt before she'd even found her feet, the petite redhead pacing around her.

"Again!"

Ainn was tough, bringing tears to Dee's eyes more than once. She pushed through, more frustrated than hurt, unused to this level of severity. She might have complained if there was anyone to complain to.

-Complain that they're teaching you how to stay alive?-

Dee blocked the swift attack, then another, and another, before seeing an opening to push an offensive.

Then, she was face down on the ground.

"I can't believe you're this slow."

"You had everyone fooled."

Dee glared at her trainers as she pushed up from the ground. Ainn threw a laugh, at her expense, towards Ellie.

Without thinking, Dee threw herself forward, barely touching the ground as she came to her feet at a sprint, forcing Ainn to defend against a flurry of attacks. Coming together in a cross-block, Ainn smiled. "I knew you were holding out."

They stepped back from each other, breathless. Dee was stunned at what she'd done when she'd stopped thinking so hard.

"Think you can do that again?" Ellie stepped in behind Dee.

Dee turned to the taller, fairer of the pair. "Let's see."

The Soldiers put Dee through the paces, working with her the better part of the afternoon before they released her.

"You really were holding out on me." Hamal's voice called to her from his perch on the low wall that wove its way through Amalthea's land.

Dee smiled so widely she thought her lips might split.

He hobbled from his perch as she got closer. She wrapped her arms around him in a bear hug, forgetting to be gentle until he flinched from her hold.

They broke apart awkwardly, Dee smiling apologetically. "Sorry. It's just really good to see a face I recognize." She looked him up and down, assessing his recovery. "I wasn't sure when they'd let you out. They said you were hurt pretty bad. Surgery?"

He nodded. "I couldn't stay cooped up any longer. Besides, I needed to make sure they were taking care of you."

Another awkward moment hit them, something in his words bringing Dee's memory to the kiss they'd shared.

-What's with the girlie sentimentality? Life-threatening situation happening here.-

He smiled his cocky smile. "I think there's much we have to tell each other."

Her eyebrows rose in disbelief. "Can that happen now?"

He shrugged ambiguously while his laughing eyes declared affirmation.

Dee's spirits soared as they made their way towards the house.

Coming in through the French doors, the pair was stopped by Amalthea, who sat in the corner of the large receiving room, camouflaged by the plants that were abundant everywhere. The Rishi stood, forcing the pair to stop to greet her. Hamal surprised Dee when he bowed respectfully.

Amalthea smiled graciously. "It's nice to see you up and about, Hamal. I hope your visit with your previous charge won't hinder anyone's plans."

Dee noticed Hamal stiffen, her attention turning to his face to see what she might read there, but his face was a blank slate. She looked from her mentor to her hostess, and back again, waiting for their eye contact to break. Whatever was said was spoken in subtext Dee wasn't privy to.

Another moment passed before Amalthea turned to Dee, satisfied by whatever she'd read in Hamal's face. The Rishi took Dee's hands. "I hear your training is coming along wonderfully. Already a breakthrough." She smiled warmly, bringing the same expression from Dee despite her uneasiness about what had just transpired with Hamal. "I've sent word to Paige that you're bringing a friend for supper. Enjoy yourselves."

As the Rishi disappeared through the adjoining rooms, the pair watched her silently, thoughts aligned differently from where they'd been moments before.

-*That was weird.*-

"That was weird, right?" She cast a glance at Hamal's stiff posture. They crossed multiple rooms and were up the stairs before Dee broke the silence again. "You alright?"

Hamal's attention was distant.

She sighed. "You can't talk to me, can you?"

Hamal looked at her, surprised.

"It's the only thing she could have been talking about. Reminding you of your duty. And the silent stare down? Why else would she need to interfere? Am I wrong? "

Hamal's eyes were locked straight ahead, not looking at her. "You're not wrong."

Dee sighed again. "Any way anyone will ever tell me what's going on?"

Hamal chuckled. "I wish I could answer that. Even I don't know most of what's going on."

"Can you tell me who attacked us on the road?"

Hamal was shocked. "Amalthea hasn't spoken to you?"

"Not really. She's explained to me that I'm safe, that I won't be here very long, though she didn't give me any context about what *very long* might mean. All my questions have been pushed off for another time."

Hamal shrugged as if this information was perfectly reasonable. "She's technically a neutral party and bound by the same rules as I am."

What no one seemed to remember was that Dee hadn't spent her life inside the circle of whatever world this was. Her frustration rang clearly in her tone. "So? What does that *mean*?"

*

Hamal looked Dee over as they reached the closed doors to her rooms, her sweat-stained shirt clinging to a body that'd only grown more toned since that first day he'd begun following her. Her gaze no longer held that tint of insecurity he'd hated. Even stuck in a place she didn't know, surrounded by beings that probably scared the hell out of her, hadn't broken her. He was proud of her.

The thought pushed a strange feeling through him. He clenched his fists at his side in a refusal to brush her hair back from her face.

He pulled his eyes away. "It means she doesn't know enough to tell you. Amalthea won't answer your questions because her own questions haven't been answered. None of the Rishis have answers."

He was glad Dee turned to push the door open so she wouldn't read the worry in his face.

The room was bright with the lingering sunlight of the fading day. Hamal swept the room with his eyes, taking in the hanging plants, the ivory furniture tossed playfully with colored pillows that matched the blooming flowers scattered throughout. Compared to his room, which contained only a bed and nightstand, this was a palace.

Hidden off to their left was a small, round table set for two. Paige stood near, smiling shyly.

Dee's eyes lingered on the table of food. "Hamal, this is Paige. She basically watches my every move and feeds me."

Hamal nodded, startled by the child's presence.

"Do I have time to shower?"

Hamal wondered who Dee was asking, but Paige's answer, in a quiet voice, almost made him laugh. "Of course. Supper is ready whenever you want it."

Dee shared a look with Hamal that said, *see what I have to deal with.*

This time, Hamal did laugh. "Right. You've got it rough."

Dee rolled her eyes as she walked into the bedroom.

Hamal was struggling. He had gone against his better judgement and allowed himself to engage in interaction with Desiree. He should have just watched from the shadows, ensuring she was safe but not letting her see him. Now, he couldn't find it in himself to leave, even as his brain listed all the reasons it was a better idea.

He couldn't leave the estate. It had been deemed too big of a security risk for anyone to come or go until they had more information on what forces were massing nearby.

His injuries keeping him from the training field left him no outlet for his mounting frustrated energy.

This was how he was explaining his emotional overload to himself.

He stood nose to the window, staring out over the green land that spread across his view. He barely saw what was in front of him; instead, he followed Dee's movements in the shower with his mind's eye.

It's because you've never had to say no. You have to say no to this one, and it's screwing with your head.

Despite his self-talk, his mind continued to drift to the adjacent room.

He'd never had a problem keeping a benign eye on what belonged to the Rishis. Dee clearly fit in this category, yet he was finding it more and more difficult to remember it. She'd stopped being his mission the day Atkins and the others had shown up. His mind should have stopped worrying about what happened to her. The reins had been passed to superior protectors. He shouldn't even be here, and as annoyed with Amalthea as he'd been for her interference downstairs just now, her visit was justified. In fact, he should thank her. She'd already known what he was still arguing to himself about.

Why had he even come here? He'd told himself it was just to make sure she was alright, but of course, she was. No one had ever been as well cared for as she would be here. He didn't need to see her to know that. Amalthea wouldn't do anything to harm the precious cargo she'd managed to secure. And, even if she had, or orders had come down the line that Hamal didn't like, he was in no position to say, or do, anything about it.

*

Dee came out of the bedroom smiling. "Compared to the guest bedrooms at my house, this place is—"

She looked around, catching Paige's eye who was resetting the table for one.

Hurt, Dee knew it was for the best. After Amalthea's silent gag order, she wouldn't have gotten much information anyway.

Even so, Hamal's absence caused a wrenching ache to form inside her. Her breath caught, and she found herself sobbing, still standing on the threshold of the rooms.

She was alone here. She was alone in a life that had become a stranger's, and there was no way for her to figure out what was going on except to sit back and wait for others to bring information to her.

-Absorb what you can for now. A time will come.-

She wasn't sure she had the fortitude for that approach.

-As if you have a choice.-

She wanted to call Mike, except that was forbidden as well. There were too many security risks with contacting him, though she had been allowed to leave him a message as they'd left town with a lame explanation of why she'd gone without first seeing him.

She thought of how confused and hurt Mike must be and her tears fell harder.

Chapter Twenty-Three

"I don't understand. You got involved, but Zibanitu can't get involved? Didn't he send Hamal, then Dimitri and Daniel?"

Dee's head hurt. She was finally having an actual conversation about what was going on, yet she wasn't sure any of the answers were helping her make sense of any of it. It seemed to her the Rishis were a bunch of rich busy-bodies so concerned with what the others were doing, they couldn't enjoy their own lives. Or let her enjoy hers.

"Hamal's part is easily overlooked. He is not one of us, so can not technically be viewed as an asset of a House. Dimitri and Daniel were sent to assist me, which is allowed, and a pair of young Soldiers sent to assist a House without its own army isn't likely to be noticed."

Dee leaned over, elbows on knees, hands covering her face. "Okay. So, the Ophi—Han?—"

"The Ophiuchus. Sabik Han."

"Sure. That guy. He's the one who came after me on the way here?"

Amalthea patiently nodded. "He sent Barnard to you. And the ambush, yes."

"But Zosma was sending those Revenants after me?"

"That is still the question to be answered."

"It was definitely not The Off—Han."

Amalthea smiled. "Oh-fee-YOU-kus. Ophiuchus."

Dee nodded, knowing she still wouldn't be able to remember the pronunciation. The word didn't flow right off her tongue. Leaning back in the chair, almost entirely laid out in the oversized seat, she sighed. "Basically, I'm not going home anytime soon."

Amalthea shook her head, face set in an expression of compassion that Dee wouldn't like her answer. "Even I wouldn't agree to let you return home at this time."

"Even you?"

Amalthea's motherly expression made Dee suspicious despite never receiving anything from the Rishi other than kindness. "I am curious about you, yes. As will the others be, when they learn of you, but I have no agenda outside of that. I wish you no ill will, regardless of what the answers to your questions might be."

"The others wish me ill will?" Dee perked as fear knifed through her.

Amalthea shrugged, a strange gesture coming from the ancient Master, so it almost took on a different meaning. What that meaning might be, Dee couldn't decipher.

-It's clear we're not getting out of here anytime soon.-

"If one of them wants you, there will be another that wants to take you from them. There are twelve of us, thirteen when you count Han, and with family, there is always at least one that has to rock the boat."

-And you thought you weren't learning anything.-

She shuddered. What happened when they all knew about her? As far as she could tell, only four Rishi knew she existed, and her life was already in chaos.

-You'll be running forever.-

"With Han deciding to play, the game may erupt into war. The very thing Zibanitu has been working against since the beginning."

-Beginning of what?-

Dee buried her face back in her hands, not sure what she was supposed to do with information that was more stifling than enlightening.

Sure, she was comfortable, for now, but Amalthea was talking about the possibility of war. Could she sit around and wait for that to happen because of her? But, where could she go?

-We could always get on this Ophiuchus' side of things.-

She didn't think that would be allowed, even if she did decide that was a good idea.

-You should have killed Hamal.-

If her inner-voice was a tangible being, she'd have slapped it. Why her head always went back to that point made her crazy. There was no way to look at any of this that would make that point valid.

-You wouldn't be here. You'd probably have gone with Barnard.-

Forced to go with Barnard.

-How is that any different than this?-

Exactly.

Rubbing her eyes, Dee looked back to the world to find that Ainn and Ellie were waiting patiently for her to recover herself.

"Ready to work?" Ainn's tone brokered no room for a negative answer.

***

Her mind whirling with thoughts of what a war between these creatures, with her at the center, would mean, she didn't notice the group that had massed at their training spot until she was on top of them.

Looking around nervously, Dee spoke towards Ellie in a low tone, "Everyone's training with us today?"

Ellie smiled. "Something like that."

-They're bringing out the big guns to show you just how powerless you are around here.-

She forced her feet to continue behind Ellie, knowing Ainn would have just pushed her from behind if she had stopped anyway. Drilling with the girls had significantly improved Dee's adeptness in the training ring, but she was still far from consistent enough to be tested. She hoped the others were only there to stare at the freak.

She donned the mantle of arrogance she'd learned from Hamal, feigning confidence. "Didn't think I was getting enough of an ass-kicking from you two on the daily, you had to bring in the rest of the troops?" She made sure her voice was loud enough to be overheard by the others.

Ellie chuckled. "Actually, no, but since you don't seem to mind the idea, maybe we'll switch the day's plans."

-*Good one. How 'bout we make it a rule not to be sarcastic with the uber-powerful, psycho Soldiers?*-

Dee made a mental note to keep her mouth shut and just do what she was told.

-*Like you'll have any other choice.*-

Her lack of control had been bothering her since she'd arrived. As well as she was being treated, she never forgot the fact that she was a prisoner. She could only do what was asked of her, not knowing enough to contradict anything she was told. Even if she could slip away, there was nowhere she could go they couldn't follow. Sabik Han probably had guys waiting right out the front door for when she did something impulsive like that. Then, she would be his, no harm, no foul.

-*Unless you plan to jump the fence right now, you might want to pay attention to everyone standing around waiting for a piece of your noobishness.*-

Her eyes moved around the ring of Soldiers, counting bodies as she did. She'd only made it to four when she realized she was staring at Daniel.

Her face broke out into a smile, and she moved to him. "Daniel! No one told me you were out and about."

He laughed, pleased by her reaction. "Why would they?"

She hugged him. She hadn't planned to, but with so few familiar faces around, it was just a natural reaction. He embraced her warmly, ignoring the catcalls from the others. "I'm not one of Amalthea's, remember? I'm sure no one thought you'd care."

"You saved me."

"I hear you saved me."

Dee's eyes swept over his neck, remembering the wound she'd thought would kill him. "They said you weren't healing."

"I guess it just took longer than they thought it would."

Dee was too happy to see him to care about the specifics.

Daniel looked over Dee's head. "I'm surprised Hamal isn't with you."

Dee shrugged, thinking of Dimitri, wondering what she could say to express how sorry she was. She was cut off from further speech when Ainn whistled loudly, bringing everyone's attention back to why they were there. "I'm glad the reunion is going so well, but it's time to work!"

Daniel rolled his eyes playfully, stepping back to his place in the circle. "Sure thing, Sarge."

If Ainn was annoyed by his flippancy, she didn't show it. "Alright, Desiree. I know you think we've brought everyone out to get a shot at you, but the real reason is so you can watch other Soldiers fight. We want you to see what you can do. Our theory is that your preconceptions are holding you back."

-They really think you're one of them? Interesting.-

A million questions came to her, but it wasn't the time for talk. Instead, she moved to take a spot in the circle, watching as two Soldiers moved to the center, long staffs held like they were born with them in their hands.

The way they maintained an above-human speed was the first thing that caught her. She knew she could move as fast, but had only managed it in quick bursts. She hummed with curiosity to see if she could do what she was seeing. She allowed the energy to echo through her legs, so she was bouncing on her toes as she watched wide-eyed the display of athleticism that defied anything she'd ever dreamed a person could do.

-I'm not sure that's what they are.-

It was a point she'd shied away from, not understanding, or wanting to understand, what these Ancient Rishis were, and by account, what the Soldiers were. By all appearances, they were human. Dee hadn't seen Amalthea do anything to suggest otherwise, despite the humming in her head that told her there was great power there. She couldn't even define what that power was, so it was just some vague concept that brokered fear.

By the time the third pair stepped to the center of the training ring, Dee was pacing the perimeter of the circle, analyzing everything she was seeing. She encoded to memory the feats of agility she witnessed, recognizing things Hamal had shown her, expanded upon by Ainn and Ellie, and again by those she now watched.

Acrobatics stitched seamlessly into the forms she'd been taught through katas opened her mind to new ways of blending styles. Commentary from those watching gave her insight into what happened in the ring as well.

"Always keep your feet. If you jump, you're much too vulnerable."

"You have to keep your opponent guessing! The leaping and spinning keeps them off balance."

"Too much ground-work. Someone'll come behind you and *tap-tap* the back of your skull."

Dee filed it all away, eyes dissecting the play in the circle.

As the last pair came to the end of their exhibition, Ellie called to Dee, "You ready for a go?"

Dee hesitated, the excitement that had built in the watching erased in the face of performance anxiety. Ellie didn't give her a chance to say no.

Dee grabbed the staff Ellie tossed her from the air. The feel of the smooth wood in her hand erased the doubts surfacing. She twirled the bo with a smile, knowing Ainn would yell at her for disrespecting her weapon, but it was time for a little exhibition. Wasn't that what this was all about?

-Careful. Don't get cocky.-

Rather than use a verbal reprimand, Ainn stepped into the circle, her staff buzzing with offensive motion to berate her student physically. Dee brought her weapon up to block, stepping and twisting as she did so, forcing muscles to respond more quickly than she'd considered allowing them before. If these Soldiers, whose every waking moment was fixated on honing themselves into the best possible fighters, thought she was more than she'd shown, she was going to trust they knew what they were talking about. Here she was going to see just how capable she was. She was going to show them they couldn't hold her. She was going to show them she didn't need protecting. She was going to show them to leave her to the quiet life she never realized how much she enjoyed.

-Right, because you were living quietly, rather than hiding.-

Egged on by the pestering voice in her head, she continued to up the ante, pushing herself until she no longer needed pushing, following the flow that had naturally set over her as her mind allowed her body to be free.

She wasn't sure how long they sparred, neither getting a hit on the other. Given that Dee was used to lasting only as long as it took her to get to her feet, this was an improvement beyond what anyone could have hoped for.

Much of her vision, a sense relied on more than any other, was lost in the whirring motion of their accelerated action, yet, there was no disadvantage. As if her muscles had sight, some foreknowledge of the oncoming blows, there was no need for her eyes to perceive what her body naturally sensed.

The fight's pace quickened. Murmurs flowed around the central pair, but neither of the two engaged took notice.

Finally, it was Ellie who called for a halt.

Panting, Dee stood, bo held with one end resting on the ground, eyes barely noting the impressed looks from those surrounding her as she relished the feeling of her body. Energized, she bounced on her toes, giving Ellie her attention, who was beaming. "Dee, never had I imagined our exhibition would bear such fruitful results. Would you like to see more, or continue playing with what you've learned about yourself?"

-*Let's play!*-

"I'd like to play a little more." She tried to adopt the severe nature of her newest tutors, but her smiling face betrayed her.

The Soldier matched her smile, pleased with Dee's answer. "Alright, then let's continue. Who'd like to join Dee in the circle?"

Daniel ignored the others whose hands rose or voices called out, instead leaping forward, sword drawn. "Had much sword practice?"

"Not much." Dee stared at the weapon in his hand, heart fluttering, thinking of the katana gifted by Hamal, now lost on some back country road. The sword stalking towards her was a different style, and she found herself curious how it might feel in her hand.

He looked to Ainn, ensuring he had permission to continue. The trainer had already pulled a pair of practice swords for them, tossing one to Dee, then the other to Daniel as he sheathed his own. Absently, Dee nodded thanks, testing the weight of the new weapon before returning her attention to Daniel. "Promise not to maim me?"

He chuckled. "No promises, but I will try very hard not to scar you for life."

She might have laughed with him, but the gleam in his eye as he began circling her was anything but mirthful. This was a solemn duel.

She spun in a slow, tight circle as Daniel stalked her, his movements smooth and fluid, sword point never wavering from his target.

Her memory flashed to the first night she'd met him. The same night she'd faced Barnard in the woods, and the first time she'd ever wielded a sword with the intent to kill. How much easier would her nights have been if she'd carried one all along? There would have been no problem killing a few Revenants.

-Or you would have accidentally slit your own throat.-

Daniel moved forward using a stuttering step to feint, a move designed to pull her head into the fight.

His feint spiked her adrenaline, as well as a tinge of embarrassment that he'd shaken her so absolutely. She scrambled to make a move. Coming at him in a blur of speed, her eyes searching for the counter she was sure he'd throw, she wasn't prepared for the simplicity of his action.

As her muscles created movement out of the disordered plan in her mind, he adjusted his position, moving only enough, right at the last moment, to avoid the hit. There was a split second when she thought she would win with a first strike.

Then, she was on her face, reminded of those first days working with Ainn and Ellie.

Leaping back to her feet, she spun to a smiling Daniel. "Not thinking is not the same as not having a plan," he admonished.

Dee stood in a fighting stance, not lowering her guard as she tilted her head at his words. "Oh?"

His sword arm dropped, his stance relaxing from his fighting position. "You reacted emotionally. Not that I can blame you, but in a fight, leave emotion off the table."

Her lips were pressed together in a tight line of annoyance. "I did not react emotionally."

His eyebrows rose. "What did you feel right before you sprinted at me with no plan of attack other than irrational outburst?"

She met his eye, her embarrassment rising. Grasping for any explanation that might make sense, she shrugged again, realizing his assessment was correct.

"You were embarrassed. I get it." He pointed his sword straight out, turning to each of those standing around them. "We all get it. We all started as beginners with the worst better than us. Being embarrassed at not knowing should be erased from your mind. How could you know? Why shouldn't you be beaten by all of us who have decades of experience over you? Why shouldn't I show you up? You should simply walk out on the field and already know how to play? You are here to learn. Learn!"

He was speeding towards her before the last word had cleared the air, but she was ready, his words wiping her mind of background distractions. All those eyes on her, and their potential for judgment, were forgotten. Regardless of other motives, at this moment, they were there to teach her. Right here, right now, she could allow them their influence as it would make her stronger, more able to face the chaos beyond this circle.

And so it went, Dee amplifying what she knew as each Soldier met her in the circle. They only stopped when the last of the sun's rays passed from sight.

Bowing respectfully to each other before wandering off in groups and pairs, Dee found herself standing in a hushed twilight, staring up at the star-riddled sky, her body aching deliciously from working so hard.

"You were great." Daniel's words implied multiple meanings. She wondered if he flirted with everyone like this.

"I think I have you to thank for that." She turned her head to look at him before returning her gaze to the sky. "Learn!" She shouted it into the night, laughing. "Everyone was inspired. And everyone remembered to give me some slack for being such a noob."

He chuckled. "Noob. That you are." His voice dropped as if talking to himself, "I wonder how many of them would understand the term."

She studied his face as his attention moved to the stars. From many of the Soldiers, there was a sense of timelessness, similar to what she felt from Atkins, but Daniel wasn't like that. He appeared no more than thirty, and until this moment, she'd never considered he might be exactly how old he seemed. His jovial nature was in contrast to the others whose stoicism allowed only focused work. Could that be due to his more modern heritage?

"How long have you been one of them?" Daniel wasn't surprised by her question, instead smiling quietly to the sky.

The remaining Soldiers continued to shuffle away. When the air surrounding them was filled with only sounds of croaking frogs and chirping cicadas, he answered, "A few decades. I'm a baby. *The* baby, actually." He laughed, turning his attention to her. "I think it was why Dimitri and I were chosen as the first to come to your aid. I'm a little more relatable than these old-timers. Plus, sending your weakest Soldier on a mission this important is counter-intuitive. My showing up is easily deflected as unrelated to the curiosity surrounding the anomaly."

His eyes studied hers with an intensity she wasn't sure how to define.

Forcibly, she maintained eye contact with the young Soldier. "So, you're Baby and I'm Anomaly."

He laughed and Dee couldn't help but join him. When their laughter faded, they were both looking back at the sky.

"So, you were also sent because your playful attitude might endear you to me?" Dee had been playing his words over in her head.

Daniel chuckled. "Playful attitude, huh?"

She smiled, eyes remaining on the sky.

"I think that's a reason, yes. Zibanitu's been manipulating both humans and—whatever it is we are—for so long I'm not sure we could measure it. There are always layers to his actions. And non-actions."

Dee nodded, wondering how he was manipulating her. Had he wanted her here with Amalthea for reasons other than to circumvent a diplomatic incident she still didn't understand?

Daniel's words gave her a thought. "So, Zibanitu's waiting for someone to make a mistake. For someone to come forward, at which point they'll be forced to explain what's going on."

Daniel shrugged. "I just work here."

She frowned, knowing he had his theories. Knowing it wasn't his place to say, despite him having offered his cryptic insights up to this point, didn't make his silence any less frustrating.

"When will you be going back?" She wasn't sure what she felt that Hamal would be leaving and she probably would never see him again.

Daniel shrugged again, looking over at her, his playful demeanor turned on full. "Why? Think you'll miss me?"

Dee chuckled, rolling her eyes. "If you can leave, maybe I can leave."

The playfulness washed from his face as he studied her. It was there, in his expression, in the seriousness of one so genial, that she saw her infinite imprisonment. He might only just work there, but even he knew what her fate would be.

"Why did you," her hands moved in front of her as she searched for verbiage, "become one of them?"

"Zibanitu keeps tight control over how large any House gets. It's rare, well—it's rare now—that Soldiers need replacing. There's not enough conflict that kills us off, so there's not much Initiating going on."

Dee frowned. "You say that like you wish that weren't the case."

He shrugged, eyes still on the sky. "I was created to fight. What does one do when their purpose is no longer purposeful?"

Dee had never had purpose. She had no way to relate.

Daniel continued. "They take humans. The better warriors they are, the more they're sought after. Then, it's like they infuse whatever they are into us and we come out like this." He lifted his arms to the side to gesture to himself, eyes falling to Dee's face, his eyes guarded against whatever emotion bubbled underneath.

"What do they do?" Dee's voice was soft, not sure if she had any right to ask.

Daniel's gaze was internal now. "I have no idea. I just know I woke up after a few weeks and I was this."

"A few weeks? Like you were in a coma?"

He shrugged again, eyes returning to the sky. "I guess. There's not a whole lot of explaining that goes on. Soldiers obey. Explaining the whys and why-nots tends to muddy the water. That's how mutinies start, and players switch sides. Not good for business, those things."

Dee's scrutiny moved from his face to the sky. "Don't want your troops knowing the heinous shit they're responsible for?"

He smiled. "Exactly. But, I knew coming in. We're not just plucked from our lives, prisoners to their will. Only after does our will become theirs."

-*Must be nice.*-

Her eyes lit with surprise, her attention returning to studying his face. "So, you knew them before you agreed to the change? You knew what they were—are, whatever."

"I still don't know what they are. Not really. But yeah, I knew they were something—else. I was allowed a genuine decision, to stay and be more than I ever could have been without them, or continue with my old life. I saw what these Soldiers could do. Watched their training. Saw where they slept. How they lived. After that, there was nothing the Rishis could have shown me that would have made me say no."

Steps through the grass, coming from the house, turned their attention.

Dee hadn't seen Hamal since he'd left her room a handful of days ago. She struggled to remember exactly how long it had been, each day here seeming a week, the last few weeks a lifetime.

Part of her was elated to see him, but that part was buried beneath another part that didn't know what she was supposed to say after he'd abandoned her without explanation. They stared at each other, his blank mask covering any clue to what he might be thinking.

She grit her teeth against the disappointment growing inside her.

*

Daniel was the first to speak, noting Hamal's tense posture, the way his eyes moved over the pair in search of something going. He hid his smile, realizing the truth of the rumored infatuation Hamal had with the anomaly, knowing it wasn't something to throw in his face unless the Soldier wanted a real fight.

The idea brought a smile to his lips, but Daniel knew better than to test the Rishi's patience with something so juvenile. Besides, what if he hurt the human?

The Soldier peeked a glance at Dee before deciding on a course of action. Was this infatuation reciprocated? Daniel was sure the plan was never for the two to become enamored of each other. But, with Zibanitu, one never knew true motive.

Dee's face was stone. The effort it took to hide what she was feeling was evident, though Daniel couldn't determine which emotions she was hiding. Did she detest the man who'd been forced to lie to her, blaming him for bringing her into all of this, even though he had nothing to do with causing it? Or was she secretly in love with her mentor?

"Hamal, good to see you up and about." Daniel's tone was friendly, genuine.

Hamal's was less so. "Daniel. Word of your impending death was greatly exaggerated. An interesting story that'll be told for centuries, I'm sure."

"Just what I need, a story of my almost dying proceeding me. Hopefully, I'll fight another day to fix my reputation to something a bit sexier."

Dee chuckled, a sound that brought a frown to Hamal's face.

Tension rose over the group.

After a beat of silence, Hamal asked Dee, "Everyone treating you well?" She nodded.

Daniel took Dee's hand, watching Hamal's face. "We were on our way to supper. Would you like to join?"

Hamal's eyes went to their hands clasped together.

Daniel watched the war in the human's eyes as he struggled with how to respond. It told Daniel all he needed to know.

When Hamal abruptly turned, walking away with clenched fists, there was no longer any question.

*

Dee wasn't sure what she felt as Hamal walked away, her hand still clasped in Daniel's, who was working small circles on her wrist with his thumb.

Snatching her hand away, she continued to stare after Hamal. "What the hell was that?"

Daniel chuckled. "Just messing with him. And proving a point to the both of usYou'll both be glad of it, trust me."

She turned to face him. "What point?"

"His feelings for you. They need to be tempered. If you share his interest, you too, need to forget it."

Dee opened her mouth to speak but found no words. Too many emotions swirled through her. Surprise that Hamal cared for her. Anger that Daniel would interfere, and even greater indignation that he would tell her how she was allowed to feel. Not least of all, longing for the thing she'd already known she couldn't have.

She kept her thoughts to herself. Daniel wasn't interfering. He was just explaining how it was. Not liking the reality of it didn't make the truth any different.

"Daniel? Who am I?"

Genuine surprise filled his face. "Honestly, I'm not sure anyone can answer that. I didn't know anything about you until I showed up at your house, dodging bullets before I was even sure I'd found the right place."

Dee smiled, remembering well her attack on him.

-And Dimitri.-

And Dimitri. One already dead because of trying to help her. How many more would there be before the end?

"You aren't one of us." Daniel pointed his finger at his chest. "But neither are you one of Them. I'd place my bets that you are something else."

Chapter Twenty-Four

Prepared for her typical quiet, solitary morning eating a quiet, solitary breakfast, Dee stopped fast when she found Amalthea seated in one of the oversized chairs that faced the windows in the living area of her suite. The Rishi sat calmly, as if her presence there was a daily occurrence.

"Come, sit with me." Amalthea motioned with a hand that lay lazily on an arm of the chair.

Hesitating only long enough to cast a sweep of eyes over the room, Dee did as she was told, falling into the chair that sat near its sister, turning her gaze to where Amalthea faced.

They stared out over the lands of the estate. Fall had fallen over the landscape to redefine color. How had she never noticed so many shades, or that green could be yellow, and red, or even brown? How bright colors were only so because of the contrast from the duller leaves.

Minutes stretched in this silent observance, until Amalthea's soft voice eased into the quiet, "It has been my pleasure to have you here. Not only have I ensured myself a place in this story but I've found you to be a most gracious guest."

Dee smiled shyly, not sure what to say.

-*Thank you?*-

"Thank you, Rishi."

Amalthea smiled back, and Dee relaxed.

As the Rishi looked her over, Dee wondered what she was seeing, or what she might be looking for. She thought to ask but held her tongue. Speaking with Amalthea was not the same as talking with Daniel or Hamal.

"As I've said, I'm excited to finally be part of one of the grand stories my brothers and sisters play out. Even so, there is no script, and as patient as I can be, I do not like to sit around and wait to see what might happen. I like to touch things, feel them, experience them. Stories are no good if they have no life."

Rising, Amalthea stood tall at the window, her full five foot two frame casting a shadow across her guest. Dee went rigid, fear born from instinct running through her. The Rishi continued to stare out the glass. "It is time to show you what this is. This world we've dragged you into. A world, I believe, you have no knowledge of, regardless of whether others think you're playing a game of ignorance."

Dee opened her mouth to defend herself. This was the first she'd heard that anyone thought she'd been lying.

Amalthea held up a hand, still not looking at her. "There is no need to explain to me. I believe you. Hamal believes you. For now, that is good enough."

She turned from the window to face Dee. "I will show you what I can about the things you've seen. It may give you some insight into our world, though there will be much more to learn." The Rishi studied Dee for a moment, and Dee got the impression she was debating something to herself. When she spoke, Dee knew that whatever it was, she had decided against it. "Eat. Get dressed. We will be hiking many miles today. I will send an escort when we are ready to go."

-*Hiking?*-

***

An hour later, Dee was walking through the very hills she'd been staring across that morning, matching steps with Daniel, her assigned bodyguard. Dee wasn't sure why she needed private security detail when they were safely on Amalthea's land, surrounded by the Rishi's Soldiers, and she didn't ask. Still, her heart hadn't lowered to a regular beat since leaving the shadows of the house.

Hamal hadn't been chosen to come with them. Or had decided not to. Dee was pointedly not worrying about it.

A few hours later, she realized she was enjoying herself. A much more meditative activity than jogging, she wished she'd started hiking years ago. How different her life might have been.

-*Sure, you'd be dead down some gorge after being tackled off a cliff.*-

Her imagination envisioned just that happening so vividly she shuddered, prompting Daniel's question, "Hanging in there?"

"I'm great, actually." She took a deep breath of the clean air to emphasize her point.

They walked side by side, behind Ellie and Vali who followed another pair Dee recognized, though she didn't know their names. Behind her, Amalthea walked with Metis, and behind them, Atkins and Ainn.

Glancing behind her to judge how quietly she could speak for the pair behind her not to hear, not entirely sure such a thing was possible, she caught Metis watching her. His carefully crafted expression betrayed nothing. Since seeing him at the battle on the road, which the others now referred to as *Roadside*, she'd caught only glimpses of Amalthea's beautiful right hand.

She wasn't sure what it meant that he was the Rishi's *right hand*. What things did Amalthea's House deal with that the Rishi would need someone to act in this manner, and how powerful was he that he could fill that role?

There were still so many questions. She was excited that this trip might fill in some gaps.

-Careful. So far, every time you've learned anything, its only created more questions.-

This was true, but there had to be a point when answers would start yielding information rather than further muddy what she thought she knew.

Daniel bumped her casually. "You're fidgeting."

"Sorry, I'm not sure I can talk without everyone hearing me."

"Would it matter?"

She thought about it. "I guess not."

She shot another glance over her shoulder to find the Rishi and Metis engaged in hushed conversation. Could she eavesdrop on them if she focused?

Another bump from Daniel refocused her thoughts on her own conversation. "Where are we going?"

"That one's easy. I thought Amalthea told you."

"She told me she was going to show me about 'the world I've been dragged into.'" Dee air-quoted.

He chuckled. "Typical. We're hiking through the hills to a secure location. We're still on her property, but removed from the rest of the estate."

"Secure location? I thought the house was secure."

Daniel swept out a hand to encompass their surroundings. "Sure, but this is secure from anyone knowing about it."

"Except us."

He smiled. "Except us."

"I'm surprised she'd let you know the location of this secret location."

He shrugged. "I just work here, remember." He paused before continuing. "I'm sure there was a conversation with Zibanitu. Hamal wouldn't come, so it had to be me."

Dee's heart dropped, and she chastised herself for it. Why wouldn't he come?

-Who cares. You should have killed him.-

If Daniel noticed her deflation he let it pass without comment.

He continued. "Amalthea wanted this to be an excursion with just her people. They proved they could defend against Han, but Zibanitu wanted someone from his House with you at all times. Amalthea knows better than to defy him, especially when she's waited so long to get in on some action."

"She said something similar to me. She *wants* to be dealing with this drama?"

Daniel smiled. "Strange, huh? But that's the truth. She's been sitting around here for who knows how long. She wants something exciting to happen. She wants to be involved in the politics among the three Houses who have yet to settle an age-old feud."

Dee sighed. More questions. She wondered if she should even try to figure out what he was talking about.

"Daniel, that's enough." Amalthea's calm voice was laced with warning. The pair didn't turn around to acknowledge her words, though Daniel bowed his head.

There was only silence after that.

Chapter Twenty-Five

Darkness bled from the earth as the sun fell below the trees, but still, the group continued forward. When the rolling, forested hills of Amalthea's estate turned to steeper terrain, Dee wondered just how far into the middle of nowhere they were going. She couldn't even guess how far they'd traveled, glad she was easily keeping up with the rest, who didn't seem ready to stop, even after the full day with no break.

A particularly abrupt rise gave way to a level plateau. Dee found herself looking across a grassy knoll onto a three-story house carved directly into the mountainside. With a concave front and tall windows showing the brightly lit interior, the house was a beacon of modernity in the center of uninhabited land. A stone pathway, wide enough for three of them to walk abreast, began where they climbed from and meandered to the edge of a platform that dropped down into a sunk-in porch that ran the width of the house. The front door, nestled among the stone front of the structure, stood framed in narrower windows.

Dee stopped to gape at the incredible feat of architecture ahead.

Amalthea, pleased at her reaction, had stopped next to her. "What do you think?"

"I've never seen anything like it. What's it doing way out here?"

"We all need our secret places." It was all the explanation Dee received before the Rishi moved on, Metis at her side.

Daniel lingered, eyes roaming the design with their own tight-lidded awe. Only when they were the last two outside did he gently push Dee forward with a hand at her back.

Expecting a cave-like quality to a house built into a mountain, Dee was pleasantly surprised by the white oak flooring, bright lighting, and colorful paintings lining the walls.

Disappointed she couldn't linger and gape, Dee hurried after Metis, who led her and Daniel up a broad set of stairs that curved past the second floor to the third. As they made their way deeper into the house, the sense of being underground grew. Dee couldn't help but feel the forest above pressing down on her. How far into the mountain did this place go?

Leading them through a solitary door at the end of a long hall, Metis explained, "You'll sleep here. You'll stay here when not training, or when not with the Rishi." His voice allowed no argument.

-*Just a more sophisticated prison.*-

Any excitement she'd had about this new adventure was gone. Dee looked back down the long hall they'd traveled, feeling isolated. Was there really that much worry that they'd be attacked, or was the security because of something else?

"Daniel is staying up here too?"

-That's *the concern worth voicing?*-

Metis pursed his lips. "Zibanitu wanted one of his people with you, so that's how it will be."

Daniel had turned his back on the conversation to study the room. She liked Daniel well enough but wasn't sure she trusted him sleeping in the same room as her.

Her eyes stayed on the Soldier's back, but her question was for Metis, "How long will we be here?"

"As long as it takes."

Dee took a breath to ask, *as long as* what *takes*, but Metis was already out the door.

Daniel continued to search the large room, pressing his hands into the walls in varies places, then jumping lightly as if to test the floor. About to ask what he was doing, Dee was saved the trouble when he turned to explain, "This room is well secured. No windows. It's not even close to the exterior so no one could consider coming through the walls. Amalthea is taking your security very seriously."

Ignoring the bout of claustrophobia that threatened her, Dee focused on another issue. "You're going to be sleeping in here with me?"

He met her eye straight on. "I bet Hamal would have come if he'd known this was how the sleeping arrangements would be."

Dee cocked an eyebrow.

His chuckle turned to laughter. "What? You think I'm going to eat you? Kill you in your sleep?"

Dee wasn't sure what she thought. She turned away from him, walking towards a door she assumed was the bathroom. "I'm going to take a shower."

"Mmmmmm."

She whirled at the hinting expression. "You stay out here."

He held his hands up in mock surrender. "Of course." He turned away. "Unless I think you're in danger."

She stared at his back, judging how safe it was to get naked behind a door that wouldn't keep him out if he didn't want to be kept out. But, what could she do? She wasn't going to skip bathing the whole time she was here. Or not change her clothes.

What was she afraid of? She liked Daniel. So, why was she suddenly nervous at the thought of him being so close to her for however long they would be here? She didn't think he was here to hurt her, did she?

-Truth is, you don't know who to trust. You don't know if any of them are really on your side. -

***

The next day, Dee found herself with the same group who'd accompanied her on the previous day's hike, making her way down a damp stone hallway that curved steeply below a structure hidden even further in the forested hills than the house had been. This structure, which looked like an old mausoleum, hid the entrance to the stairs they were now on.

As they continued to descend beneath the surface of the world, Dee's mind whirled with ideas about what she was being led to see.

-No one's going to find your body down here.-

She refused to let her thoughts linger on the idea that she was being brought to her death, though that kernel of thought couldn't be completely silenced. She focused on taking step after step through the dim, tight corridor that stretched down, forever curving so she could never see where they were going.

Daniel was ahead of her, Metis behind, with Soldiers bookending them. For a secured area, they were treating this as a dangerous place.

-The things you don't know...-

There was a lot she didn't know.

What was Amalthea going to show her? Was this where Soldiers were made? Maybe they were in a hidden passage that led to another compound.

Dee's nerves were frayed by the time they moved into a large chamber, its vaulted ceiling lost beyond the shadowed light of sconces she wondered who had lit. The space was roughly forty by sixty feet, bare of anything but dirt and spiders, who retreated from the newcomers with unnatural speed. Dee barely noticed, too busy peering through the dim space towards the iron door that lay on the opposite side of the room.

When that very door opened after a series of clangs from sliding bolt locks, she jumped. Something beyond the door let out a moaning howl that echoed around them. Skin crawling from the noise, Dee barely noticed the emaciated figure now scuffling towards them until the door was shut, erasing the awful sound. The figure stared straight down, and Dee wondered if he would run into them.

Amalthea stepped ahead to greet the figure, who stopped in front of her. The frail man bowed from the waist, his eyes never coming up from the floor. "Everything is as you asked, Rishi."

"Thank you, Waverly." She turned to catch Dee's eye, motioning her forward. With a gentle hand on her arm, she guided Dee towards the iron door, following closely behind Waverly as he led them back the way he'd come.

Thankfully, the moaning had stopped, so the group was greeted with silence when the door re-opened at Waverly's tug. Before Amalthea could make a move to follow the strange little man through, Metis was there, apologizing as he pushed ahead of her, Atkins close on his heels.

Dee watched Amalthea's face as the Soldiers carefully pushed her aside, waiting for some sign of anger or annoyance, but the Rishi showed neither, merely allowing them in front of her, an amused expression covering her face.

Noticing Dee's watchful glance, she turned to the girl, smiling. "They think I'm an old lady, unable to take care of myself. I indulge them. It is what they have trained for after all. They forget I could take all of them if I had a mind to."

Dee believed her. A different kind of chill washed over her. She knew the Rishi wasn't just some middle-aged lady by the power that hummed in Dee's skull, but after being surrounded by both her and her Soldiers for so long, this warning system had became a dull hum she ignored.

Dee made a note not to ignore this crucial point. Of all of them, it was the Rishi who was most dangerous, not her Soldiers who played at protecting her.

When the all-clear was announced, Dee's stomach fluttered, wishing she'd asked precisely what it meant that Amalthea was going to *show* her. What was down here, hidden away, that the Soldiers wouldn't let them enter without first checking that it was safe? Hadn't the skinny man just come from here? Was he not what he seemed either?

The first thing to hit her was the noise. The howling had commenced as if cued by their entry. Now in the same room as the source of the sound, the volume overwhelmed her nervous system. She hunched in on herself, her steps slowing. Behind this howling, interlaced like some melody coined in Hell, were the growling snaps of some animal.

Looking at her feet, as if changing the direction of her sight might dampen the noise, Dee noted the floor strewn with straw. Curious by this, she allowed her gaze to dart around, glad for something to focus on other than the painful noise overwhelming the room.

Much smaller than the cavern they'd just come from, the room was separated into six cells cordoned by metal bars. A center aisle from the door cut through the center of the room.

All thoughts blown from her mind by the incessant raging that filled the air, Dee didn't think to look at what might be in these cells until she heard Amalthea speak. "We'll start with the Burn, please, Waverly."

-Burn?-

Dee closed her eyes against the noise to better focus on Amalthea's words. When her eyes opened, she found Amalthea had moved to stand close to the bars of a cell where a human man lay on the stone floor. Thrashing and screaming, his movements cut his skin against the broken floor, so blood was smeared throughout the cell.

Horrified, Dee watched as the cuts quickly healed themselves, only to form anew when the intensity of his convulsions punched new wounds into his skin. Moving closer, her steps brought her next to the Rishi, though her mind screamed for her to flee the gruesome sight. Gulping loudly to swallow her sobs, she couldn't stop the tears that welled in her eyes. As much as she tried to tear her stare away, her eyes seemed caught, unable.

"What's wrong with him?" Her voice was choked around the sob lodged in her throat.

Amalthea smiled sadly, turning to Waverly. "Do it now, please."

Waverly was ready with a hypodermic needle. His nod brought two Soldiers to the cell to grab the mans legs, pulling him towards the bars so Waverly could insert the needle into his thigh. The man never stopped his thrashing screams or made any sign he was aware of the group around him.

Dee shuddered, a tear falling from her eye. She didn't bother wiping it away.

When the plunger had released the liquid into the Burn, he quickly fell silent, movements ceasing apart from an occasional twitch.

"Only a few of us are able to create Soldiers. None of us has ever truly figured out the why or how of it. Of all the Soldiers you will come across, only a handful have been with us since the beginning."

Dee continued to stare at the man in the cell, listening to Amalthea's words, trying to link what she'd seen in front of her with what the Rishi was telling her. "Not all who risk the change from human to Soldier survive. Most don't actually, and it is not something we ask of anyone lightly."

Dee nodded, remembering Daniel's perspective on this. "This man agreed to become a Soldier." She stared harder, thinking of all the Soldiers she'd met, most of whom, by what Amalthea was saying, had been taken from their human lives and enhanced. Daniel had called it *Initiated.*

"This is what happens to those who don't become Soldiers?" Dee's voice was steadier now that the room was quiet.

Amalthea turned her full attention to her guest. "Sometimes. What I mean to show you are all possible outcomes of the transition."

Dee turned, finally looking at what she'd ignored.

Across from the cell that held the Burn was something she recognized. The creature who accounted for the growled snarls she'd heard earlier.

"That's a Revenant." Dee had taken a step towards it.

-You were right about them having been human.-

Dee shuddered to think a person, agreeing to become something more, would wake up as one of these things. She hoped there was no memory buried inside the snarling beast.

Amalthea nodded. "It is. There are varying levels of intelligence in these, but generally, they're animalistic creatures who hunt any warm-blooded thing."

Dee swallowed hard. Sadness morphed to anger at the thought that someone's life had been taken from them for a promise that might not have been real. They were then used as someone—something—saw fit. Manipulated into a kind of slavery, and for what?

She couldn't keep the anger from her tone. "These things were sent after me. Who would use them for a targeted purpose if all they would do was kill anything in their path?"

"This is a question we are looking into."

Dee stared hard at Amalthea, attempting to judge if it was genuine ignorance of the situation, or if information was being purposefully withheld. Dee wasn't sure which was worse.

-Great. The blind leading the blind here.-

The Revenant, deciding its time of quiet was over, launched itself at the bars, hitting with enough force to show how well built each cage was, sending a spray of spit towards the pair. Dee stepped back, but Amalthea held her ground, looking pityingly at the creature who'd once been human.

The Rishi continued to stare at the enraged Revenant as she spoke. "Waverly is another. Sometimes, instead of enhancing the human form, the transition diminishes it. Most of these die soon after they wake, usually from some sickness they contract their bodies can no longer fight off. Waverly is one of the rare ones who has managed to survive this particular adaptation."

Dee watched Waverly as he moved between a string of monitors set up along the back wall. She wondered if he hated these Rishis who'd taken his life, even if he had agreed to it. Did he remember who he'd been, longing for a life he could never return to? Daniel had explained that most Soldiers began as exceptional humans. She wondered who Waverly had been before his change to the frail being he was now forced to suffer.

Amalthea had crossed back to the cell next to the Burn, where a girl seemed to sleep peacefully. "Some go to sleep and never wake, sometimes living in this comatose state for decades before finally fading away. None have ever woken, but we can't bring ourselves to kill them before they die on their own." Her voice dropped to a whisper. "You never know when that first one will rise."

The Rishi stared into the cell for a long time, and Dee wondered if the girl was someone Amalthea had been fond of. The idea made her think of something she hadn't asked. "How do you determine who will go through the transition? How long do you know them as humans before they're allowed to know what you are? How long do they get to decide if they should risk their lives to become..."

"More? Better? Raised up? Something greater?"

Dee nodded, wondering what the odds were that any of those things were met, rather than the horrifying changes she was seeing. She stared silently at the girl who seemed at peace in her dreams.

-*You think she dreams?*-

Dee didn't want to think about it. She asked the first thing that came to mind to distract from the tearing sadness of all she was shown. "How do you feed them? How do they live so long?"

Amalthea, eyes still focused far away, shrugged noncommittally. "It's as if they're in a state of timelessness. We never feed them, yet still, some live many, many years."

Amalthea turned again to move across the center of the room. Dee pushed herself to follow, ignoring the Revenant still attempting to force its way through the bars, its spitting ferocity unnerving.

The next cell she was brought to contained a very awake, very conscious, very annoyed man sitting very straight on a cot at the far side.

Amalthea held the glare of the prisoner.

-*If looks could kill...*-

After a few tense seconds, the man in the cage spoke, his body held rigidly, words overly enunciated as if bracing himself in strict control. "Rishi, is all of this necessary?"

"You tell me, Pax."

Pax stood as if pulled by a rubber band, eyes drifting to look at Dee before returning to the one who'd imprisoned him here. "At least get me away from this frothing zombie. Please." He fell to his knees with the last word, hands gripping the bars in front of him, head bowing to look at the floor. While his body language suggested penance, his tone was full of hateful disregard.

Amalthea said nothing, inspecting the man as a mother who watches her child try to talk themselves out of a punishment they justly deserve.

The Revenant lunged at the shared bars, startling Dee's eyes from the man kneeling in front of her. Before her eyes had focused, her head was slammed into the iron that separated her and Pax. His act of contrition, with the help of the Revenant's convenient distraction, allowed the prisoner the opportunity to grab her, pulling her towards him with a quick jerk that left her face cracking against cold iron.

Dee barely registered the pain exploding across her face as she grabbed the man's hand in a wrist lock without opening her eyes. Twisting it, he fell back to his knees, screaming as she popped his wrist joint so his fingers went slack. Her other arm came through the bars to grab him by the neck, fingers splaying around his throat, squeezing as she yanked his face into the bars.

As suddenly as it started, she was pulled away, two pairs of arms relocating her to a distance away from the cell.

Looking up to a blurry room through eyes filled with tears, she knew her nose was busted. She tasted blood. Licking her lips, she assessed the damage.

"You did good, kid." Atkins handed her a towel.

"Oh yeah? Maybe shouldn't have gotten close enough to get my face bashed open." Talking brought more tears to her eyes, so she closed them angrily lest they spill down her face.

Daniel stood next to Atkins, laughing tightly. "That's true, but I bet you'll never let it happen again."

Atkins nodded, a short drop of his chin. "No better teacher than experience."

Dee was too busy glaring across the room at Pax, who, she was glad to see, was holding his arm to his body, face bleeding from multiple cuts, throat red and bruising, to notice the genuine compliments she was receiving.

Daniel had another towel and was carefully brushing blood from her forehead. "Never a dull moment with you, is there?"

She smiled, an expression that morphed into a grimace as the movement of her lips re-split the cuts that were already healing. "It's not my fault. All this keeps happening because of you crazy—whatever you are."

He chuckled, eyes looking her face over. When he was sure she didn't need any further attention, his gaze met her eyes. "Your face is going to turn a nice color of purple, then green, then yellow, not much different than it was a few days ago actually. It'll be a good story to tell."

"As long as we have that."

"Yes, we will have that." His gaze had taken on a heated edge she knew wasn't allowed, from his own mouth. She went rigid with surprise when his hand came up to her face to run a finger carefully down her nose. "How you do it... I understand Hamal better now."

She held his gaze as he back-stepped, before turning smartly to assess what was happening in the room.

Did that just happen?

-Which part? Getting your face bashed in, or getting the moves put on you from the very one who said to keep it impersonal?-

Her face hurt too much for her to think about it. It was ridiculous. Why would Hamal or Daniel make their lives so difficult for her? It wasn't like she was the only girl around. There were plenty of female Soldiers who were way more badass than she was. Not to mention more accessible.

-You're the new girl. The notoriety will pass, and they'll forget you.-

Amalthea was moving towards her. Dee couldn't see into Pax's cell, now surrounded by so many Soldiers. Had Pax signed his death certificate with his stunt?

"My apologies, Desiree." Amalthea's hands rested on Dee's shoulders, eyes assessing her face for injuries of the spirit as well as the already-healing physical ones.

Dee's eyes flickered beyond the Rishi to Pax. "Apparently, it was a learning moment for me."

Amalthea chuckled. "I do believe I just heard Atkins crack a smile. Well done." She winked before turning to the others. "We're done for today."

Dee noticed four of the Soldiers stay behind as she was flanked by Daniel, whose hand at her back pushed her along behind Metis, who followed Amalthea.

Dee turned her head to ask Daniel. "Who was Pax?"

"That's for Amalthea to tell." Daniel's answer was clipped. Not sure if it was his way of distancing him from her, or if something else had ruffled his feathers, Dee was too ready to be away from the underground dungeon to cess it out.

Chapter Twenty-Six

Wrapped in a towel, Dee avoided glancing at Daniel who was perched in the corner, flipping through a book she could tell he wasn't actually reading. She'd evaded the shower for as long as she could, even after the Soldier had taken one of his own before brazenly meandering around the room stark naked, ignoring the look of awkward terror that had preceded Dee fleeing to the hallway.

"I can't guard you if you're hiding out there!" He'd called, but she'd refused to come in until he showed her he was clothed.

She could tell he was still laughing at her, even as he pretended to keep his attention on the book in his hands, one leg bent casually, so he was the poster boy for unobtrusive.

She had planned to dress in the bathroom, but of course, she'd forgotten an essential element of her outfit. After staring at the door, she'd finally acknowledged there was no other way around her predicament except to come into the room with only a towel between her and prying eyes. It wasn't that she was a prude, there were just lines one shouldn't cross.

-*Oh, really?*-

"Amalthea asks that you join her for supper, with her sincerest apologies."

Dee jumped. Metis, standing just inside the door, had been completely overlooked in her distraction.

Heart thundering in her throat, she sent Daniel a silent curse that he hadn't warned her they had a visitor. She felt his silent laughter fill the room.

Focusing on Metis' invitation to circumvent her embarrassment, she wondered if her nerves could handle whatever else the Rishi might wish to show her. The bruises she'd sported on her face during the trip back from the underground cavern had healed, but that didn't mean she was eager to have them replaced so soon.

-*It's not like you can turn her invitation down.*-

She knew the Rishi genuinely felt guilty about Dee getting assaulted on her field-trip, but she also knew that wasn't the only reason for the invite. There was still much that hadn't been covered.

Dee forced words through a constricted throat. "Of course. When—"

"As soon as you're ready. I'll wait outside for you." Metis's eyes never left her face. Dee was almost grateful for his stale manner after the bemused attitudes of Hamal and Daniel.

She didn't move or speak until the door had closed behind him. "He doesn't like me much."

Daniel tossed his book on a nearby table. "He doesn't like anyone much, though I think it's more that he's mastered the art of indifference. It's not his place to opinionate. He comes across like a dick, but really, he's pure neutrality."

"Hmmm." Dee turned from the door to shuffle through the clothes hanging in an armoire almost twice her height. The outfit she'd picked to lounge around in wasn't going to cut it for a meeting with the Rishi. That there were so many clothes, all in her size, was a point she accepted without thought. That question didn't take priority over all the others.

-What does one wear to dinner with a Rishi in the middle of a forest in the center of nowhere inside a mountain?-

Daniel's arm reached over her shoulder, and she froze, heart thudding at his closeness, brain whirling that he'd moved from across the room without her noticing. She really needed to return to a more conscientious awareness of them.

"Wear this." He pulled out a green dress, sheer outer layer trimmed with a twilling of silver that gave the illusion of leaves blowing in a breeze.

Voice like steel, she sneered as she turned to look at what he'd chosen. "You're a fashionista, too?"

"I'm not sure fashionista is a word." He ignored her attitude, instead grinning with the laughter that hadn't faded from his face since she'd fled from his nakedness earlier.

The smile in his eyes helped loosen her own. "A female-fashion-guru, then?"

He let the laugh leak from his face into the air. "I've picked up a few things here and there. I know what Amalthea likes, and she'll appreciate your homage to the green things she loves so much."

Dee nodded, taking the dress from him. "Thanks."

"My pleasure." He returned to his perch and the book he'd been flipping through.

She was staring at him, unaware she was doing it until his gaze rose to meet her own with a smile. "Regretting not staying around to check out the goods?"

Flame flashed over her face. She whirled around, almost losing her towel again in the process.

Daniel's laugh rang out even through the closed door.

***

Picture windows opened to the night allowed the mountain breeze to waft over them while an undisturbed sky full of stars flickered in the background.

Unfortunately, Dee was too distracted to appreciate the setting. It took all her energy to keep her voice calm. "I appreciate you showing me all of this, but I'm not sure I understand the context. What the Soldiers are, how they're made, that isn't what a Rishi is, is it?"

Amalthea smiled. If she sensed Desiree's mounting frustration, she didn't let on. "No, we are something else entirely. That, we will get to, I promise you. Just, not quite yet. I wanted you to know about the Soldiers because we feel you are some branch of them."

Dee stared off, the meal in front of her long cold, while she traced her memories back to that blank spot in her past. Her last lucid thought was of her and Steve standing in the kitchen of the tiny apartment they shared with Kim and Ray. Had they been cooking? It didn't matter. Steve had been about to tell her something, then Ray had banged through the door, filling the space with his overwhelming energy.

Then, nothing. Just heat and flames and confusion.

She shook her head to break free from the thoughts, bringing her attention back to Amalthea. "There's this huge chunk of time I don't remember. I was in my apartment with my roommates. Then I was outside some house in the middle of nowhere as it was burning to the ground."

Amalthea leaned forward. "Who took you to the house?"

Dee clenched her eyes shut as if the act might trigger an answer. "I don't remember. I'd never seen the house before. I don't even know if I would recognize it if someone showed me a picture. I only saw it engulfed in flames."

"No one was with you?"

She opened her eyes. "Just me."

"How long were you there?" They were questions that had already been asked, but the Rishi seemed to think some kernel of information could filter through.

Dee's shrug told that this wasn't that time.

It was Amalthea's turn to look off. "It would be strange that you were given the Initiation in some unknown location. The Rishis who transfer humans to Soldiers have specific space for this, and I know none was ever some house in the middle of nowhere. That one would try this in such a removed location, if that's what this was," her eyes came back to rest on Dee's face to emphasize this point, "suggests a Rishi we've never known to succeed in an Initiation has finally mastered the skill. That, or something entirely new has been discovered. If there was an accident, it might make sense that you got away from them. Maybe they thought you'd died in the fire. Maybe it took them this long to find you."

-Way too many maybes for a conversation supposed to be making things clearer.-

Dee sat forward, playing with the food in front of her as she mulled over what had been said.

Amalthea had another question. "Where were you staying before you woke up at that house?"

"Where?" Dee glanced up from her plate.

"What part of the country? I assume you were still in the United States."

Dee nodded absently. "Northern California."

The Rishi received the bit of information as if it meant something to her, but changed the subject. "I showed you a Burn, a Coma, a Revenant, which I know you were already quite familiar with, and a Flawed. That was Pax."

"A Flawed?" Dee sat up in her seat, eager for some concrete information to sift into her meager file of data.

"Yes. One who survived the transition but with no augmentation occurring. They're extremely rare and are always given a position within the House. Pax grew bored with his assignments, so came to me with information on his former Master. He'd release the information to me if I would give him a more stimulating position."

"You imprisoned him because he was a traitor?"

"The timing was perfect to show him off to you." The Rishi smiled warmly, as if the fortuitousness of the universe working in her favor was something she'd planned.

Dee rubbed her face. "He seemed stronger than a normal guy would be."

Amalthea shrugged. "Possibly, but not enough to pass the Soldier's test. Nor was his mind gifted to be used in any other capacity."

"His mind?"

"Another variance of the Initiated. Even Soldiers' minds are enhanced with their bodies, and sometimes the mind's enhancement overshadows the physical. These typically become Messengers, though their use has significantly decreased, as most Rishi's won't allow another House's messenger into their domain."

Amalthea answered the question Dee's raised eyebrows implied. "These Messengers' minds have been enhanced, so they possess some level of psychic ability which we train them to use in manipulation."

"Okay…?"

Amalthea smiled kindly. "For example, a Messenger might have been sent to you so that you would agree to go with them to meet their Master. Barnard is one of the best Messengers ever to have been let out into the world. His talents, combined with a Soldier's training, have made his use most effective in the past."

Dee thought back to the day on the road when Barnard had held his hand out to her. There had been an active compulsion to go with him. Was that this Messenger trick, or just her wanting to explore all her options?

Amalthea smiled as if sensing what she was thinking of. "Yes, I imagine he used his skill on you then. You are either stronger than most, or he was gentle, unsure how your brain might react."

Dee looked up. "What could have happened?"

"Lesser humans have become enthralled, another reason the use of Messengers has fallen out of practice. Some have been known to start cults of fanatic followers."

Dee could see how that might be dangerous, as well as annoying, to the Masters who'd now have competition for leadership.

"Okay, so," Dee counted on her fingers. "Waverly."

"Pallid."

-Really, with these titles?-

"Right, Pallids, Comas, Burns, the Flawed, Messengers, Soldiers, Revenants. Seven possible outcomes when someone decides to be Initiated."

"Death is another possible outcome."

"Of course." Dee let out a flustered breath. "Eight outcomes then. And the running theory is that I'm a Soldier."

Amalthea nodded hesitantly. Dee sensed the Rishi didn't think she was a Soldier but wasn't ready to share her opinion on the matter.

-What else is new? -

Dee couldn't let it lie. "You don't think so?"

The Rishi smiled, the motherly warmth that so easily flooded her demeanor wrapping Dee in comfort. "I am loath to say what I think at this point."

Dee sighed. "Will you tell me about the Rishis?"

"No, but others will. We will visit them soon. It is their skill to tell stories, where it is my way to show. The past is difficult to present in tangible terms, so I leave it to others who are better suited for such things."

"Another field trip?"

"Yes. One I promise to be much less violent."

Dee laughed, touching her healed face, even while her insides screamed in frustration.

Stumbling: Book One on The Fool's Path

Chapter Twenty-Seven

Dee was distracted, mulling over the lack of information she'd gotten from Amalthea, so that she almost missed Daniel's question. "Learn anything useful?"

Her distracted answer of *maybe* drew a laugh from him. "You're fitting right in."

"Hmm? Oh? Oh, right." She grinned. "Yeah, sorry, but really. There's not a lot of actual answers going around."

He nodded, pacing quietly at her side while her thoughts returned to their spinning.

-Amalthea doesn't think you're a Soldier, implying you're more. If you were less, she wouldn't be so interested.-

It wasn't a fact, but it was a possibility. If she were more than a Soldier, there were still things inside her she hadn't tapped into yet. The notion made her buzz with excitement.

"Daniel? You think we can go for a hike?"

"A hike? It's dark."

"Don't tell me you're afraid of the dark."

He grinned. "You know better than that, but I don't think it would go over well if we went traipsing through the woods when you're supposed to be under heavy guard."

"Is there really anything to worry about out here?"

"I couldn't say. And even if I could say, I wouldn't."

She pouted for a few steps before another idea came to her. "You think anyone would be up for some training?"

He smiled broadly. "Of course they would. We were, literally, created for fighting. There's not one of us who doesn't hate to stand around waiting for something to happen."

*

A half-hour later, every Soldier on this field-trip, other than those on some security detail, were gathered in front of the house where just enough clear space allotted a decent sized training area before the plateau plummeted steeply down the mountain.

"Restless already, Noob?"

Dee laughed at the comment. Apparently, Daniel had told someone about her noob comment, and she'd found herself with a new nickname. It sounded like Vali, but she couldn't be sure. It didn't seem like him to make a joke.

"Something like that."

-Let's kick their asses.-

She felt the excitement of her inner-voice, finally loosed from its shackles by her expanding perspective of what she might be. Willing to believe she was something much more than she'd ever thought, it was exhilarated at the opportunity to let itself out of its cage.

Stepping to the center of the half-circle of Soldiers, wielding the practice sword she'd used the last time she'd fought in the practice ring, Dee waited to see who would be the first to join her. Surprisingly, it was Atkins, whom she'd barely seen since he'd held her hostage at Amaltheum.

-Let's take a crack at that one.-

She'd heard the rumors, seen the way the others watched him when he was near. Nodding to the voice in her head she analyzed the way Atkins felt, attempting to differentiate what made him more than the others through the way he hummed in her skull. The warrior nodded back, thinking the gesture had been for him, which was fine. It was an appropriate greeting for the sparring ring.

Atkins moved forward quickly but not so fast as to overwhelm her, so she knew he was going easy on her, testing her. His attack was styled differently than anything she'd seen from the others, so rather than engage, she flowed smoothly away, allowing herself time to read his movements before coming up with a plan of attack.

Atkins smiled at her evasiveness. "Well played, Ms. Galen. Learn first. Engage when ready."

They were still moving around each other, Atkins continuing his probing attacks while Dee eluded them. "What if I'm never ready?"

"Then your opponent will slaughter you." His voice was conversational, instructing.

"Should I run?"

His eyes flicked to her face before returning to her movements. "Sometimes, that is the right decision. Sometimes, it is just another way to die."

She knew he still hadn't begun to show her the magnitude of what he was capable of. Remembering Daniel's words about not being afraid to be embarrassed because one couldn't learn without putting yourself on the line, she engaged, moving as quickly as she ever had.

FEEL.

It was like her consciousness coursed from her brain to extend through every cell of her body, so she was anticipating his movements, forcing him to move further into the best of himself as she easily drifted around his attacks, blocking when necessary.

Press.

Another calibration of senses and she was pressing forward, forcing the greatest of opponents to defend himself against her blur of offense.

Flow.

No longer were the words in her head but rather a song that hummed through every synapse, sparking inside her blood. She sensed and obeyed, saw and reacted, until she was proceeding with a surge that made it impossible for her to be hit.

Atkins' amazement was palpable, so heavy that it rang against her thoughts, wrestling her from her heightened state until she was forced back into defense. The loud crack of their practice swords rang out to echo back at them from the hills.

Dee laughed at the sound, enjoying it so much she purposefully matched him strike for strike, so their fight became a song of percussions. Then, as if given some cue only the two could hear, they came to a stop, panting breathlessly.

Blinking quickly, Dee looked around at the semi-circle of staring faces whose expressions told all she needed to know.

Daniel's voice broke the silence. "Curiouser and curiouser."

She remembered him saying the same thing when they'd first met.

She smiled, meeting his eye, finally remembering where she'd heard the line before. That one of these Soldiers, creatures beyond human, had quoted *Alice in Wonderland* was the irony of the year.

-There's always more than what is first revealed.-

Her inner-voice was a philosopher now?

Ainn walked to the pair. "A sudden growth in your skill seems..."

The Soldier didn't finish her sentence, so Dee did for her. "...like I've been hiding it all along?"

The Soldier said nothing but the distrust was apparent on her face.

Dee smiled sadly. "I might think the same if our positions were reversed, but, please, believe me, that's not the case. You did this. You and Ellie and Daniel. You said my lack-of-belief in what I can do might be holding me back. Something Amalthea said earlier made me wonder if there wasn't more I could find."

Ainn stared at her with blank eyes, studying her students' face for any sign of deceit. Dee met her gaze, reading the mistrust that lay within. "Is there any way for me to prove this to you?"

"No." There was no hesitation in the response.

Two steps forward, three steps back.

She'd found her confidence among her betters. She'd found they weren't better, as well as finding a piece of herself that had been elusive. But in that, she'd isolated herself even more. Looking around at the group who'd maintained their positions in the semi-circle, postures denoting their readiness for a fight despite their blank faces, Dee suppressed a sigh.

"I think we're done for the night," Ainn decreed. No one contradicted her, though Dee felt the disappointment in many of the Soldiers who'd never gotten the opportunity to train with her.

As the others dispersed, Daniel moved towards Dee, eyes on Atkins. "A fine display, Atkins."

In spite of the somber tone, Atkins' attitude wasn't affected. In fact, he seemed as jovial as Dee had ever seen him. "My thanks, Daniel. It has been a long time since I've played." He smiled a full mien that lit up his face. "It was fun."

She smiled back, something inside her loosening that Ainn's examination of the event wasn't reciprocated by him. "Yes, it really was."

"I think you call it a rematch? I'll ask for one soon."

Her smile broadened. "Sounds good to me."

She and Daniel watched the Soldier walk away until they were the last two outside. When all was quiet, Daniel turned to her. "You understand what you just did, right? Why everyone is so freaked out?"

She shrugged. "Atkins is really good."

Daniel laughed. "That's putting it mildly. He's one of the best of us. In any House. He might even be able to beat Caster."

"Who's Caster?"

He laughed. "Oh, there's still so much for you to learn about us."

"Yeah, no kidding. Maybe you could tell me some things."

His laughter stopped. He turned to studying her face while she pointedly ignored his. His voice was a whisper. "Don't do that."

"Don't do what?" She wasn't looking at him.

"Don't get mad. Especially don't get mad at me. We're all bound in some way. Some more than others."

"Sure, sure." She started walking towards the house, ready for another shower. Maybe even a hot bath in the deep tub she'd been eyeing since arriving.

Daniel grabbed her hand, pulling her back to him, so she tripped, hand landing flat on his chest reactively to stop her forward momentum. She looked up into angry eyes. Eyes that made her sad, rather than frighten her. "I'm not mad at you. Relax."

She shifted to pull away, but he caught her hand to his chest, holding her there.

His voice was low, eyes peering through her. "Don't be angry at all. Not at this. Be angry that they'll take you, cut you off from your life, even as they suggest you asked for it. Even as they suggest you couldn't survive without them."

His words froze her, her attention moving from the heat of his hand over hers to the pressure behind his gaze. Running his words over in her head, she remained motionless against him, staring up into the lightest green eyes she'd ever seen. "Your eyes. I never noticed their color before."

He let her go so abruptly she stumbled forward. He was already halfway to the house when she turned. "I'll have food brought up for you." His words were clipped.

-What?-

"Umm, okay. Sure."

She stared at his retreating form, continuing to wait for some explanation even after he stopped just outside the door. Holding it open, avoiding her look, he lingered like a good bodyguard.

With a loud sigh, she moved to the house.

Chapter Twenty-Eight

His raging garnered so much attention that he found himself face-to-face with Zibanitu himself. The Rishi's stare studied the human's face as they stood eye-to-eye in front of the lenses that projected them to each other.

Hearing Amalthea had taken Dee to see the Twins was enraging enough. Hearing Zi's people had been barred from going sent Hamal over the edge. It was bad enough he'd been unable to watch over or guide her once they'd reached Amaltheum. He'd pulled away when told to be careful where his human senselessness was leading him. That was what Amalthea's speech to him had told him the night he'd gone with Desiree to her room.

He could have lived with distance, if at least able to keep an eye on her. Having her taken entirely from his sights was maddening.

For three minutes Zibanitu studied Hamal, whose skill at remaining passive under such scrutiny was being pushed to its limit.

Hamal had been counting the seconds off in his head to help keep him from saying something out of line, which, on this matter, would have been anything he had to say. His mission had been completed. The only reason he was still here was a matter of security. No one was being moved from this location at this time. That he was facing the Rishi was both a relief and an embarrassment.

Hamal's eyes snapped to the Rishi's face when Zibanitu finally broke the silence. "I understand you have concerns about the girl."

So, she was still just *the girl*. Hamal didn't like what that might mean. If she was still nameless, she still wasn't important enough to fight for if something went wrong.

"It's not my place to have concerns."

Zi actually laughed, teeth showing white against deep bronze skin patched with pale creams. His skin exactly resembled vitiligo, its appearance so similar as not to need its own description. As far as Hamal knew, he was the only Rishi to exhibit a skin coloring other than the smooth bronze of the others.

Hamal's eyes widened in surprise at the reaction, gaze forced downward so his expression might not show, lips pressed together in concern. He couldn't recall a time when he'd ever seen the Rishi appear to indulge in delight. He was at a loss.

"You speak truth, Hamal, yet it has come to my attention that you'd risk us all for erroneous attachments."

A slow inhale kept his displeasure of the Rishi's words off his face; biting his tongue kept his words to himself.

Zibanitu wasn't content with silence as an answer on this. "Are these concerns correct? Or has my time been wasted with inaccurate gossip?"

Hamal didn't have to look up to know the smile that had been on the Rishi's face was gone, replaced by annoyance that bordered on anger. Hamal had managed never to have this anger pointed at him, and he wasn't about to let this be the first time. The time for silence was over. "You sent me to watch her, then to protect her, I—"

"Protecting her was your own decision. An unsolicited conclusion drawn outside the scope of your mission parameters."

Hamal took a deep breath. Despite his words, his voice was even. "Your parameters were crap, and you know it. You sent me to handle it exactly the way I did. You sent me because I was the only one who could have handled it this way. She'd be in The Ophiuchus' hands right now if not for my interference."

Zibanitu studied Hamal again, maddening the human with his inscrutability. Hamal had seen Zi hand out a death sentence in the same breath as praise, and wondered if that might not be his fate now. He wasn't helping his position by mouthing off to the one referred to as the Air God. He hoped his unique relationship with the Rishi, one that resembled uncle and favored nephew, would help his case here. Even Michael Corleone had his own brother killed.

"Your interference did save the girl from his hands. We would never have regained the opportunity to figure out what she is if that had come to pass. Your decision-making skills under pressure have always been excellent." Hamal held his breath, waiting for the shoe to drop, eyes peering at the screen that showed Zibanitu's face. "It's your decision to call on another House that has me second-guessing your motives."

Hamal laughed, a burst of sound that seemed loud, even to himself. He cut off the noise before it could grow to fullness. "You aren't second-guessing my decision. If that were true, we'd have spoken long before now. It was the right call, and you know it. You even sent Dimitri and Daniel to help us. It's my decision-making abilities at this exact moment you're questioning because you've heard rumors about me having feelings for this girl. *This girl* who's so important that no one will call her by name, or risk their asses to help."

He clenched his hands tightly, fingernails pressing into his palms. That hadn't come out like he'd wanted. There were too many words that illuminated the lie he'd been telling himself. He didn't have to meet the Rishi's eye to know he'd over-explained the truth of the problem and in doing so, given away another fact of the matter.

Surprising Hamal again, the Rishi chuckled softly. The sound that was almost kind, pulling Hamal's eyes to the face broadcasted through the large screen. "Sometimes, there are things we can't plan for. Sometimes, things happen outside the design that makes the pattern, itself, better."

Zibanitu lowered his chin in a more relaxed posture as Hamal thought on his words, not sure he should believe their implication.

The Rishi was speaking before Hamal could decide what the implication was. "Hamal, it's important to me that you know I understand. I also need you to understand that it matters not. However this had gone, there would have been nothing you could have done to help her. No manner of interference from me would have kept her away from the others. Calm your anger. Sit tight. She'll be back to you in a matter of days. I won't interfere with you resuming your shadowing of her, but, for your own sake, until we know what she is, keep some distance."

Hamal's fists clenched tighter. His elation that he be allowed to stay at her side quickly squashed. Still, this stipulation wasn't as bad as the realization that he was in over his head even farther than he'd considered. What could he do to help her against superior beings? He reminded himself that Zibanitu's rules were to protect him, not cause him pain.

Despite this, the words still came out of his mouth, "I don't think I can do that."

Zibanitu's eyebrows shot up, shocked to be so blatantly contradicted. "What do you think you will do?"

His tone was part mocking, part warning. Hamal ignored both. "I'll continue the mission you put me on."

"Gather information? I have better spies than you on the job now." Hamal knew the only reason the Rishi allowed the conversation to continue was a morbid curiosity to what the human would say to justify his self-destructive attitude.

"I can watch out for her. Keep her safe. Teach her."

They both knew he couldn't keep her safe and there were others who could teach her much more efficiently. Still, the point was used for argument's sake. "Teaching?"

Surprised he was allowed to continue, excitement bolstered his words, so he forgot the inherent lie in them. "You expect her to navigate your world, but she has no idea what's going on. She needs someone to teach her."

"She is being told what she needs to know. It is not your place to tell of things you do not understand."

Hamal held Zibanitu's gaze, knowing he was pushing his luck well beyond a place he'd ever been but unable to hold back now. His stare dared the Rishi to stop him.

This challenge sat the Rishi up straighter. "Hamal? What are you asking of me?"

"I don't know exactly. I didn't know I'd be making this argument. I didn't know I wouldn't want to give her up. My plan was to ask to come home." He clamped his mouth shut against the words that tumbled from his mouth. Vulnerability was not something he shared with Zibanitu. Not anymore. Not since he'd been a child.

"Maybe coming home is exactly what you need." The Rishi's voice was quiet, soothing.

Hamal said nothing, hearing the truth in those simple words, but not wanting to admit it, to himself or otherwise.

Silence stretched between them.

"There is another way." Hamal barely caught the words, so softly were they spoken. His eyes shot up, surprise covering his face. It had been in his mind to ask, but he didn't know how. That the Rishi would bring it up without Hamal's direct prompting said much.

Still, Hamal needed to know what had initiated the sudden change in the direction of the conversation. "Why now?"

Zibanitu looked away, staring at something off-screen. Hamal thought he caught a glimpse of real emotion shadowed in the look, but it was gone before Hamal could be sure. "I would not risk you, but neither can I stop you from following your path."

Hamal was quiet, swirling the words around in his head. Zibanitu could very well stop him. It was the Rishi's way, to control what he could. That he'd used this phrasing meant Hamal was being offered a gift only a rare few ever received. He was being offered the ability to choose.

Zi let him have his moment of thought before continuing. "Be sure. Surer than you've ever been. There are many ways her path may lead, and even I am not sure of their direction. You might not get what you desire if you choose the dangerous path. In patience, you may. Coming home does not mean erasing yourself from her life, or that you can't revisit this decision at a later time. You will always be the first who made contact with her. You will always be a part of her story."

"If I survive."

The barest flinch of a nod validated Hamal's point. "Even if you do not, those things will still be. If you survive, if you successfully achieve what you are suggesting, you may still be too far from her. If you manage to be by her side, you might be farther away than you are now."

It was a fair point. A point he hadn't considered. Could he watch her, be by her side, forever on the sidelines as her shadow, as Metis was to Amalthea?

"I could wait."

"You could wait."

Hamal smiled at Zibanitu repeating his words, as Dee was prone to do. She did it to assist her learning. Zi did it to emphasize that which he wanted someone else to learn.

"I could wait." Repeating it, the words didn't sit right. He was already going crazy not knowing what was going on with her. Could he wait longer? Could he remove himself entirely before coming back with a clearer head?

If he decided on taking the Initiation, he might be out of commission for weeks. He might be out of commission forever.

But, if he stayed as he was, he was guaranteed to be out of commission as far as her life was concerned.

"Why did you agree to let her meet the Twins?" The words slipped out as his brain was distracted by other things.

Surprising him, Zibanitu answered. "The Ophiuchus was close to breaching Amaltheum's security. We needed the girl out of there. Amalthea wants the Twins to tell our story. It was the perfect cover and the perfect place to go while a military of this might closed in."

Hamal looked up, worry-turned-anger burning in his eyes. "The Twins don't have a military. It's just the two of them! They won't be able to stop him if he attacks there."

"There are a few more than just the two of them. Besides, don't underestimate them. Not that it will matter. By the time the Ophiuchus knows where we've sent her, she'll be on her way back to a reinforced compound."

"You need to—"

Zi cut him off, the fatherly figure morphing instantly to the Rishi Hamal knew to be wary of. "Careful, human. You are dear to me, but not so much that you may throw your judgmental questions around so flippantly. You've been given enough liberties with this as it is. Porrima would seek your skin if she heard even a portion of this conversation."

Hamal stood motionless, afraid to even blink. He'd forgotten himself and hoped he wouldn't pay dearly for it.

Chapter Twenty-Nine

The city sprawled as far as the eye could see. She'd never seen anything like it. An enormous contrast to the small town she'd spent most of her life, Dee found Sao Paulo unreal.

Her face pressed to the window of the private plane, eyes straining to see past the aircraft's wing as she swung her gaze from side to side. She stared across an endless sea of buildings, patches of trees as lakes of life in the topography of cement and steal. Single story buildings, a sandbar among the taller skyscrapers, were a dense layer of residency she couldn't imagine living in, their squalor a harsh juxtaposition from the towers of mirrored glass rising around them. Her house in the woods, so much open air surrounding it, would be alien in this place.

Excited by the news they'd be traveling, Dee'd held the emotion back, afraid she'd be sequestered away in some deep, hidden fortress, surrounded by security that wouldn't let her engage in the world around her. Still, she allowed herself indulgent ideas of sightseeing as the plane coasted over the new city on its landing path.

As they touched down, it occurred to her that not only was the urban landscape far removed from her father's house where she'd grown up, it was also the opposite of what Amalthea called home. This brought up more questions about the Rishis. Obviously, they weren't all the same.

The idea made her more nervous.

The chatter of Alnath, the female Soldier assigned as her personal guard for this trip, citing facts about the city they were about to land in, became a hum in the background of her thoughts. She'd let Amalthea's motherly nature calm her to a sense of safety that might not exist. Hadn't her promise of safety proven untrue when she'd visited the cold underground where Dee had been shown the risks of Initiation? What new danger might she run into here? And why had it taken until their arrival for her to consider it?

-Maybe your lack of control over anything going on? You stopped paying attention.-

Dee closed her eyes against the memories of The Ophiuchus' roadside attack that had left one of those sent to protect her dead, and two others near death. Was a similar ambush waiting here?

Or, what if the Twins she was about to meet decided they didn't like her? What if she didn't like them? What if they thought she should die? Would Amalthea's people be able to stop them?

She closed her eyes, swallowing around the tightening of her throat. Breathing slowly, she turned from the window to face Alnath, whose replacement of Daniel was still taking some adjustment. Zibanitu's people had been forbidden into the Twins' territory. As Amalthea had seemed unconcerned by this, neither had Dee, until now, when questions she should have thought of earlier cluttered her mind.

"...it the New York of Latin American."

Dee nodded politely to the well-muscled woman whose long hair was pulled back in a tight ponytail. Alnath noticed the distracted look and stopped talking, before deducing, "You're nervous."

"That obvious?"

Alnath nodded. "Only because of the change in you from three minutes ago. You were excited. Now, you're not."

Dee's eyes skimmed over the plane's occupants. "What if they try something? Do we have enough people to keep me safe?"

"Keep you safe from the Twins?" The Soldier chuckled. "All of Amalthea's people combined couldn't keep you safe from the Twins. Even The Ophiuchus won't try something against those two."

Dee's nervousness was quickly turning to panic.

The guard lowered her voice. "I think that's part of the reason the Rishi was eager to get you here. Apparently, she trusts the Twins enough to risk their fickle nature, knowing it wouldn't be much longer before The Ophiuchus was pushing against her walls."

-Nice to find one of them so eager to explain what's going on.-

Dee barely registered the plane landing as her thoughts turned to what might have been happening outside Amalthea's walls while she'd remained inside, convincing herself things were going to be alright.

-I think we've left the eye of the storm.-

Dee gulped. If that were true, they were walking into catastrophe.

Coming out of the plane to two sleek limos waiting on the tarmac, Dee was held back by Alnath. They watched as their luggage, and most of their entourage, piled into the two cars. When the pair of limos pulled away, Alnath led Dee, with Amalthea, Metis and Atkins, to a third limo that had pulled up in the others' wake.

Alnath held the door open for Dee. "This will take us to our transportation."

-This isn't transportation?-

Dee climbed into the luxurious car ahead of the rest, noting Amalthea's uncharacteristic quiet. She had left Dee to her thoughts for most of the flight. Was it that she understood the girl needed space rather than oppressive overlooking or was something bothering her?

It was just another thing to make Dee nervous.

When the car came to a stop, still on airport property, near a helicopter, Dee understood what transportation Alnath had been talking about. The whistling blades of the helicopter erased Dee's long-assumed notion that all helicopters were loud, annoying beasts. A red carpet set a clear path to the open door of the metallic bird from the limo.

Dee had never been in a helicopter and her body thrummed with nervous excitement. The sleek, long-nosed design was far removed from the egg-shaped metal bin she would have pictured, its size clearly able to hold their entourage with room to spare. This wasn't a craft to pack passengers in like sardines.

Climbing inside, her chin hit the floor.

-*Who knew there was a market for luxury helicopters?*-

White leather covered two large swivel chairs and a 'L'-shaped couch stationed behind the pilot's seat so its short end was to her left spilling around to the far side of the door. Following Amalthea's direction, she took the bucket seat to her right so she was seated across from the Rishi. The Soldiers perched themselves on the couch.

Dee looked around, stunned at the space available inside the machine. This rivaled the comfort of the private plane she'd spent the previous ten hours in.

"This is yours?" Dee couldn't help but ask.

Amalthea smiled, enjoying the girl's wonderment. "No. The Twins sent it for us. Traffic through the city is impossible. Helicopters have taken over as the chosen means of travel. For those who can afford it anyway."

Alnath added her two-cents. "And for those who can afford it, these birds are so quiet, there's no longer need for us to wear head-sets to talk to each other. Technology is wonderful."

Dee stared at the ground as the helicopter took off. How the pilot knew where to go was a mystery. From above the city, everything looked the same to her. Noting the streets jammed with unmoving cars, she was glad for the use of the helicopter. Hours in a car to go a few miles didn't seem enjoyable, especially after having sat on a plane for most of the day. She wondered how the others, forced to travel in the limos on the ground, were faring.

Amalthea 's voice pulled her attention from the passing view. "We'll be landing soon. There will be plenty of time to freshen up before making our dinner reservation. I thought a relaxing evening for us might be nice before you meet the Twins tomorrow."

Dee relaxed, ecstatic the meeting was delayed.

The sun was setting as they made their descent. Dee continued to stare into the city, watching the electric lights from bridges and skyscraper come on to battle the coming night. The shift in panorama morphed the city into something new. Something more glamorous. Would they be here long enough for her to explore?

***

Dee enjoyed a quiet shower in a lavish suite she assumed was the penthouse of an opulent hotel.

Coming in from the rooftop, she had yet to descend below the top floors. She understood how easy it might be for one living so far from the rest of a population to grow disconnected from the rest of the world. Looking out from her lofty height, she almost forgot her own troubles.

Pressing her forehead to the glass that ran from floor to ceiling, she shouted in her mind, -*I'm the king of the world!* -

Abandoning the lofty view, she made her way into the living area of the suite. Nodding a greeting to Alnath who remained positioned by the main doors, Dee made a slow spin, taking in the room she hadn't bothered to examine upon entering. White with gold trim was everywhere. Walls, floors and ceilings, highlighted with cherry wood furnishings told of a price tag even Dee's fortune would have balked at paying. Surrounded by white carpet, Dee was afraid to walk through the room for fear of leaving a trace of dirt.

A quiet knock on the door revealed the presence of Paige, who Dee hadn't seen since she'd left for the mausoleum of frightening Initiates. Dee smiled a warm greeting, surprised how much she was glad the girl was here, even as she wondered about how the child's life worked.

-*Don't overcomplicate your life. Worry about child labor issues after you've secured your own position.* -

Paige all but ignored Alnath, who'd opened the door to let her in after a complicated exchange of passwords.

-*Are they always so paranoid, or is there something we don't know?* -

There were so many things she didn't know, Dee didn't let this one add to her stress, instead focusing on the girl who'd entered the room. "Paige, it is great to see you."

The girl blushed. "Rishi said you would need help preparing for supper." The child looked Dee up and down, frowning at the towel wrapped around her head, the too-big robe barely held on by a hastily tied loop.

-*Supper? No room service then?*-

Dee sighed, disappointed she'd have to wait even longer to eat. She was sure by the time food was actually placed in front of her, her stomach might have eaten itself and it would all be for nothing.

Following the girl to the bedroom, Dee allowed herself to be primped for an evening she hadn't anticipated. Paige surprised Dee with her expert hands, watching as the girls tiny fingers folded and pinned her shaggy mess of hair to elegance. Perfectly applied makeup turned her features up, so she barely recognized herself.

"Paige, why all of this? What's happening tonight?"

"Just supper downstairs."

Dee raised a manicured eyebrow. "All this just for dinner?"

Paige shrugged, showing no signs there might be a hidden agenda she was privy to. Dee sighed. There was still so much to understand. Learning about the Soldier's Initiation was interesting, but it didn't really help her figure out what was going on, or what her link to all this really was.

She closed her eyes as Paige finished her makeup, forcing her memory to those painful moments of blazing fire. The information they were all looking for was there, she was sure of it, but how could she remember something that was a complete blank?

"Time to get dressed." Paige's quiet voice pulled Dee back to the room, her growling stomach reminding her how long it had been since she'd eaten.

Dee stood mechanically, opening her eyes as she turned away from the mirror to watch Paige unzip a garment bag laying across the bed. A brilliant blue dress, a perfect match to the color of her eyes, was hidden within.

Sliding the dress over her head, a strapless silver bust line fell away in layers of blue material to her feet. She couldn't remember ever having worn something so elegant. She twirled in front of the mirror despite herself, noting how the dress highlighted her toned shoulders and arms. The intimidation she'd been feeling amidst all this glamour fell away, as it turned to intoxication. She could easily get used to this. For once, she didn't feel like a stranger in a strange land.

Dee turned to face Paige, who held out a pair of silver heels to her. A look of concern covered her face. There had never been a time when she'd found the urge to wear shoes that seemed more trouble than they were worth. "I don't think I'll be able to walk in those."

Paige's look told Dee the shoes were non-negotiable.

The shoes strapped around her ankles in crisscrossing hatches, the six inches of spike at her heel scaring her more than meeting any Revenant in the woods ever had. Taking Paige's hand skeptically, Dee was shocked to find she had no issue walking. Her intense training with the Soldiers must have some alternative benefits.

Dee stared at herself in the mirror. "Wow, Paige. You're an artist."

Paige's face lit with appreciative pride, and Dee continued staring, unable to stop herself from spinning her hips back and forth so the layers of fabric on her skirt swayed around her.

When a knock came at the door, she froze, suddenly fearful to leave the room, knowing everyone would see right through the facade Paige had created. What did she know about moving through the uber-wealthy? Everyone would be able to tell she was a phony. That she shouldn't be there. Sure, her father had money, but they'd never kept the company she would find here.

Taking a last look at herself, she squared her shoulders and stepped towards the door.

Chapter Thirty

Vali joined Alnath as her escorts, both dressed to impress in stunning evening wear. Dee wondered at the practicality of their outfits, even as she hoped she wouldn't need the extra protection.

Alnath noticed Dee frowning at her shoes and laughed "Don't worry. They're really not a hinderance. When I was human, you wouldn't catch me dead in heels. Now, I don't even notice the difference between them and regular shoes."

Dee might have doubted her, except for her own comfort in heels three-times the height of her guard's.

Moving through the hotel, Dee wondered who the staff thought she was. Judging by their prostrating, they seemed to think her some kind of royalty. Or maybe that's just how those who could afford such posh living were treated. No wonder there was such a disconnect among tax-brackets.

Surprised to be led all the way to the street, then out to a waiting car, she almost forgot to grab as many details of her surroundings as possible. The city lights were dazzling, though not so different as any other metropolis from this vantage. She sat between her guards, the traffic much easier to navigate at night than during the day, so they moved easily to their destination.

Entering the restaurant, Dee saw that an entire section was cleared around the table Amalthea sat at, her guards positioned subtly throughout to blend in with the wait staff and other diners. Metis and Atkins sat at the nearest table behind Amalthea, who stood to hug Dee warmly as she approached. "You look beautiful."

"Thank you. The dress is beautiful, and Paige's skills are magnificent."

Amalthea smiled as if the compliment was hers to accept, allowing Metis to hold her chair while she sat. Vali did the same for Dee before moving to his place nearby with Alnath. As he walked away, Dee allowed herself to look at him. So concerned until now with everything else distracting her attention, she'd barely noticed this second addition to her personal guard.

She remembered him, vaguely, from her rescue on the street, and had seen him among the faces who'd watched her on the training grounds, though she had never sparred with him. His blue eyes, lighter than her own, pierced the room with no hint of the mirth or mischievousness Hamal and Daniel shared. A small scar marred his top lip, setting his mouth in a constant sneer. Dee got the impression this sneer would have been a part of his expression with or without that scar. While Hamal's arrogance carried welcome, Vali's revealed his contempt for those around him. Or maybe he just wasn't fan of guard duty.

A waiter appeared to pour Dee a glass of wine. She tasted the liquid around the tightening of her stomach. Even around her nervousness, she appreciated the wine's flavor. Things really were better in luxury. She'd have to learn how to spend her money.

Amalthea appeared to enjoy watching Dee take delight in this new experience. If she sensed the girl's unease, she didn't mention it. "Coming to the city is not usually an idea I back, but, since it seemed the right call, I thought we'd at least take our time to enjoy it. Tomorrow I'll introduce you to the Twins. Who knows how long they'll draw out their telling. Or, if they're in a foul mood, we might not get a story at all." She twirled her glass of wine. "However we find them, our time here will not be wasted."

Dee's shoulders tensed. Amalthea gave a smile meant to relax her. "There's nothing to be nervous about, child. The Twins have managed to hold their own House under circumstances that suggested impossibility. They will not risk another tribulation, regardless of how interesting they might find you."

Dee knew better than to overthink what she was being told. Amalthea trusted where they were, so Dee should too.

-Right, because we trust those who're giving us advice on who to trust?-

Continuing to wrap herself further in this impossible situation, she allowed herself a genuine smile. At least for the evening, there would be nothing to worry about. She took a breath, forcing the tension out of her shoulders, ignoring the impulse to roll her neck.

"I would like to apologize that Hamal or Daniel weren't able to accompany us. We all see how fond of them you've grown. It was the Twins' express wish that none from any House but my own join us."

Placing her wine glass on the table, knowing getting drunk would not be a good idea, Dee smiled courteously. "Alnath has been great company. And Vali seems more than competent. I don't know that I'd have been better off with either of them here instead."

Amalthea laughed, a heartfelt sound that, at first, set Dee's nerves ablaze before she realized it wasn't mockery the Rishi was bestowing. "I'm sure Vali appreciates your sense of his competency." She even winked.

Dee reached for her glass hoping no one noticed the tremble in her fingers.

Settling back in her chair, the Rishi nodded, moving backwards in the conversation. "It would reflect badly on them if something romantic were to happen, but I think sometimes we forget the value of such things. As long as they're valued for their own sake, of course, and not used to confuse the mind."

Dee blinked stupidly across the table.

-Is she suggesting you have sex with them as long as you don't allow it to turn into a relationship?-

She thought that's exactly what the Rishi was suggesting. Her blush brought more gentle laughter from across the table. It was the last thing she'd expected to hear. It was the last thing she wanted to talk about. Boys were the last thing she needed to be concerned with when the state of her life was still up in the air.

Trying to think of a way to change the subject, her mouth was speaking before her brain caught up to what she was saying, "Daniel said such a thing was forbidden."

"Forbidden? Did he use that word?"

Dee tried to remember exactly what he'd said. "No. He said if I had feelings, to forget them."

Amalthea nodded. "Yes, feelings cloud things, but a physical act is not the same as feeling from the heart."

Dee understood the point, but didn't have much experience with it.

A wash of power flooded her senses, overshadowing whatever else Amalthea might have said. Dee searched the room, eyes wide, searching for the source. She gripped the side of the table to keep her from sliding beneath it to hide. Her eyes moved to her guards to see if they'd picked up the source of this new power.

Dee had grown so accustomed to the tingling of energy in her head from so much time around Amalthea and the members of her House that her radar had been repressed. It was because of the *newness* of what she felt that it filtered through. Someone, or something, she hadn't come across was drawing near. Someone who was powerful enough to be Masters of their own House.

-*It could only be the Twins.*-

Amalthea watched one of her people, a Soldier Dee hadn't even noticed planted near the front of the restaurant, move to the lobby. Another followed. This second Soldier re-appeared after seconds, looking first to Metis, then Amalthea, hand gestures explaining what was going on.

Dee barely caught the exchange, not knowing the secret language anyway. Her attention remained on the entrance.

Amalthea rose from her seat. "It looks like we'll be having company."

Dee's breath froze in her lungs. Three Rishis in the same place? How had she allowed Amalthea to talk her into this?

Vali moved up to take a seat at the table next to Dee while Amalthea, escorted by Atkins, moved off.

Vali's eyes scanned the room, never ceasing their search for danger, even when he spoke to her. "Remain seated. The Rishi will greet them. Rise when they come to the table."

Dee dropped her chin in curt acknowledgment, panic continuing to wrench the breath from her.

Could she escape? Her eyes flew around the space, realizing she had no idea where to go even if she escaped the restaurant. There was no chance she'd find her way to safety.

The suspense of waiting pushed against her.

The world seemed to pause in shared suspense as two of the tallest, most striking men Dee had ever seen glided into the dining area. They resembled Dee so closely, she was nervous they were here to tell her she was their long-lost sister. Long dark hair flowed around their shoulders, accenting deep blue eyes set into clear skin—skin much lighter than the other old-ones she'd encountered, though still maintaining a hint of the unique copper-hue they all shared.

Their power cascaded over her as they moved closer, and if Dee hadn't been so mesmerized by the sight of them, she might have curled up in fear.

They greeted Amalthea with warm hugs, enfolding her shorter stature even as both pairs of eyes searched out the anomaly they'd come to see.

Amalthea smiled encouragingly at Dee as she led them back to the table, her guards spreading quietly back to their posts, noticeably more uptight than before. Dee noted the Twins' lack of bodyguards. Was it because of how powerful they were? Or were their guards more subtly integrated into the surroundings?

As they approached, she stood, remembering Vali's instructions.

Amalthea smiled widely, enjoying her opportunity to introduce them all. "Desiree, meet Caster..."

The twin to Dee's left stepped forward, bowing gracefully from a height over a foot taller than her, taking her hand gently to lay the barest trace of a kiss.

Amalthea continued. "...and Pollux."

The second twin bowed, stepping closer to the girl than his brother, meeting her eyes with a penetrating gaze she couldn't decipher.

-A warrior's appraisal or a suitors lust? -

"We are very excited to have you here, Ms. Galen." Pollux's voice was barely loud enough to penetrate the ambient sound of the surrounding tables, most of which were still quiet as they continued to stare at the striking group in their midst. He took her hand as well, laying a kiss into her open palm, a surprisingly intimate gesture that washed the tension from her stomach.

Dee looked shyly away from his gaze, not sure if she held the polite smile she was attempting, or if it morphed into a grimace.

Caster cocked an eyebrow at his brother.

Dee's eyes were drawn to Caster's face, curious about his reaction, but there was too much going on for her to linger on the question.

Metis had moved to stand behind Amalthea's vacant chair, tension showing in his grip on the fine detail of the seat though his face was nothing but a mask of calm. The Twins' charm had alleviated some of her panic, but seeing Metis' reaction brought it soaring back.

Vali, clearing his throat quietly behind her brought her attention to the table. Pollux waited for her to sit, his hand on her chair to assist her, an expression of patient mirth on his face. Embarrassed, Dee sat quickly, wishing she could slide under the table and hide.

-Nice. They're all laughing at you. Caster thinks you're a naive little girl and Pollux thinks you're daft. -

Dee mentally rolled her eyes, wondering if maybe this wasn't how she wanted everyone to view her. Might they let her go if she seemed too ditzy to pose a threat, or whatever it was they were worried about from her?

"Your message suggested you wouldn't be available this evening." Amalthea leaned into the table as she spoke, not in the least put out by the unannounced change in plans.

Pollux leaned back, swirling the wine that had just been poured, allowing his brother to have run of the conversation while his eyes continued to study Dee.

Castor's voice was smooth, suggesting perfect control. "It was necessary to judge the merit of your request."

Amalthea frowned, sending an alarm through Dee's internal system.

The Rishi's voice remained even, though her usual warmth was lacking as she responded. "The merit of my request might have been considered before we came all this way."

Pollux smiled as if from some private joke, monitoring Amalthea for a moment, whose eyes blazed as she stared his brother down.

The silent brother leaned Dee's way, still swirling his wine, whispering so only she could hear, "My brother knows how to push her buttons. Sometimes, I'm not sure he even means to do it. She'll either explode in a rage or relax in motherly patience."

He raised his glass to point to the pair glowering at each other across from them. "Just watch."

Dee followed his gesture, noting Amalthea's deep frown challenging Caster's calm gaze.

Caster's face morphed to laughter. "Oh Amalthea, you're too easy. I'm shocked you weren't prepared for us."

Amalthea's lips pursed, not amused, but letting her anger sizzle away. "Assumption, my boy. Ass-umption."

Now Pollux laughed. "And the ass you typically are, brother."

Caster feigned a frown, shooting it his brother's way. "Right, I'm the one known as the ass." He shook his head, turning his attention to Dee. "Ms. Galen, you're proceeded by a very strange reputation."

Dee stared back at Caster with a blank expression. "Oh?"

He turned back to Amalthea. "Eloquent."

Amalthea laughed gently, chiding the twin. "Give her a chance, Caster. Until a few weeks ago, she was living as a modern girl from a small town in the United States. No one's ever taught her eloquence, or communication, or anything really." She shot Dee an apologetic glance. "No offense, Desiree. It's not your fault."

Dee drained her glass, fighting to keep her frown from taking over her face. Was this what the trip would be like? Passive aggressive shots at her?

Don't be embarrassed for what you've never learned. Daniel's words echoed in her head. She sat up straighter. She wouldn't let them bother her, especially if that's what their goal was.

The Twins shared a look Dee didn't understand. Then Caster spoke to her again. "Amalthea's brought you to hear our story, but first, I would ask to hear yours."

Dee looked at Amalthea, frantic pleading in her eyes. There was nothing to tell. Didn't the Twins know this?

Amalthea tried to come to the girls rescue. "Her memory is gone. Her story lost even to herself."

"As you've said, but still, I wish to hear it from her." Caster's eyes never left Dee's face as he communicated with Amalthea. Pollux leaned back.

She looked to Amalthea, but there was no help to be had there. She was going to have to explain to this group what she remembered, even if it wasn't much.

Not sure where to start her story, Dee took a breath. She'd always hid pieces of the story, never sure how the listener would react. Here, she decided to just tell the story as she remembered. Maybe it would even help her jog more of her memory.

-*Maybe these aren't the guys to be remembering for.*-

She was afraid of this, but she needed to move forward, rather than continue to play this game of circles.

She was looking at her hands clasped on the table as she debated how to handle this. Finally deciding, she picked her gaze up to meet each Twin in turn. "Two or three years ago—"

"Two? Or three?" Caster interrupted.

She took a breath, closing her eyes to count the time.

Her father had died in November. She lasted in his house until the following summer, when she'd bolted for the other side of the country. For three years she'd moved around with Kim, then Steve and Ray. When Mike found her, half-dead on his porch, it'd been two years since he'd last heard from her.

She choked a sob back, realizing just how much time she'd lost in whatever game she'd been pulled into. Locked away with all her other memories, she'd never let herself think of the details that might strip her of the precarious hold she maintained on her sanity.

When she opened her eyes, only a sheen of tears glimmered. She was proud when no trace of warble was in her voice. "Two years. I can't remember two years.

"So, three years ago, I was living in Northern California with some friends. We'd been moving around together for about a year and a half, finding jobs that paid just enough to pay the rent, and still keep us regulars at the local clubs. That was why we lived, to drink, and dance, and forget the world."

She half-smiled, remembering Kim and Ray, then Steve's face as they'd looked in the syncopated strobing of the club lights, all sound drowned out by the deep thrumming of house music. Nostalgia made those days seem glamorous in her memory, rather than the stressful, avoidance-ridden reality they were.

"I remember being home with Steve when Ray came in. I don't remember where Kim was. Maybe at work?" She chuckled. "That's a shocker, but it must have been where she was."

Dee closed her eyes, fighting against the blank gap that came next. "Then, the heat of the fire. Waking up in the grass, in the backyard of some house I didn't recognize. I sat there for a long time. I think it was a long time. Just staring at the flames. Eventually, I got up and started walking, coming to a town where I stayed until I was attacked."

Amalthea's head perked at this. It was a detail she'd always left out. That she'd been nothing more than a bum living on the streets never seemed relevant.

-Except it was there you were first attacked. It was there someone first found you.-

"I don't remember the specifics of that either. I remember being attacked, something coming at me from behind. Then, it was gone." She closed her eyes in the hopes the memory would be clearer. "No, that's not right. Then I'm home. Well, not home, exactly, but the place I was staying. I don't know what happened to my attacker. I don't know how I got from the street to my bed.

"I was hurt pretty badly. A lot of blood from scratches all over me. I had no one to help me."

She paused for a moment, collecting herself. It was the first time she'd ever talked about it. It was the first time she'd really remembered sitting in that grungy room, bleeding, not knowing who to call or where to go. How long did she sit there before she decided to make her way back to Mike's? How long did she travel before she made it back to her hometown?

Something tugged at her memory, but like a word on the tip of her tongue, the more she chased it, the less clear it became. "I figured they'd all died in the fire." She regressed, not sure why this part seemed important. "Ray's truck was in the driveway. I remember that. We went everywhere in that beat up truck. The four of us barely fit, but we did it. The four of us went everywhere together. If I was there, and the truck was there, we were all there."

She smiled again as a memory of her sitting on Ray's lap, Kim trying to keep her legs out of the way so Steve could shift gears was conjured in her mind. Ray had tried copping a feel like he always did. It was his game, trying to get the girls in bed with him. Sometimes it was endearing. Mostly, it had been annoying. She remembered she'd accidentally jabbed him in the throat with an elbow.

"Luckily Mike hadn't moved out of town. He says I showed up half-dead on the doorstep. That was last summer."

Caster looked at Amalthea, as if to ask if that was all she knew. Amalthea's look must have assured him it was, since he asked nothing. The brothers matching postures reclined in in their chairs, swirling their drinks as if of one mind.

Dee forced her eyes to dance around the grand restaurant while she waited for someone to comment on her story.

Caster spoke softly. "How did you get to Mike's?"

Her stomach flopped. She'd just been thinking about how she couldn't remember this.

He noted the confusion in her face, pressing her with a flippant tone. "Did you drive? Walk? Hitchhike?"

"I really don't remember." Then, more to herself, "Why don't I remember that?"

"You started in Northern California, then made it to Upstate New York with almost no memory of any traveling. You remember seeing Ray's truck in the driveway, though you say you woke up in the backyard."

Dee shook her head, eyes staring into the past, tears glimmering in her eyes. The shock of all that had happened had been repressed for so long that talking about it was taking its toll her. It was definitely not the time to be succumbing to a loss of her senses, not when surrounded by these ancient beings.

"Where did you stay between the fire and your return home?" Caster's voice was quieter, more soothing, as if he knew she was on the brink of losing it.

"I just stayed in that dirty room. I slept all the time. Sometimes I left to get food. I have no idea where I was. I cried about my friends. I cried because I was so confused about what had happened."

"Explain." Caster swirled his wine. Pollux had put his glass down, leaning forward towards her.

She barely noticed. "Explain?"

"Yes, explain what you were feeling. You woke up outside of a burning house you suspected your friends were killed in, then you walked to the nearest town after no one came to put out the fire, and you never told anyone. You stayed in a place you didn't know. You must have talked to someone in order to have a place to stay. How did you pay for it? For food?"

She hadn't called anyone. Hadn't told anyone. Were her friends' families still wondering what had happened to them? Had anyone ever found that house with the three sets of burnt bones lying beneath the rubble?

Her stomach was suddenly sick with grief and regret. "Oh my god. I never thought to tell anyone. I didn't know what to say, so I never did."

"Explain your feelings of confusion."

"My feelings?" She caught herself from letting out a hysterical sob. Tired of talking about things she had never wanted to think about, she managed to find a response besides *go to hell*. "I was confused. Lost." She took a breath, closing her eyes to immerse herself in the memories, forgetting her surroundings. Forgetting even Pollux's weighted gaze on her.

"So tired." She was whispering. "Afraid. I don't know what of. Maybe that someone would find me and think I had something to do with the fire. Was that why I didn't tell anyone?" Her words were for herself now, questions she should have asked long ago finally finding an outlet.

Her eyes remained closed. Tilting her head, she continued to feel what she'd been in those times. "Sleep. Dreams of—someone, standing over me. Watching me. Tired. Lonely."

She took a frustrated breathe before opening her eyes. "That's all I remember. Being tired was the highlight. So tired I didn't get out of bed for days at a time."

"And you never saw what attacked you?"

She shook her head.

"Could it have been a Revenant?"

It wasn't the first time the thought had occurred to her. "Maybe."

"If it was, then whoever found you in New York had most likely found you before. I'm not sure what it means that it took them so long to re-discover you, but it does add more weight to the idea that one of us was with you at that house that burned. That one of us was doing something they shouldn't have."

Caster looked at Amalthea, who returned his gaze. The two stared at each other for a moment and Dee wondered if maybe they were speaking telepathically.

Pollux continued to study her, while Dee sipped at her refilled glass to give her something to do other than squirm under his gaze.

When Pollux stood and put a hand out for Dee she didn't bother to hide her surprise. His words surprised her even further. "Desiree, would you care to honor me with a dance?"

Dee looked around. There was no one else dancing. The classical music playing was loud enough to hear, but nothing to inspire dancing. She was sure the activity would bring more attention to their group. She glanced at Amalthea, but she and Caster seemed locked in some silent conversation.

Pulled to her feet by the less disparaging of the brothers, Dee stood. She matched Pollux's steps away from the table. Nervousness replaced her annoyance.

Pollux seemed to read her hesitancy. "When you spend money like we do, they allow you certain indulgences. No one will mind watching such a handsome couple dance between the empty tables."

Taking Pollux's hand, she was guided gracefully to an empty space, noticing a maitre d' motioning for staff to come take the closest table away so they'd have more room. Pollux didn't seem aware of the activity. He wrapped his arm around her waist, his light touch respectful. His towering height forced Dee to either stare into his chest or crane her head backwards to see his face.

He was a fantastic dancer, leading her around the space the tables had just occupied as if they were seasoned pros.

As the song blended into another, Dee allowed her fears and apprehensions to fall away.

"You move like a trained killer." His words startled her. She looked up, allowing him to catch her eye.

He laughed at the shock in her face. "This is the greatest of compliments, Desiree. My brother and I were trained for killing. Somewhere along the way we discovered that the best killers are also the best dancers."

Dee couldn't help but grin.

Daniel's words flashed through her head: *You realize what you just did? He might be as good as Caster.*

In conversation about the best, the Twins were the ones to beat.

She thought about how skilled of a warrior he must be and if she could feel that in the way he moved now—the arm around her, the grace that led her—even as she remembered her manners by accepting his compliment. "Thank you, but I'm not sure I'm deserving of such a high compliment."

"No? Why not?" He spun her in a clean turn before pulling her back to enfold her in his arms. The movement took her breath.

-Really? You're going to get all hormonal with another one of these guys?-

She couldn't keep the frown from her face, and hoped Pollux wouldn't notice. In the next step, she was twirling out, then back to their original posture.

"I've only just begun to train. I haven't even begun to learn."

He smiled. "Maybe not, but I've seen you. Your battle with Atkins was magnificent."

The look on her face asked the question as her stomach flip-flopped.

He laughed gently. "No worries, Ms. Galen. Amalthea has been keeping a close eye on her charge. She sent a video for us to view when she appealed to us to help you."

Dee didn't feel much better knowing she'd been being watched so closely, especially knowing that a video of her had been handed out. Who else had Amalthea been sending updates to?

-*Zibanitu, for sure.*-

The smile left her face. "Why did Amalthea appeal to you?"

"She thinks we might help you understand what you are by explaining what we are."

Dee's brow furrowed. "She already showed me the Initiates."

Pollux chuckled. "Yes. But they are not what we are."

She paused for a moment, thinking on his words. "You think I'm like you? Not the Initiates?"

He shrugged.

"What are you?"

"You will have to wait for that, but I will say, now, that there is not a word for our race in your language. Or any language in use. Anti-Diluvian covers it, but is more a general term than one that pertains to just us. *Us* is not widely known, so language hasn't needed to encompass our existence. Your scientists throw out any evidence that suggests a race as old as us ever existed. How could there not be extensive archeological evidence, they ask. We are fine with these delusions."

The scope of time he was talking about made her head ache. How did one live so long and not go mad? Two-hundred thousand years since the birth of homo sapiens? Was that right? The Rishi's were older than that?

And he'd mentioned Anti-Diluvian. Before the flood? *The* Flood? She recalled that every culture's origins had a story of a great flood that wiped out the Earth so life could start anew.

Her head was spinning. Vaguely, she noted Pollux's contented smile as he led her back to the table.

Holding out her chair before taking his own, Pollux's thanks for the dance brought her from her thoughts. She forced a smile to mask her face, surprised to find the truth in her words, "I should thank you. I didn't even know I could dance like that. It was—nice."

He smiled, grinning wider when he caught his brother giving him a look. "Brother, relax. It was your boring conversation that sent us away."

"Boring conversation? We might be looking at the first flare of war in centuries."

Rather than cast a pall over the table, the news seemed to excite the dancing twin.

Amalthea was shaking her head. "Boys, let's not anticipate the worst."

"If The Ophiuchus is moving on others, especially against those who have never played at war, the rest of us will be there to stop him." Caster was adamant.

"I thank you for your chivalry, but let's keep talk of war for another day." Amalthea's voice was firm. Dee wondered if she caught a hint of sarcasm there as well.

Food was served and Dee gratefully dove into her plate. After a few bites she felt brave enough to join the conversation. "War? Because of me?"

Caster played with the food in front of him. "Curiosity is a tantalizing thing to those like us who find the repetitive patterns of man exhausting. You are a curiosity never seen."

-Anomaly.-

"So, basically, you'll be fighting over possession of me?" Dee didn't have the knack of keeping her voice conversational when she was angry.

The three looked uncomfortable at her choice of words, though none made a correction. She put down her fork. "If I had gone with Barnard, none of you would have even known about me, would you? Only Zibanitu, who wouldn't have risked sending anyone after me."

Pollux sat up straighter, looking to Amalthea for confirmation.

The matriarch nodded solemnly. "I would have known, only because Hamal called Atkins. He may or may not have told me what he knew. But, your point is valid." She turned her attention to the Twins'. "Barnard was sent to acquire Dee in New York, but Hamal had already called Atkins in to help. Atkins told me, I called Zibanitu. Zibanitu sent Daniel and Dimitri, and here we are."

Pollux's voice was thoughtful. "We knew Barnard had been sent with the team to take her on the road, but we hadn't been told about this earlier visit." His attention turned to Dee. "What did Barnard say to you? Why didn't you go with him?"

Dee shrugged. "It never occurred to me Barnard wasn't there to kill me in New York. When he came to me on the road, I thought about going with him. I wondered if it would stop all the fighting." She frowned. "I guess maybe I should have gone with him."

"But you didn't."

She shook her head thinking, *I'm here aren't I.*

Pollux's stare was intense, but Dee met it. "Would you if he caught up to you again?"

"Not if it wouldn't stop the fighting."

Pollux smiled wickedly. "That time has passed."

Chapter Thirty-One

She wasn't sure what she expected, but it wasn't this. Walking into an ancient Roman theatre nestled within a sleek, modern skyscraper was the last thing she'd anticipated.

Another helicopter ride over the city had brought them to the Twins' home and Dee wasn't ashamed to admit how surprised she was that their center of operations was in the heart of such a major metropolis. Her idea of the Rishis all hiding themselves away in remote corners of the world was obviously incorrect. São Paulo was hardly a quiet place to be reclusive.

She was chaperoned on one side by Atkins and on the other by one of the Twins' own Soldiers, Leda, whose towering five-foot-ten seemed much more intimidating than Atkins six-foot-plus. Her blue-black hair and impressive muscularity had Dee wondering if maybe Wonder Woman wasn't based off this breathing being next to her.

Following her from the elevator, Dee's eyes looked up to a ceiling that stretched forty feet over them. Twenty feet ahead, the floor sloped downwards, thick steps sculpted from smooth stone holding dual-purpose as both stairs and seating which leveled off at an orchestra pit that took up the half-circle before the stage. Stretching the width of the room, at least sixty feet, the stage yawned, its stone design matching the rest of the room as if carved from a single, gigantic boulder. Rising up from the stage were eight columns that seemed to hold the high ceilings from tumbling on the visitors. The stonework was threaded thinly with silver and gold veins that sparkled in the light that had no source Dee could find.

Atkins' gentle push at her lower back got her moving. She wasn't sure how long they'd let her stand there, gapping with her chin to her knees, blocking their entry into the grand room but it was long enough that Leda had stopped to wait for her.

In Dee's first few steps she noticed the blackness of the stone, and the many-size pockmarks that covered it. It reminded her of lava rock she'd seen once, though that had been anything but smooth.

Amalthea and Metis stepped past her, unimpressed by the sights or their sense of propriety wouldn't allow such blatant expressions of awe. Either way, Dee found herself stepping slowly, eyes unable to stray from the grandness surrounding her. So much was her attention taken, Atkins finally placed a strong hand on her elbow when she almost fell for a third time. The wide thickness of the steps was hard enough to manage without roving eyes making her clumsy.

Her mind balked at the idea that they were inside the glass-lined building the helicopter had landed on, but, short of some transport technology she'd never heard of outside science fiction, that's exactly where they must be.

Three-quarters of the way down to the stage, Dee stopped, mirroring Amalthea as the Rishi chose a seat. Pillows had been stacked and arranged for them and Dee wondered just what sort of storytelling she was about to witness. Her attention settled on the stage, imagining how grand a production would look in this venue.

Dee noted how Amalthea lounged in the fashion of old Rome. Too out of her element to get so comfortable, Dee sat forward so her elbows rested on her knees.

Atkins and Leda had moved away to stand just above and to each side of Dee so the guest of honor was sitting alone in a sea of black rock.

Invited by the silence, Dee said, more to herself, "I can't believe this place is hidden inside a skyscraper in the middle of the city."

Amalthea nodded. "Things are easily hidden when no one knows to look."

-What else is hidden in plain sight we've been missing?-

Dee didn't have time to wonder. The lights dimmed. Two stage lights burst to life to shine on the pair who seemed to materialize on stage.

As if a reflection of each other, the Twins stepped forward, movements so synced Dee's brain was legitimately convinced she was watching one person and the reflection of that person, rather than two separate beings.

The doppelgängers stopped at the edge of the stage, attention turned to Amalthea. They bowed low, their movements slow, before rising in uncanny synchronization to turn their full attention on Dee.

She couldn't look away, feeling the dual weight of that ancient experience press against her, long, dark hair framing bright faces, large, blue eyes staring piercingly into her. They had a strange beauty, humming with underlying notes of violence momentarily calmed.

Dee shivered as another second stretched.

In these moments, the giant room, already silent, seemed sucked of sound. Her breath held, heart hammering as she waited for what was to come.

When the Twins spoke, her skin rippled with goosebumps, their voices blending together as one, maintaining the eerie illusion that they were one being temporarily split into two.

"Forgetting and remembering. Two sides of the same coin. Linked passages in the brain that obliterate self, sense, being."

Dee swallowed slowly, panicked she might make too much noise, unable to look away from the pair of eyes that held her as if trapped. She fidgeted in her seat, leaning backwards as if the greater distance would render her safe.

She realized she was wringing her hands. She clutched them together before wiping her palms across her thighs. Breathing was difficult. Had she blinked? She did now.

Silence stretched again.

In this silence, their words echoed in her head, so she postulated their meaning.

Forgetting and remembering; the same?

She understood forgetting. Would remembering be the same? How could it?

"In forgetting, how does one not change? In forgetting, how does one not lose all they were? Do we become something else in the forgetting? Is who we were lost, pulled away by those things departed?"

Again, their voices blended as one, inciting more goosebumps, on a lesser scale. This time, Dee found she could relax, allowing the strange monologue its place in her thoughts. Her eyes lost their startled glaze, her posture loosened, so her attention was completely on what was being told.

"Remembering adds, morphing self to something else. Changing it. In both, there is alteration."

Another pause.

Then, the images came, implanted in her mind from some unknown source. Her eyes darted to Amalthea to see if she was seeing the same things. The Rishi's eyes met hers for a moment, face unreadable before she smiled a gentle smile, a look that told Dee all was well.

Dee relaxed into the visions, even as she continued looking at the Twins on stage. Her curiosity won out over her fear.

The story unfurled with no more interruptions.

The theatre was gone. There was only the past unfolding in her mind's eye.

She saw an Earth spread with green, thick leaved plants, taller, wider, more massive than any she'd ever seen. Even the green seemed different, each abundant shade more vibrant than the colors she was used to.

Gently placed among the landscape, a great city sprawled high, thin skyscrapers sectioned at junctures where wide platforms connected them to others. Long, bracing legs reached to the ground where gardens and forests were unaffected by the metropolis sprawling around it. Here was a city in symbiosis with the land.

There were people, all with the bronze skin shared by the ancients she'd met. They were happy. There was peace.

Something in her vision shifted. This peace was threatened, though she couldn't explain what had changed to shatter the bliss. She saw a figure, away from the cities, arms raised to the sky, others flocking towards him.

This was Sabik Han. The Ophiuchus.

A part of her thought to be angry at him, but that was the influence of past conversations reflected in her. The Sabik Han she saw now was another version of him. A version whose curiosity, whose thirst to know, whose desire to look in, rather than out, ruled him. The Sabik Han before the hate of the others crashed around him.

Another was there. This one's skin spotted with splotches of paleness. Zibanitu had spoken for the others even then.

Their conversation turned to argument. Han didn't agree with Zibanitu. He left the cities. He left them all to search on his own for that which he felt in his heart was there to find.

Bliss returned, though an undercurrent of violence threatened. That was the Twins watching, searching for what Han might do, even as the others pretended all was well.

Dee felt herself smiling as she watched these mental pictures of an ancient time. Even before they found immortality, they were long-lived. Had those flocking towards Sabik Han been the first of what Dee had been born from? Or were they another race of beings who'd had their time on this Earth?

Her mind had wandered. A spike in her heart rate hit her before her mind comprehended what was changing.

War.

It came quickly to those who weren't privy to the politics, but to the few who watched the path unfold, it was no surprise.

She saw the Twins in their glory.

Standing at the front of armies, they were the generals trained to lead warriors and fulfill the plan set by the Council, who'd chosen this route to combat The Ophiuchus' moves.

Dee's mind raced. What had Sabik done? Had she missed something? Had they skipped a part of the story?

She watched as armies clashed. Millions died, yet the fighting did not stop. Years. Decades. Still, war waged.

Tears fell down Dee's cheeks as her heart ached from the losses. Choked sobs caught in her throat as she was pulled through a time she'd never imagined yet was emotionally tied to in a way she'd never felt in her own life.

Dee watched two events unfold. First, great weapons were loosed, rocketing the Earth to charred ruin. Nothing remained but pits of molten rock, charred landscapes, and scarred ground. An entire planet scorched to nothing.

In this other scene, Dee watched Han, standing naked, arms reaching over him in a large 'Y', his powerful form exuding a calm serenity that juxtaposed the thrumming energy building around him.

They will make us forget. We should not forget.

It was a voice she didn't recognize but knew. It was the voice that had spoken to her through Barnard's welcoming hand, offering her a home.

His mouth opened to let out a chant which created a strange reverberating melody through the rhyming cadence of a language Dee didn't recognize.

She didn't need to understand the words, his intent penetrating her mind from the word-spell the Twins weaved.

Tying himself to the Earth, so not to forget, so not to allow their technology to supersede what they were, what they could be, he would force the others to see what he intuitively understood. He would force this connectivity through them all, tying them directly to the heartbeat of the universe. He was sure that would bring a lasting peace to his people.

But the bombs were already going off, counteracting his mission. Bombs that stripped all evidence of their great technologies, sending all his people had built to smoldering dust. Nothing could survive what this war had wrought.

Despite the destruction that obliterated all that existed, a small island of hope remained where Han stood. The others converged there, staying just ahead of the blasts erasing them from existence.

Han's chanting grew incensed, the power crackling in the air so Dee was sure gravity had lost hold on her hair where she sat. Whatever magic, or science, Han was casting had taken on a power of its own.

Commotion flooded Dee's senses. There was no understanding the source, her eyes searching the space beyond Sabik Han for insight to what was happening.

The Twins were there, facing the still-naked sorcerer. Time had skipped, so Dee wasn't sure how they'd arrived. There were others, many, many others, behind the pair, but she couldn't see them, only feel them in the memory of the story.

Few words were spoken, though Dee sensed communication happening in the long stares the trio gave each other.

Then there was fighting.

Fluid agility whirled as the Twins fought to take out The Ophiuchus before this last piece of Earth was ground to dust.

A mortal blow put Caster on the ground, Pollux now fighting to keep Han from finishing him, rather than kill the one who'd doomed them all. One brother alone could not best Han, and they all knew it. Only as one had the brothers had a chance to end this.

Dee felt more tears. They were Pollux's emotion made tangible. The emotion overwhelmed her as Pollux's frustration turned to fear that his brother would die. She chocked on this fear; *his* fear. She came to her feet, so wrapped in what she was seeing and feeling.

As the Twins had appeared, so too were others suddenly there. Ten bodies, six females, one Dee recognized as Amalthea, and four males, circled Han, who stopped. He was so still Dee was sure he'd been trapped somehow.

A moment before the spell hit, the leader with the marbled skin turned, yelling a command. But it was too late.

Those caught in the spell's radius were brought to the ground, forcefully pressed tightly to the Earth.

Those outside the spell were caught in the blast of the atomizing bomb released by the leader's last command. As the blinding flash lit the world in bright oblivion, those pressed to the Earth were saved.

Saved from death but forever forced to live with what they had wrought.

Dee's awareness came back to the theatre slowly, eyes blinking fast in confusion as she was forced back to the room around her.

She was standing, Atkins at her elbow, ready to assist if she moved to fall. As her brain acknowledged this, her legs collapsed her back to her seat, eyes continuing to blink around the overflowing emotion of all she'd been shown.

Remembering Caster bleeding out on the ground, her eyes darted to the stage, where the Twins remained standing together, watching her, waiting for her senses to fully release her back to the present. She held Caster's gaze, than raked her eyes down over his form, as if something in the way he stood might explain his survival.

Remembering Pollux's pain, her eyes turned to him, and they shared a relieved smile of shared experience.

Blinking again, she took a deep breath, then another, recalibrating back to her own skin.

Finally, she turned to Amalthea. "I see why you wanted them to tell this story. That was—incredible."

Amalthea nodded, a weight to her look that set Dee's radar screaming. "What is it?"

"Their storytelling was in the nature that we can speak to one another. Only those of us who've survived since that day can use this telepathic speech. None of those we've ever created has ever had this ability."

Dee frowned.

-*She's telling you you shouldn't have been able to see the story.*-

Dee looked at Amalthea, fear shining from her eyes, even as she attempted to keep it hidden behind a mask of contemplation.

Amalthea opened her mouth to comfort the girl, just as Pollux stepped from the stage to offer reassurance. Both were stopped when the elevator door opened, its motorized function echoing in the stillness of the room. Not turning to the sound, still too dazed, Dee felt, rather than heard, the frantic approach of one of the Twins' people.

"Zosma—"

The word, a name, filled the room.

Pollux leapt to action, as Caster shouted a command to hidden guards, cutting off the rest of the message.

But there wasn't enough time. Soldiers had surrounded them, repelling from the ceiling as others moved in from hidden doorways near the stage and around the perimeter above and behind them.

It happened so fast, Dee barely recognized something unplanned was occurring.

"I think you have what is mine." A deep, booming voice filled the room, cutting through the chaos of so much motion. The stillness held for a breath before erupting in anxious calamity.

-Are we being overrun? Seriously? -

Dee turned to the voice that rose from the shadows; a voice that claimed her as his own.

His red hair was neatly cut, while his large eyes flashed arrogantly on an attractive face. He was thin, but the command that blazed around him had Dee wondering if that thinness wasn't a disguise his clothing offered him, and underneath was nothing but hard, sinewy muscle waiting to be released.

The implication of his words infused her shocked brain, and her attention on him changed to wide eyed surprise. Was he someone who actually knew the answers to her questions?

-Wouldn't that make him the one who did this to you?-

She stared up at this new Rishi with adrenaline spiking through her veins. How was she supposed to react? Was it time to run? To fight? Part of her wanted to step forward and barrage him with questions.

The Twins had pulled weapons, moving to stand between Amalthea and Desiree, Pollux close enough to Dee that he could protect her if necessary. Atkins stood just ahead of her, blocking her view of Zosma, who towered over them all from his vantage at the top of the theatre steps.

Amalthea's fierceness met him with challenge, "You have no right to be here. Zibanitu will end you for this."

Zosma laughed at the implied threat. "Zibanitu can do what he likes, but he won't be able to fault me in this when I show him the truth to my claim."

Seeming to float up the steps, defying the girth of her frame, Amalthea spit her next words. So venomous were they Dee wondered if there weren't some long standing personal feud between the two. "Your claim means nothing. If your claim were so polished she wouldn't have come to me!"

"Careful your temper doesn't get you into more trouble than you can get out of. You may have fallen across this bit of drama, but don't think it means you're worth any more than you ever were."

Not even Metis' hold could stop the matrons fury. Castor called out to her just as she reached the top landing where the newcomer stood, but she was too far gone.

Dee hadn't realized she carried a weapon. It was out, slicing downward with an incredible speed that further revealed the power hiding beneath her motherly frame.

Flinching at the blow she was sure would land across Zosma's face, he managed to block and parry the onslaught. Caster and Pollux, waiting to see how the lady would fair, were suddenly on the landing with her, three to his one too great of odds even for him.

Showing the agility he possessed, Zosma vaulted backwards to surround himself with his own Soldiers whose weapons were aimed and ready.

Despite the large space, it was suddenly crowded as more Soldiers from contending sides faced off. A barely contained potential energy charged the room with an almost audible hum, causing Dee's hand to itch for a weapon. She cursed the decision that she not be allowed one, and held out a hand to Atkins.

Not bothering comment, the Soldier handed over a long knife Dee hoped would be enough. She shifted the weapon in her hand, getting a feel for the grip before settling it firmly in her palm.

Amalthea continued to seethe at the group of invaders. Still flanked by the Twins, none moved forward.

It was Caster who broke the staring match. "If you leave now, there will be no harm done."

Pollux shot a hard look at his brother. "No! Harm has been done. We can not let it lie!"

He stepped forward to begin an attack, but a stern, clipped syllable from Caster stopped him. "Just a moment, brother." Caster's voice echoed throughout the cavernous room. She noted Zosma's eyebrows rise in barely masked contempt. "We should at least offer the intruder the chance to explain his breach of our laws."

Pollux turned his attention on his brother with a smirk, calming slightly.

If Dee didn't know any better, she might think the Twins were baiting Zosma.

Castor continued, speaking directly at Zosma through the wall of Soldiers who'd lined up between the Rishis. "What is yours, as you claim we have, that has allowed you to risk war by breaking into our space?"

Zosma met Amalthea's smile, then held each of the Twins' eye. He raised an arm, single finger pointing through the crowd on the landing to Dee. All attention turned to her.

He didn't wait. Zosma sprung, vaulting towards the trio, his own Soldiers moving with him to clash with the army waiting to defend their Masters.

Dee found her feet leaving the ground, just as she noted Atkins, Leda and Vali crossing swords with Zosma.

How had he gotten so close? How had he gotten through an army of Soldiers, then Amalthea and the Twins?

Carried like a sack of bones, she struggled to get free, until Pollux's command stilled her fight. The world spun by in her upside-down position, preventing her from checking on the condition of the others. Amalthea's shout convinced Dee the Rishi was still okay.

Had she been calling for Pollux to stop?

Gunfire erupted.

Dee squeezed her eyes tightly, clenching her body in anticipation of getting shot.

-Well done. If you can't see, the bullets can't hit you, is that it? Maybe wish hard enough and you'll teleport right out of here and into Mike's living room. Tap your heels three times and all that...-

But there was nothing else she could do. Pollux carrying her off had negated any ability she might have of assisting in her own escape.

-You could tell him to put you down. You could fight him. Maybe you should kill him like you should have killed Hamal.-

*

Amamlthea whirled on Caster as gunfire filled the room. "Where is he taking her?!"

Caster barely glanced at the Rishi, whose rage pushed against him. "My brother is prone to overreaction. She'll be fine. He'll keep her safe."

Amalthea seethed, ducking around the flurry of projectiles, even as Metis was there to ensure her safety. Glaring at the spot she'd last seen Desiree, she gathered control of her anger. Matching her speed to the frenzy of activity around her, she turned to the fight, thoughts still on the girl she'd promised safety to.

Caster was moving through the chaos, following, albeit much more slowly, the path his brother had taken with Dee. The secrets buried within this building were vast, security in their own right, though the fact that Zosma had managed to infiltrate so deeply made her afraid it wouldn't be enough.

Chapter Thirty-Two

"Keep your feet."

Dee barely interpreted the words before she was spun from Pollux's shoulder, managing to stay upright as her feet met the ground, their speed never slowing.

She hadn't seen much of where they traveled but guessed they'd ventured down a number of secret passages leading through mostly unused portions of the building. Whether or not she'd find herself hiding out in a secret corner of São Paulo, or somewhere new, she would have to wait to find out once their frantic retreat came to an end.

Using that skill that allowed her to know when they were near, Dee was made aware of Zosma's approach. He'd caught up to them, despite Pollux's hidden doors and switch-backing escape.

Assuming Pollux was aware of the approaching Rishi, she kept the knowledge to herself. When he didn't appear to be changing speed or direction or doing anything that might stop the invader from catching them, she called out her insight to him.

He looked back without slowing, head cocked over his shoulder so she could see the incredulous smirk on his face.

She frowned. He didn't believe her.

Stopping abruptly in the stone passage got his attention.

Forced to stop, or leave her behind, he whirled. Her back pedaling was the only reason he didn't scoop her back onto his shoulder. Seeing she wasn't backing down he stopped coming after her. "You're serious."

Dee was too relieved to be mad he hadn't believed her. "Yeah, I'm serious. He's behind us, catching up."

He studied her face a moment longer before shrugging. "Very well."

Pulling his sword in his right hand, a long knife in the other, he paced past Dee, waiting for their pursuer.

Somewhere along the route Dee had lost the weapon Atkins had given her. She cursed her uselessness. After so much time being trained by the best, even showing the best she could hold her own, she continued to be the damsel.

Her inner-voice was cut off before it began by Zosma's appearance. Raging forward with an energy that surprised her, Dee was taken aback. Was it all really because of her?

A sword materialized in Zosma's hand. He stalked forward, halting ten yards from his quarry. "Pollux, you served me once. Would you really try to take my life now, over some girl none of us know?"

Pollux's voice was icy calm. "You claim to know her."

Dee's muscles tensed in anticipation of a fight.

The intruder tried a different tact. "I'm not sure I understand this play of yours to whisk the girl away. Your brother seemed surprised. Very unlike the two of you not to be in perfect sync."

"There was a slight deviation from how we thought the day would go." The Twin barely moved, patiently waiting for an attack. Dee was surprised Pollux himself hadn't attacked, wondering if he'd decided playing offense was less prudent with her standing there.

Zosma smiled, almost laughing, drawing Dee's attention from her guard. If he was mad at the unfolding events, he was hiding it well. "Yes, I imagine you didn't see this coming . You realize how weak your House really is now. How easily I could come through and take all of you if I wished."

"Yet, you don't. Why is that, I wonder?"

Dee wished she could see the Twin's face to see what look smoldered behind his eyes even as his voice remained calm. Whatever was there brought Zosma forward in a flurry of anger, so easily parried, it was the Twin's turn to laugh. "Careful your anger doesn't ruin this moment for you. Or, is it already ruined since I'm the one with the prize?"

Zosma backed away. "Where will you take her? There's no where I won't find her. Not again. Not after all the time it's taken me to relocate her."

"Which begs the question: Why has it taken so long to find her if she's been yours all along? It's not like you to keep such poor care of what is yours."

Zosma managed control, frowning at Pollux's words. Dee was surprised when he responded to Pollux's insinuations. "It is unlike me, isn't it? A gross failing on my part. So long had I gone with poor results that I no longer paid attention. When this ones numbers came back more promising than any other, I raced to find out the details. Little did I know, I'd been lied to by the ones who'd been in charge that installation. A false identity had been given."

The anger in his face was enough to send a shiver through Dee, and she wondered who it was that had been brave enough to lie to him.

Not dissuaded by Zosma's tale, Pollux mentioned conversationally, posture still set for battle, "Either way, we might just call finders-keepers."

"Finders-keepers?"

Pollux laughed at Zosma's confusion. "Finders-keepers. Whoever finds becomes the keeper."

Zosma's frown deepened. "Not in this. In this there will be no keeper that is not me."

He pressed forward again, this time intent on breaking through to the girl who watched, overwhelmed by this new player and all he claimed. Her mind raced backwards to the night of the fire, willing her brain to give up information that might corroborate what Zosma was suggesting.

"You did this to me?" Her voice was a croak, forced to life through fear and confusion.

Pollux perked his head but didn't turn around. Zosma's eyes found hers behind her guard. His voice softened. "I have sought long and hard for you. We lost much in that fire. We thought you'd been lost, too."

Dee was staring at Pollux's back, eyes still not seeing the space around her, only the burning inferno that had taken her friends. "You found me."

"We weren't sure. We were never sure. Hamal's scheming got in the way of too much."

Now, Dee's eyes flashed upwards, meeting the fatherly gaze of the man who was looking at her like she was his long-lost daughter. It wasn't the look she'd expected and it tempered her anger so the volume in her voice was lowered. "You tried to kill me."

"If you weren't what we thought—"

"—those things would have killed me!" She cut him off, taking a step towards him in her fury. "They almost did. If not for Hamal…" Gritting her teeth, she screamed in her head. She would not break down. She would not lose it right here.

-At least you're not throwing up in the bushes.-

Her hands clenched. In her mind, she flew forward, clawing at his face with enraged passion. In reality, she maintained her stance behind Pollux, afraid to let loose her will in fear the Rishis might be forced to kill her.

"I have all the answers you seek. I can show you those things you've forgotten."

Dee looked up, caught by the idea that she might learn the truth, but also stopped by the very same thought. Did she want to know how this was done to her? Did she want to see those last moments of her friends' lives before the fire took them all?

-He tried to kill you! -

Head bowed with the weight of an impossible decision, she whispered. "Why didn't you just bring me to you? Why this convoluted game?"

Pollux chuckled, answering for him. "Because he was scared of our reaction. Of all of us. If he'd simply picked you up, everyone's spies would have known and we'd have been all over him, forcing him to show us what he'd found."

Zosma stepped forward, face snarling. "You would have had no right!"

This time Pollux actually laughed at him. "Except you didn't do it. You knew we'd all heard the rumor about your science. Your blood experiments that Zibanitu outright forbade. You knew we'd all put you down for it. You knew you'd never survive what would follow."

The end of the corridor erupted in fighting. It was Zosma's men pushing through the Twins' defenses to follow their Master. Caster's voice called, "Zosma, it's over. Surrender to us and avoid this fight."

Zosma turned perpendicular to the Twins. Giving Caster an imperious look, he threw his head back and laughed, a full-throated sound that belied the attitude he'd been giving off as Pollux outed his cowardly schemes. "Surrender? To you? Have you forgotten it was I who elevated you to what you are?"

Caster paced carefully closer, sword in each hand pointing just away from his body at the floor. "You may have taught us the art of war, but it was never you who put us here."

Zosma frowned, as if reminded of some truth he'd rather forget. "You worked under me. I brought you up. I raised you from nothing!"

Dee's eyes widened as the Rishi seemed to lose himself in his own rage, but it was quickly controlled.

She'd taken a step back without realizing it.

Caster continued to force Zosma's attention on him. "Yes, you did teach us. Cared for us. Then, you abandoned us to fend for ourselves when we were blamed for failing to win *your* war. We owe you nothing!"

This last word was punctuated by the perfect sync of brothers rushing forward.

In her head, Dee clearly heard Pollux's voice command her to run. Without thinking, she did, turning to follow the corridor wherever it might lead.

She ran. The sounds of fighting behind her growing quieter as she moved farther through the darkened corridors of the Twins' secret underground world.

-Why always underground? -

She didn't know how she knew she was underground, but she was sure of it just the same. She'd come a long way from the towering helicopter pad on the top of the skyscraper.

She took random turns as her feet propelled her, not sure where she was going, but even less sure it was safe to stop running.

-You've been running for over four years. Maybe it's time to stop.-

As the words echoed through her mind, her sprint slowed to a run, then a jog until finally she was still, standing silently in the dark.

She hadn't been running. She'd been avoiding. Avoiding what'd been done to her.

But, even before that, it had been the same. Since her father died.

The tingling in her skull pierced through her. She turned, knowing one of them had caught up to her.

The question she couldn't answer was, which one was it?

Chapter Thirty-Three

"You're not surprised." Her tone held an edge only someone not used to being taken advantage of could hold.

"We had to draw him out."

"You let him know where we were going?" There was incredulity now, with the slightest hint of temper flaring. "How did you know it was him and not Han?"

Zibanitu looked away, disgusted by the use of the name that was blasphemous in his House. Composing himself, he turned back to the irate Rishi filling the screen in front of him. "I didn't know. Now I do."

"You risked her. You risked all of us!" Shock overrode some of the anger. She didn't even try to hide the expression from her face.

Zibanitu allowed an ironic smile to play over his features, voice remaining level. "Risked you how? What could be done to you? Zosma wouldn't dare, even if there was some danger he could serve you."

"But, the girl—"

"The girl is his prize. He wouldn't risk her either, of that I was certain. Now, he will be forced to explain his case to the Council where we'll hear firsthand what he's been up to." A touch of annoyance that he was forced to explain himself laced his words.

She breathed relief. The slight that he hadn't let her in on his plan overridden by the knowledge that the girl was safe. "So, you know where she is."

"No."

Amalthea was stunned speechless, a feat that hadn't occurred in a thousand years. She sputtered, trying to formulate a cohesive thought.

Zi smiled kindly. "You thought the Twins were in on it? No. Their role I did not anticipate."

Amalthea nodded, thoughtful, long years teaching her how to remain calm in the face of such sudden, unfortunate news. "Pollux was quite taken with her."

Zibanitu raised an eyebrow at this, but didn't ask further after the point. "I had expected Zosma's success in capturing the girl, but this is an even better outcome. They can't stay hidden too long and it makes our bargaining power stronger. Also, it pushes the fighting farther to the future."

"You anticipate fighting for her?"

He gave her a penetrating stare. "Would you have let it go?"

She squared her shoulders. "I would not let it go."

They locked eyes in a look of understanding that reminded Amalthea of why he had become their head. Even in the moments he seemed to act outside of reason, or practicality, or even feeling, he chose the best path for the long game. Only once had he ever failed them and that couldn't be placed solely at his feet.

He nodded. "When the others hear, I feel they will all want their time with her. A curiosity like this will garner everyones attention."

Epilogue

It was dark.

Not complete blackness. He could just make out the edges of the door across the room.

He closed his eyes, forcing memory from behind the fog in his head.

There was no recollection of where he was, or how he'd gotten there.

He opened his eyes, exploring the space in the hopes that something might spark his memory.

Slowly, he sat up, listening for some sound that anyone was near.

There was only quiet, his body rustling against the stiff sheet draped over him a loud jolt to the deathlike silence around him.

Sitting with his legs on the floor, hands pressed into the bed at his sides, he closed his eyes again.

Shouldn't he remember where he was? Shouldn't he remember *who* he was?

His head lifted as the door opened…

A Very Special Thanks

To my sister, Kim whose enthusiasm for this story kept me going when I'd forgotten it was supposed to be fun.

To Stephanie and Mom, who read it when it wasn't quite ready, but said it was fine all the same.

To Christina, who showed everyone at work and found me new fans.

For Dad, whose subtle excitement for my work was as loud as the rest.

To Jason, who deals with me at my most crazy, and adapts as needed. He cooks for me too. And of course, designed this fabulous cover.

To Bethany, who gave great feedback and sacrificed much of her own time to help me see what I'd missed.

To Nicola Rose (@nicolaroseauthor), my first real IG partner. Thanks for cheering me on… and of course feedback… and making this creation better.

To Benjamin Kinney, who came into the process late, but made it the best it could be.

NanoWriMo: where I learned how much I could actually get done and that this dream could be a real thing.

To the wonderful #amwriting #writersfollowwriters and #ishouldbewriting community on Instagram where I find daily inspiration to continue this journey. May your muses continue to sing.

To those on Unsplash who graciously allow us to use their photos for our own creative endeavors.

Of course, to all the readers who took a shot on the unknown by following me on this adventure. If you haven't already, you should grab your travel pass to get an exclusive ticket to more free adventures on my website: CMMartens.com

Find more C. M. Martens:

CMMartens.com

IG: author_CMMartens

Twitter: AuthorCMMartens

Goodreads: CMMartens

FB: authorcmmartens

Sign up for a free travel pass to explore Cindy's parallel worlds:

CMMartens.com/freechapter/

C. M. Martens is an avid reader and coffee drinker. In a past life she was a personal trainer and nutrition coach. You'll often see her with a book on Clearwater Beach in sunny Florida, where she currently spends most of her time when not cooped up in her office spawning new adventures. Unless it's Summer. Then you'll find her traipsing the hills of central New York.
Always with a book.
Always.

Stumbling is her first novel.

Discover more of her parallel worlds at: CMMartens.com

Whether you loved it or hated it, consider writing a review. More reviews means more exposure which means more people who will find this book to read. It's the greatest gift you can give any author.

Desiree's story will continue in **Falling Forward**, *Book Two of The Fool's Path* due out December 2018.

Turn the page for a sneak peak

A whirlwind.

It was the only word she could think of to describe the past week. A week of rushing from one place to the next. Hiding in shadow. Avoiding contact with everyone including random strangers and known associates. Her cell phone was miles behind her, atomized by Pollux's foot. All part of some forward direction whose endpoint was never divulged.

If Desiree ever thought life as a fugitive might be romantic, she was long past it. A full nights sleep had been a thing of fantasy. Hot food a myth. Jumping at shadows was more than an expression. The palm of her hand was imprinted with the handle of the long knife Pollux had procured.

She'd learned not to ask questions. She'd stopped attempting small-talk. There was never answer or response.

So, she'd resigned herself to this scary world where she was hunted. Those days at home, training with Hamal, wondering when the next thing might come after her was nothing compared to this.

Then, they'd arrived.

All was quiet. All was serene.

After three days, Dee was bored to tears.

This morning of the tenth day, up before dawn, wrapped in a heavy, home-spun blanket, Dee stared out over her new world. Settled close to thirteen-thousand feet above sea level, the view was spectacular.

The wood-planks of the balcony where she stood, red paint clean and fresh, kept her from plunging to the mountain valley below. A year ago, the height might have forced her through an exercise in panic control, but she'd found so many other things to worry about since then.

-*Hamal would be proud.*-

Dee smiled sardonically at the voice in her head. As awkward as the last encounter with her mentor had been, she couldn't help wonder how he was doing. What he was doing. With too much time to think, she'd struggled to keep her thoughts from slipping to obsession. Her safety in question and her life on the line, she knew Hamal shouldn't occupy any of her thoughts. It was most likely she'd never see him again anyway.

Ignoring the hint that she should think of other things, her eyes lost focus on the surrounding majesty so she might better focus on her memory reminiscing their time together. He'd taught her so much, all at massive risk to himself.

Unbidden, the kiss they'd, literally, fallen into came to mind. Would things have been different if they'd let their attraction pull them closer? More likely than not, Hamal would be dead.

She ignored the constriction of her throat at the idea, Daniel's words on the matter coming to mind: *His feelings for you. They need to be tempered. If you share his interest, you need to forget it.*

Hamal washed from her thoughts by the only other she'd consider friend, Daniel's presence had helped her more than she'd like to admit during her stay at Amaltheum. That she hadn't been able to say goodbye to either before she'd left for São Paulo weighed more heavily on her than she'd like to admit.

She gripped the banister, using the discomfort of its icy exterior as an anchor to bring her thoughts from their inner-reverie and lifted her eyes to the panorama blossoming under the rising sun. A part of her hoped to never leave this mountain retreat.

It was a third Rishi's House she stood in. As far removed as the Twins' had been from Amalthea, she couldn't get enough of just staring out the windows. There were moments here, full and unhindered, that she forgot her troubles, her mind lost to the majesty of her surroundings.

The group of circular buildings nestled in the crevice of the mountain was a marvel. Her brain struggled to envision its construction, but the peacefulness of being so removed from others explained why the difficulty was worth the undertaking. Here, Dee had learned to breathe deep and free again.

She leaned forward to better catch the wind in her face.

A bright red awning stretched over the terrace she stood on, its bright red color matching the banister she held on to. Below her, marring the perfect view, was the bright red roof of a lower building. Nestled into the crevices of the mountainside, Asellus' compound was a marvelous feat of architecture, and the perfect place for Pollux to have brought her.

The wind lashed again. Dark hair that had grown to her shoulders over months in pseudo-imprisonment whipped her face so she ducked her head instinctively into the blanket wrapped around her, her thoughts as wide as the view around her.

The Rishis had a weak truce. That much had been explained. But this last attack, the attack that had Pollux scrambling to relocate her across the world, had broken that truce. What that meant for her, she didn't know. What it meant for any of them, they wouldn't tell her.

Asellus, a matronly woman whose kind expression had set Dee right at home here, had refused to speak of it, and the Twins had followed suit. Despite the looming threat of an ancient race bent on destroying her, or not, Dee had managed to repress her stress. Instead, she let the serene safety of this place soothe her. She let her simmering rage dampen. She let the idea that things would be okay, really okay, settle in her thoughts.

Dee didn't understand how Zosma had gotten inside the Twins' domain. She didn't understand how these Rishis could be so bad at keeping her safe.

On multiple occasions, her inner-voice had prodded her to take her life into her own hands, but without trusting she could do that, contemplation was as far as that topic ever got. There was still too much she didn't know to risk going off on her own. And what would she do? Try at the normal life her and Mike had talked about? The life he thought she was off starting at this very moment. If he knew what she was really doing...

The banister underneath her hand groaned against the pressure she applied.

Using her mastery of compartmentalization, she blocked how awful she'd been to him, burying it until after her current predicament was figured out. *What's done is done*, her father used to say. *Now, what will you do?*

She spun from the splendid scenery, chased by guilty thoughts and the rising sun that told her she was late to the day's first meditation session.

The simple room that was her sleeping quarters enveloped her in the warmth thrown off by the refrigerator-sized hearth. Asellus had never bothered to update this place with central air, and whatever system provided the electricity was spotty at best. Dee had learned not to rely on having much light once the sun was hidden behind the looming mountains, or to expect the temperature to be anything comfortable.

Another compartmentalized thought slipped free, the answer to which might solve all her problems: —*-Or compound them into a suffocating heap.*—— Zosma had claimed he was responsible for what she was. His booming voice in the theatre of the Twins' urban home had triggered nightmares she'd thought long behind her.

The idea that she had been created left her numb. Anger and regret, guilt and sadness warred inside her, negating each other until she was left wrung out. She should be furious at the one who'd claimed her. She should rage against what he'd done to her. Instead, she just wanted an explanation. She was tired of running, tired of the stress of the unknown.

At least the question of who was after her, and why, had been answered. That the other Rishis were interested in her was a side-effect of this. Like any other siblings, one couldn't have something without the others wanting it as well.

She bristled at this, frustrated annoyance quickening her movements so she was throwing clothes as she dressed for the day.

If they were all blood siblings, or if it was just a word they used to streamline conversation, she hadn't been brave enough to ask. Based on their dysfunctional familial relationships, she believed the point to be real.

-And some of them think you're the newest addition.-

The idea made her head hurt. With all she'd discovered she could do, with all she now was, learning she was a part of some ancient race of crybabies hadn't been on her radar of possibilities.

All she now was.

Her eyes swept the sparse room as the statement echoed in her head.

All she now was.

Her endurance and speed had matched Pollux's who was one of the most renowned among the renowned.

Before that, she'd sparred with Atkins, another whose prowess on the killing field was only matched by a select few. She'd even killed a couple of the Ophiuchus' Soldiers, another feat that told of her extraordinary abilities. In a matter of months, she'd gone from a spaz throwing up in the bushes to a warrior who could stand toe-to-toe with the best of the best.

A wash of empowerment pulled her posture straighter.

She hadn't respected Hamal's perspective at the time. She hadn't had the awareness to understand what he'd been pushing her for. Too busy hiding, she hadn't been capable of tapping her potential or even understanding what that potential could be.

The calibration of this potential continued to be retooled. Training continued to be the focus, as it had been at Amaltheum, and as it had been when Hamal had moved in with her.

Pollux, at times energetic and excited about his task of continuing her training, at others, almost fearful of her mortality, hadn't given her a day off. Not that she minded the distractions from too many thoughts that dragged her brain to insanity. She especially didn't mind being honed into someone who could protect herself.

Soon after their arrival in the mountains, Caster had caught up with them. Reunited with his brother, Pollux was pulled from his tendency to stress, though it seemed only because that was Caster's role. His apathetic watchfulness was the balance to Pollux's eager instruction.

Together, they'd been showing Dee a laundry list of new tricks.

In direct contrast to her physical training with the Twins, Asellus was teaching her the art of sitting around. At least, that's what Dee had thought of it at first. After only a week, she could admit the benefits she was learning from calming her mind, from becoming the master of her thoughts rather than a bystander pulled along by the constant directional changes of her psyche.

There was still a long way to go, but the nightmares had calmed, and her ability to let thoughts float away rather than catch her up in their mess was enough to make coming here worth it.

Asellus was a quiet woman. As tall as the Twins, her round face, older than the others, held small features. A busty upper body balanced out her willowy frame and the same motherly demeanor Amalthea had carried shown from her caramel eyes.

Despite her calm demeanor, Asellus wasn't patient with Dee's ideas on appropriate sleeping times. Dee's usual late night to late morning schedule was fast obliterated in this place. If Dee didn't show up by dawn, someone would be there to pull her out of bed.

She knew that from experience.

Dressed in thick woollen socks, tight leggings under baggy fisherman's pants and a dense, coarse wrap-around jacket, Dee made her way to where Asellus would already be in session.

The one-hundred-and-eighty-degree panorama allowed dawn's light to brighten the room. Dee hurried, knowing she was on the brink of lateness, laying her warm outer layers out on hooks set near the door for this purpose. She glanced up, glimpsing the Rishi's knees hanging over the edge of the lofted second floor where the matron was already meditating. This second story, dedicated solely to contemplation, was where Asellus spent most of her time and where Dee spent each of her mornings.

Through Dee's first week, this exercise in stillness had been uncomfortable. Her brain didn't understand it. Her body didn't recognize it. There was no explanation for what she should be doing. Sitting and staring out the window seemed like a monumental waste of time. Her body would pull her to standing before even half-an-hour had passed. Nervous energy, spawned from thoughts she didn't want to face, made it impossible for her body to sit still. Compartmentalized thoughts were too eager to slip their cages when faced with nothing but blank time.

On the third day, she'd decided not to show up.

When a small, weathered woman had come to collect her, speaking a language Dee had never heard, Dee knew this non-activity activity was non-negotiable. Rather than continue to argue with a woman she couldn't understand, Dee had followed with leaden feet, mind stewing in the vat of her frustrated attitude.

She'd come a long way in the week since then.

Today, it was with a light tread that she climbed the narrow staircase pressed against the mountain-side wall and a light heart that pushed through the demarcation of quiet that hung in the air as her head cam through the floor. She wondered if this dense cloud of serenity wasn't some kind of magic spell. Or maybe, it was just some residual projection from the Rishi's constant attendance. Either answer Dee would have believed.

Pollux had joined them this morning. He sat with closed eyes, legs folded in lotus position, facing the Eastern window so Dee was looking at his right side.

Asellus' position was at the Northern station of the landing, so close to the edge of the railless floor a quick glance would convince someone she was floating. Dee pinned her eyes to the back of the Rishi's head, knowing the matron's eyes would be open, staring blindly into the sky in front of her.

Dee hadn't gotten over how creepy this was. She didn't understand how Asellus could be so detached from the world while still conscious of all that went on around her. Dee could barely sit still and concentrate when her eyes were closed.

As she moved to what had become her spot, she smiled, remembering those first days when she would show up here with delusions of demanding answers she imagined were rightfully hers. Every morning, these questions would fall away, erased by the peace of the room that overrode her grand plan.

It was this calm Asellus was trying to teach Dee how to hold onto, even after she left this space. It was this calm, Asellus explained, that would allow Dee to glimpse the true state of the universe.

Even now, after learning to enjoy these morning sessions, Dee wasn't sure she understood what the Rishi meant by this.

Dee's smile morphed to a grimace when she thought about the day of her meltdown. It was that third day, the day she'd been dragged from her bed despite arguments for why she wouldn't benefit from whatever this was, that burned her with embarrassment.

That morning, volatility was held from boiling over through effort that had her limbs trembling. The soothing nature of the room assisted in keeping her caged anger from exploding, but, like a spiteful toddler, Dee had refused to sit as was required.

Her inner-voice had egged her on, its position that she was long over-due for an explanation compounded by the idea that she should no longer be content to live by the dictums of whatever inner-squabbling was going on with the Rishis. At first, not as confident in her abilities to not die as her ego, she'd held back. But, pressed under the pressure of the Rishis meditative silence, her thoughts had continued to snowball until Dee finally exploded in a geyser of emotion.

Asellus' calm mask had turned to watch her rage with sympathetic eyes without interruption or interjection. Pollux, standing from his relaxed repose at Dee's loud words, had remained at the far side of the room, arms crossed over his chest while leaning casually against the wall, eyebrows raised in a mixture of disbelief and mirth.

His amusement at her expense had redirected her rant towards him. A tightening around his eyes as he absorbed her scathing remarks was all there'd been to determine that they'd had any effect while he held Asellus' silent direction.

Their silence had pulled the wind from her tirade. With no feedback to respond to, embarrassment settled over her until it stifled her bluster to oppressed quiet. Deflated, too mortified to walk past the pair whose non-response was more impactful than any words could have been, Dee followed Asellus' gesture to take a seat with minimal hesitation.

Wallowing in the shame of her rage, Dee had found her first moment of detached perspective.

When the Rishi finally spoke, Dee's eyes had been following the soar of a giant bird floating on the wind. She kept her attention on this rather than turn ashamed eyes to Asellus.

"It is more difficult to see oneself as individual in this place. A conducive point for this task."

The kindness of the Rishi's tone had Dee hold back the lashing words that sprang to the tip of her tongue, her tenuous calm overridden by the wash of frustration that forever circled her mood.

-What the hell is she talking about? Just kill them all and be on your way.-

Reigning in the bite of her inner-voice kept Dee distracted from contemplating the possible sense that might lay in Asellus' words.

When the hush continued past comfort, Dee squirmed against the pull to speak. She'd said more than enough. Her ferocious rant still hummed in the air, and she had no idea what to say to such a nonsensical statement.

Asellus spoke again. "It is something even we have forgotten. Existence plagues us all."

She pointed a long finger ahead of her, tracking the motion of the bird Dee watched. "The Hornbill does not worry about its place. It simply carries out its duty, knowing in its essence those things it must do to flow with the world around it."

The Rishi lowered her arm and tilted her head as if studying some new curiosity. "Human nature has always acted at direct odds with that innate sense of belonging. A nature that has bled to infect those of us who remain." She sighed and added softly, "So far we have fallen."

Her attention had turned back to Dee, voice pitched like she was giving away some secret. "There was a long time that I was hopeful for our return to who we were. Now, I feel we are too trapped in this construct to ever escape."

These words had brought Dee's attention from the window to Asellus' face, hoping to catch context for what the Rishi spoke of in her expression.

-Is she a little bit mad?-

The idea generated another level of anxiety to settle in Dee's mind. She'd thought there couldn't be more apprehension, but this adventure was teaching her never to construct ceilings for anything. Regarding her emerging powers, this was a good thing to learn. Concerning the crazy surrounding these Beings, not so much.

Dee resisted the urge to glance at Pollux to see if his expression would help her decide how many grains of salt she should add to the words she was hearing. But Pollux wasn't necessarily on her side, so she'd refrained.

A staggering wash of loneliness had threatened her at that moment. Hamal's presence had given her a sense of companionship. With him, she'd no longer had to hide what she'd become. He'd been more familiar with what was going on than she had been.

Then, Daniel had stepped in to buffer her next layer of assimilation. She'd even begun to feel like she might fit in somewhere. While at Amalthea's, Daniel had played a critical part of raising the blinders from Dee's eyes about what she might be.

Things in São Paolo had happened too quickly for her to have time to be lonely.

She was good at being alone. She was an only child. Her mother died so long ago she couldn't even miss her. She was independent. Her introverted nature had kept her removed from the socialite-narcissism that was common of her generation. She'd been close with her father and had found a friend in Mike when she was at the age when true best friends found their roots.

Even so, there was a difference between being introverted and being sequestered. Especially when surrounded by the knowledge that her life was in the hands of these extraordinary Beings who may, or most likely not, have her best interest in mind. It would have been nice to have had someone to look to for support on her level.

"What does your life mean to you?"

Caught off guard, Dee's tongue froze in her mouth.

What did her life mean to her? Was the Rishi asking if she cared if she died? Or was it a question of purpose? Either way, she wasn't sure how to answer.

"I know I don't want to lose it." Dee stammered out a response.

Her answer from that day echoed in her thoughts in the present. She really didn't want to lose it. She didn't want to die, but she also didn't want to live under the thumb of another. She wanted to *live*, rather than hide and run and be protected from constant unknowns.

As she took the half-lotus position that was comfortable to her, she noted the others' hand positions. She mimicked the mudra they'd formed, curious at its use. Fingertips of each hand held together, she laid hers in her lap, rather than attempt to keep them raised at heart level like the Rishis.

There had been a classroom session after her rant day. So much information about mediating, there was little of it she could have recited back. The focus on seeing and feeling the world around her was outside her sphere of understanding. Maybe outside her care to understand.

She did remember the hand positions were called mudras, though she didn't remember what any of their uses were. Connection with the Divine. Connection with the self. Connection with other things she hadn't even tried to retain. At the time, there'd been no sense that she would care about any of this sitting around.

Now, only a week later, she wouldn't consider giving up the practice.

After a few deep breathes, she closed her eyes, changing her breathing pattern so she was holding each breath for a couple of seconds before forcefully exhaling. Feeling as centered as she had learned to be, she switched this pattern to steady in-and-outs, paying close attention to those moments in-between, when the breath ceased as the inhale turned to exhale.

Her mind wandered, thoughts of her journey with Pollux filling the blank slate of her mind.

The farther they'd traveled from São Paulo, the more withdrawn the Twin had gotten. Forced to accept his quiet introspection, wondering if maybe the separation from his brother wasn't causing it, she refused to consider it was regret for saving her that plagued him. Whatever it was, the infatuation he'd held for her at their first meeting was overshadowed by it.

A bell chimed, its echo shattering her thoughts, a reminder to focus her attention on her breath. *Some days will be more comfortable than others*, Asellus had told her. Evidently, this was a day for distraction.

Inhale.
One.
Two.
Three.
Four.
Five.
Pause.
Exhale.

One.

Two.

Three.

Four.

Five.

Pause.

Answers.

Dee continued to expect them and continued to be disappointed. Worried about finding out what was going on, she hadn't wasted time considering how to disentangle herself from a web she could barely make out the threads to.

Now that things were more explicit, in their convoluted way, she thought her priorities might have to change.

-Or be created.-

The point from her subconscious was valid. There had been no priorities before, only an apathetic attempt to do as she was told in the hope she'd be freed because it was the right thing to happen.

The bell chimed again and her attention snapped from introspection to breath.

This time, a smile tugged at her mouth that a mere instant had passed before her thoughts fell to distraction.

"The trying is causing your failure. Relax, and let the mind do what it will. When you find yourself drifting, don't judge it, don't be angry about it, don't be humored by it, simply bring your thoughts back to the breath."

Dee didn't open her eyes. Instead, she pictured Asellus' patient manner explaining a thing the Rishis had long mastered. As old as she was, Dee wondered if maybe Asellus hadn't invented the practice.

It was this vastness of time that stretched back to the Rishis origins that Dee's thoughts moved to now. She allowed the abstract of the infinite draw her mind to blankness. She let the beat of her heart draw her focus, so she was pulled into a peaceful state as exhilarating as it was calming.

Her heightened hearing made the sound of her heart easy to find, its steady drum anchoring her attention in her chest. She envisioned the circulation of blood the organ drove. This circulation expanded to a sense of a greater connectedness to her surroundings. The movement of the liquid in her system synched with the movement of the wind outside and the water cutting through the mountains and on and on.

The tendrils of oneness crept on her so she barely noticed its genesis, but was reminded of what the Twins' had shown her about their origins.

The image she'd been shown of Sabik Han was of a large, bronze-skinned man whose well-defined physique screamed strength. It hadn't been his perfect form, naked to the world, that drew her attention, but rather, the feeling of what he was trying to do. It hadn't been well explained in the telling, and Dee wondered if the others even knew what the Ophiuchus' goal had been. Whatever it was, it had failed, and the direct result was their immortality.

Tying them to the Earth. She remembered that point distinctly. The point that Sabik Han had thought their technology was taking over what they were and wanted to fix it.

The bell chimed again.

This time Dee was brought back to her focus with no aggravation or laughter to further distract. Her sense of calm remained as her awareness floated on the reverberating sound that faded to silence.

Silence.

Tying them to the Earth.

Breathe in.

Breathe out.

Silence that was akin to darkness, as the warmth of a thick comforter covering one from a cold night fell around her. Darkness, as chased by the light, when the realization that all is well, that all is on its path and no other way could be or has been.

Tied to the Earth.

Golden silence. Teaching silence. Silence connected directly to the source, to that energy that threads the world and its creations as one.

Minutes or hours or decades might have passed, there was no deciphering.

In this time, darkness faded to the brightness of new dawn, hope and the promise of granted dreams.

Breathe in.

Breathe out.

This fading linked directly to her awareness of her physical body seated in this physical place as the sanctuary of her mind let her ego resume its life in her.

Tied to the Earth.

The blankness of her mind conjured an image of the planet as seen from space, the moon's grey sphere just visible near its green and blue parent. Waves of energy were observed, though she couldn't explain what form they took that she was able to perceive the invisible lines that moved around and through the sphere in circular patterns that spawned and vanished at the poles and equator.

Zooming in, pinpricks of illumination, their locations changing, sometimes in line with these energy patterns, sometimes taking their own path, were seen.

As in a dream, Dee understood what she was looking at as some intuitive force inside her awakened. The Rishis were tied to the Earth as literally as a tree was rooted to the ground, or as the oceans pulled their vivacity from the planet's core. This literal connectedness explained their power. Able to pull directly from the vast potency of the world, their power would be infinite, as would their life.

But as powerful as they were, they were far from omniscient and their strength, while impressive, wasn't as scary as this connectedness suggested.

Was this what Asellus had been rambling on about when she said: *our return to who we were*. Had their power waned over their long lives? Had this oneness been lost, setting them adrift from what they'd once been?

The bell chimed.

Dee's thoughts shattered to blissful calm.

Her own connectedness expanded.

As if some exterior layer was cracked, Dee poured outward, tendrils of herself sparking against the ebb and flow of the world around her.

Overwhelmed by the sudden shift, her nerves tingled, and her breath caught, but she refused to let go of whatever it was she'd found.

Except, it was a fleeting thing. Whatever shield she'd cracked reassembled itself and cut her off from this greater macrocosm.

Heart pounding at the strangeness of where her awareness had drifted, Dee accepted its passing, knowing she would search for it again. Knowing she would find it again.

Silence.

Breathe in.

Breathe out.

Made in the USA
Columbia, SC
23 June 2019